THE WOLFMAN

A TOM DOHERTY ASSOCIATES BOOK
NEW YORK

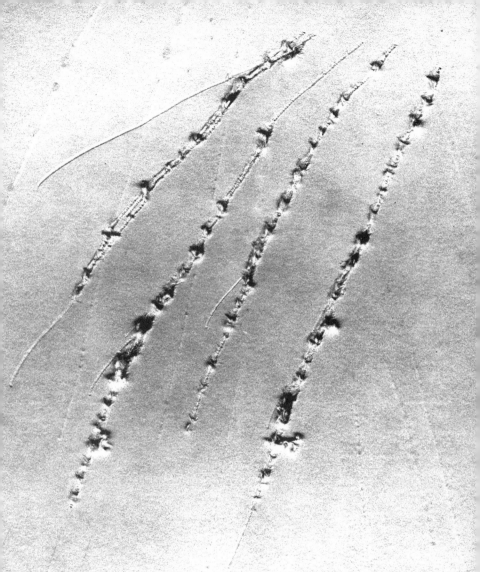

THE WOLFMAN

NICHOLAS PEKEARO

THE WOLFMAN

A Tor Book
Published by Tom Doherty Associates, LLC
175 Fifth Avenue
New York, NY 10010

www.tor-forge.com

Tor® is a registered trademark of Tom Doherty Associates, LLC.

Library of Congress Cataloging-in-Publication Data

Pekearo, Nicholas.
    The wolfman / Nicholas Pekearo. — 1st ed.
      p. cm.
    "A Tom Doherty Associates book."
    ISBN-13: 978-0-7653-2026-1
    ISBN-10: 0-7653-2026-6
  1. Werewolves—Fiction. 2. Drifters—Fiction. 3. Serial murderers—Fiction. 4. Tennessee—Fiction. I. Title.
    PS3616.E357W65 2008
    813'.6.—dc22

                                      2008003984

First Edition: May 2008

Printed in the United States of America

0 9 8 7 6 5 4 3 2 1

EDITOR'S NOTE

I had the great fortune of meeting Nicholas Pekearo two years before he died, and right off the bat, I knew I liked him. In the span of just a few minutes, we managed to find common ground. We both loved the horror films of the mid to late 1970s and the early 1980s. We both grew up reading comics. Hell, we even liked the same novelists. I was told he was a cop, but when I asked him about it, he sort of chuckled and went on to explain his role as a volunteer police officer with the Auxiliary NYPD. At first I really didn't get it. I asked him silly, childish questions, like "Do you carry a gun?" and "Have you ever been fired at?" He laughed them off, explaining that as an Auxiliary police officer he did much the same stuff a paid cop would do, that he didn't carry a gun and wasn't assigned a bulletproof vest but had saved up for one on his own. It finally sunk in when he admitted that the police volunteer work served as a great inspiration for his writing. More important, he felt that he was doing something right with his service, that it filled some sort of void. He was giving back to the community that nurtured him.

As an editor, I get a lot of folks who ask me if I would look at their work, and it's hard to say no. But most of the time, they're just blowing hot air and never hand anything over. So when I asked Nick for a look at some of his writing, I figured the odds of his showing me anything were slim. I was wrong.

He first hit me with a novel he called *The Savior* (which I found out after his death was his second; his first he called *Redbird*). It was a first-person serial killer story, and the narrative unfolded through audiotape confessions of the killer's crimes. It was dark as hell, often funny, and altogether brutal. It was rough, as Nick was still learning how to tell a story in novel form, but the voice was amazing. He had the ability to create these sick and wounded characters but somehow give them souls, ones that you felt might be worth saving, regardless of their crimes.

We met again and I proceeded to break down my reactions to *The Savior.* He fielded my criticism like a pro and quickly started telling me about the new novel he was working on, which would eventually become *The Wolfman.* He imagined *The Wolfman* as the start of a series that would take the main character, Marlowe Higgins, an essentially kindhearted man burdened with the werewolf curse, on the road as he coped with his affliction and tried desperately to find a way to reverse it. And no matter how much he fought it, every full moon he would have to kill. I thought of it as the Incredible Hulk with a raucous metal attitude. Like Bruce Banner, he would travel from town to town, trying to run from himself but constantly finding trouble—sadistic serial killers, neo-Nazi vampires, demented wizards, and insane alchemists. Those were just some of the encounters Nick envisioned for Marlowe. It simply sucks he never got to take Marlowe that far.

On the night of March 14, 2007, Nick was shot and killed while on duty as an Auxiliary officer in the neighborhood he grew up in, New York City's Greenwich Village. A madman entered a restaurant, armed to the teeth with over ninety rounds of ammunition. He killed the restaurant's bartender, then took to the streets of Greenwich Village. Nick and his partner, Eugene Marshalik, attempted to stop him after he crossed their path. They pursued the armed killer, though they themselves were unarmed. The killer unloaded. Nick was shot six times: One bullet was stopped by the vest he wore; the others weren't. Eugene was shot once in the head and died in the street. In a matter of moments, the madman was gunned down and killed by the NYPD. Nick died later that night in the hospital where he was born.

Just four days before he was killed, I had dinner with Nick and he gave me his latest round of revisions on *The Wolfman*. Apart from our author/editor relationship, Nick and I were becoming great friends. In the months it had taken me to read and respond to his first draft of *The Wolfman*, Nick had gone ahead and written another novel, *The Invisible Boy*, about a tortured teenager who shoots up his high school, which he had handed me in January. That's how prolific he was. He never stopped writing. That was his dream. His mother told me that when he was a child and was asked what he wanted to be when he grew up, among "a pizza pie man" and "a stunt man," "writer" always found its way onto the list. As an adult, he set his sights there and never looked back.

It goes without saying that Nick was a hero that night on the streets of New York. But his heroism, for me, goes beyond that sacrifice. Every time we met, he reminded me of why I got involved in book publishing: to tell great stories and meet great people. Nick was well on his way to a terrific career as a writer, and the best was yet to come. It is with great pride that I present to you Nicholas Pekearo's *The Wolfman*. You did it, Nick. Here it is. . . . Rock on.

THE WOLFMAN

PROLOGUE

Let me paint a picture for you: The full moon was bulbous and yellow like the blind and rotted eye of a witch that peered down from the murky sky with bad intentions, and a million little stars shone down on the sleepy Southern town of Evelyn. The breeze was gentle and cool, carrying on it the scent of flowers and wet earth from the recent rain spell. The only thing missing was the children singing hymns, and I'm sure it would have been enough to make someone happy to be alive.

Bill Parker was driving down Old Sherman Road, a four-lane blacktop that went right around the edge of the whole town in a near-perfect circle. Driving in the dead of night was one of his many compulsive habits, but this one was rather bad. He did it often, about four nights a week, and I say it was a bad habit for a very specific reason.

Unfortunately, I won't tell you what that reason is just yet.

Everyone in town knew he drove when he couldn't sleep. His neighbors on Bunker Street knew it because his beat-up Oldsmobile starting up in the middle of the night would, with the exception of the crickets, be the only noise on the block.

The cops knew his routine too. They'd pulled him over for speeding at two, three in the morning more times than they could count, which may or may not have meant anything, considering the kind of town it was, but still. The number was considerable. They let him get away with it after a while too. They knew he'd never stop, but aside from that, Bill Parker wasn't the kind of guy that most cops wanted to ticket. He was, after all, an important member of the community, being the coach of the baseball team over at Bailey High and all. I think a lot of the cops felt that if they gave him a ticket it would jinx the team. They lost just about as often as there was a virgin birth.

Hell, even *I* knew about Bill Parker and his odd driving habit. I only knew him as an infrequent customer at my restaurant, but gossip travels through the air in small towns like the smell of burning leaves.

Bill Parker always had a lot on his mind. He was the kind of guy that seemed to relish his worries, and if he ever found that he only had two or three things in his life to worry about, that would worry him too. He'd go so far as to turn little things into life-or-death situations.

Let me relate to you my one dealing with him, and you'll see what I mean. Bear in mind this was about a year before he died. One time he came into the restaurant and ordered a sandwich. Roast beef, perhaps, though I never really cared to remember what it was exactly. Details were never my strong point, me being a broad strokes kind of guy myself. Anyway, he ordered this sandwich and I figured, well, this here's a man that deserves a damn good sandwich, seeing as how the team he coached had just scored yet another victory, so me being the kindly sonofabitch that I am, what did I do? I put the fancy mustard on the sandwich for him—the kind with all the little seeds and herbs and so on in there.

Bill Parker went and flipped his lid when he took a bite of that sandwich, like the balance of the universe had been shocked into an irreparable state. Like the Earth itself had been thrown off its axis and was now on an inevitable crash course with the sun.

"Jesus Christ," he shrieked. "What are you trying to do to me?"

He acted like I'd put battery acid in the fucking thing.

I apologized, of course, and went on and made the man another sandwich. This time I used the regular mustard, the kind that looks like yellow paint but can sometimes smell like someone had pissed in their pants.

I thought nothing of this incident—it was like watching a

woman fuss over a broken nail in a room full of amputees—
because the fact of the matter is, if anyone on this stinking planet
has anything to worry about, it's me.

Fuck it, the point of it all is that Bill Parker was the kind of
man that couldn't sleep at night, and in some crazy way, driving a
few times around Old Sherman Road like it was a goddamn race-
track when everyone else was sleeping made him feel like everything was going to be okay. That's why he was driving that night.

He was not yet forty, but Father Time had not been kind to his
face or his features. He'd lost most of his hair when he was still
young enough to look like he couldn't buy alcohol, but the missing hair from his head slowly resurfaced on different parts of his
body, like his chest and back. Behind that hairy back he was
called "the Pad" by a lot of the kids at the school. "The Pad" was
short for "the Brillo Pad."

When Parker would make one of his young charges run a few
extra laps for some form of tardiness or other, the student would
later remark to a friend of his, "The fucking Pad had another wild
hair growing somewhere today."

Bill Parker didn't know the students had come up with a name
for him until he heard his colleagues refer to him as "the Pad" in
the teachers' lounge one day. He pretended he didn't hear them
because that's the kind of guy he was.

All that body hair must have kept him pretty warm, because he
was always sweating at least a little. It was by the grace of God
alone that a girl named Mary Beth had thought enough of the
man to marry him and go through the pain and the grief of having his children.

His wife proved through the years that she had the strength
and determination to keep the house up and running and the kids
well-dressed and fed, but Bill Parker let it all go, and focused on
his work at the school. Whereas Mary Beth fought hard to get her
librarian's figure back after giving birth to two chunky boys, Bill
Parker put weight on and never lost it. In fact, it was as if the extra

weight he'd put on was lonely, so he added to it now and then so it could have some company. At first he claimed the weight was from what he liked to call "sympathy pains," but that stopped working as an excuse when Mary Beth got back into her old jeans, and the boys were old enough to carry on a meaningful conversation with the minister from the Lutheran church that Mary Beth always tried to drag her husband to. The fact was that Bill had gotten complacent in his marriage.

I digress, back to the picture: Bill Parker checked the time on his cheap watch. It was getting on to two o'clock in the morning. That made it Tuesday, exactly fourteen weeks since he came home from work one evening to find that his lovely wife had taken their two boys and moved to her parents' house over in Edenburgh.

Bill sighed.

It didn't feel like it had been that long, but enough had happened since then that he knew his calculations were correct, like his realization that he didn't know how to operate the washing machine in his basement. Now that he was all alone, his wardrobe took on the appearance of ill-handled rags, or a collection of aging bathroom mats at a free clinic. The undershirt he was wearing was clean enough, but the daylight-blue pajama bottoms he had on reeked of meals he couldn't remember eating.

He decided that he'd make one more loop around Evelyn on Old Sherman Road, and when he got home, he'd try to pick up all the beer cans that littered his two-story home like mouse droppings.

He'd at least try.

Bill Parker frowned, thinking about what he'd done, probably, and continued driving east. He'd just passed Larchmont Street. On his left were the blocks of little one-story homes, all wood and dust and ancient glass. On his right were the woods—deep and dense and always stirring. The woods pulsated and moved like the ocean at night. You couldn't see it, but you could feel it, like something bad was about to happen.

On this night, the woods were blacker than the sky. As Bill Parker drove along, he looked up at the moon and smiled. Something about it made him feel at peace, I suppose. At that point he reached down with his right hand and turned on the radio. It was already set to KBTO—Evelyn's classics station—and once he raised the volume, he knew he was listening to Johnny Cash's "Daddy Sang Bass."

That was fine with Bill.

Up ahead, something moved. Bill Parker put his eyes back on the road, and that's when he saw it.

It sprang from the black woods like a mountain bird, as if that dark wall of leaves, branches, and limbs had rejected this thing and violently spat it out on the pavement. Bill Parker caught sight of it in the bright glare of his headlights and hit the brakes hard.

At first he thought it was a deer, but the creature didn't look like any deer one would be familiar with. In the back of his mind, he wondered what the hell it was he was looking at, but there was no time to think of such things.

Bill made a noise like a woman as the car skidded along on melting rubber tires, and just when he thought he was going to make violent contact with this thing on the road, it leapt up and came down on the hood of his car. The sound of it was as if someone had dropped a piano. Bill Parker saw that this animal had two feet, not the four that he was expecting, even hoping for. Bill's mouth fell open, not making a sound this time.

It was a look the beast had seen a thousand times. In another day and age it may have relished the fear it provoked, but now it was all business. The beast gave Bill Parker a look like he was a nail that needed hammering.

What Bill Parker saw wasn't a man by any stretch of the word, but that's all he could think of. The beast on the hood of his car was crouched down and leering in at him through the dirty windshield with bloodred eyes. Judging from the size of it, Bill figured it had to be about seven feet tall. It was backlit by the moon, so he couldn't make out any fine details, but he could see that it was covered in hair, almost like it was an honest-to-God, look-it-up-in-the-dictionary kind of animal. He also saw that the beast had nails at the ends of its fingers that were so goddamn big they could cut through a tree. Over the hum of the motor, Parker could hear the monster breathing. Deep, seething breaths. Like he owed the thing money. The beast growled, raised one of its fur-lined arms, and punched a hole through the middle of the windshield. The tiny shards of broken glass pelted Bill Parker like raindrops. He let out a guttural cry. Before he could do anything one might call "useful," the beast had dug its nails into the meat of Bill's left shoulder and was making progress on separating the arm from the rest of the body. Bill screamed again. He wasn't sure what he was looking at, but it soon dawned on him that his life was dangerously close to being a thing of the past. Thus, as he told his team, it was time to get busy.

He slid down in his seat and ducked to his right, trying to break the beast's grip, but he couldn't. Blood came out of him in spurts along the dash. Red waves caught the moonlight. Bill Parker could feel the heat of the blood as it rolled across his chest and neck in waves. All the while he screamed, and, little by little, the beast inched its head through the space where the windshield used to be. The smell of sweat and wet animal hair filled the interior of the car. As Bill Parker breathed in shallow gasps, the stench of it almost made him sick.

He struggled a few more inches and opened up the glove box. Behind the cube-shaped box of tissues, the rubber gloves, the baby oil, and the car manual was a small, black handgun. It was a peashooter by my standards. I was in the army and I used to pick my teeth after meals with bigger guns than that. In fact, I think most ladies in bad areas would have been embarrassed to carry around such a thing. Our friend Bill apparently didn't have such prejudices.

He raised the gun and aimed it at the shape above him. He

fired once and saw a brilliant crimson mist saturate the air. The beast howled and drew back. Its grip on Bill's shoulder loosened considerably. Bill fired three more times in rapid succession, and a spray of blood rained down upon him. The beast fell back, rolled across the hood, and in the night, Bill heard the thing hit the road in front of the car.

If not for Johnny Cash, it would have been perfectly quiet. Bill Parker was breathing heavily, but it took a minute for him to notice it. After that, he heard the crickets in the night, the hum of the motor, the wind playing with the leaves, the sounds of the night birds as they hooted and swooped past trees and snatched away their furry little snacks.

Bill listened intently for the sound of footsteps, the sound of a door opening across the road, of someone's concerned voice, but he heard none of it. Not a single sign of a helping hand. Solace would have no part of him. He would have given up the use of his legs just to hear one measly person ask him if he was okay.

He listened for the sound of the creature's pain, the sound of movement on asphalt. He didn't hear any of that either.

After a spell, he deemed it safe enough to move and opened the passenger door. He got out slowly. He had his gun drawn and pointed, but his hand was shaking so badly he wouldn't have been able to hit one of the houses across the way even if he wanted to. He came around the open door without closing it. The headlights brightened the cracked and sun-bleached road ahead of him. All else was darkness.

There, lying motionless in the road, was the creature. Its blood glistened like heavy red wine, like a rich merlot, on the hood of his white car. The blood steamed, and Bill didn't know why. He touched the hood of the car, and the metal wasn't that hot at all. It barely qualified as being warm. Bill swallowed and turned his gaze back to the beast. He didn't want to get too close, but his curiosity was working on him like all hell. It was almost like he was rubbernecking at his own demise.

He took a few more steps and took in the sight before him. He had never seen anything like it before, except maybe in some crazy old horror movie the kids once made him sit through. Hell, he probably thought he'd just killed Bigfoot. He read about such things in the cheap newspapers he bought at the supermarket.

He took another step. Blood pooled at his heel. He looked at the houses, saw not a single light brighten a single room. There was maybe only one other time in his life that he felt so helpless and alone, and the thought of that one other time made him shudder. He probably thought about getting himself to the hospital, but what would he say?

A new worry gripped him: that he'd get battered with so many incessant, insensitive questions at St. Francis that he'd end up dying before they even got the chance to go to work on his unique and ghastly wounds. Apparently, it was never bad enough for Bill Parker to find something new—even hypothetical—to tense up about.

Some people might have found that quality endearing about him, I don't know. I myself wasn't a big fan of his, which I'm sure is quite clear at this point.

He looked down at the creature before him, studied it for a moment, and maybe after just a few seconds, he thought he saw its hand move. Bill Parker took a step back and rubbed his eyes, smearing blood across his face like a mask. He wasn't sure if his mind had just played a trick on him or not. He couldn't be sure of anything anymore.

He looked again and saw the beast's chest rise, then fall, and finally heave with labored breaths. Smoke rose from its slackened, toothy mouth as if a candle had been blown out somewhere deep inside it. Bill stumbled back till he was against the open car door. He heard the beast breathe again. He heard his own blood dripping, splashing against the cracked tar, the black ring that held the wilderness back from the town it surrounded—the little town that grew up in the middle of it like a tumor.

The beast's eyes opened, all bloodshot and inhuman. It raised its head, and those awful, haunting eyes peered into the soul of

Bill Parker. It was in that gaze that he saw his own death. Bill Parker turned and ran.

Bill Parker disappeared into the woods. Branches beat against him like skinny arms, clawing at his skin, his clothes, and not far behind, he could hear those same branches twist, crack, and give way for the creature that pursued him. He could hear its howls reverberate off the trees, off the bones in his ears. He could hear them echo across the night like battle horns. His speed was gone, and all the strength he had was left as a trail of crimson drips behind him.

The salt in his sweat made him squint, and before long he could hardly see where he was going, but it was too dark for it to matter that much. He felt the ground shift beneath him, and he realized he was starting to head down a long slope, so he sped up and let gravity do some of the work his legs could hardly handle. Wind licked his face, and he smiled. He wasn't sure why.

His ankle got caught in a web of crooked vines growing up the side of an oak tree. He fell face-first in the black and moistened soil and rolled the rest of the way down the slope. When his back finally came to rest on flat land, he realized that his body hadn't registered the pain. He didn't feel the throbbing in his arm anymore, and he didn't even feel the slightest ache from falling so hard.

He knew then that he was dying.

He turned over and dragged himself over to the base of a very tall pine tree. In the darkness, he couldn't even see the top of it. In a matter of time, he thought, he might be able to climb that tree to heaven. He scooched himself till his back was against the tree, and then he waited. There was nothing else to do.

In the dark, he heard it coming. He knew it was over. Just as night turns to day, I know that he knew there could be only one exit from those woods, and that was in a bag, if he was lucky. In his head, he asked God why such a fate would befall him. He knew why, deep down, and I truly believe that's why he began to cry.

The beast's job was easy. The gunshot wounds it had sustained were already a distant memory; the entry holes the bullets had ripped into its hide were at this point nothing more than pinpricks on its surface. All it had to do to track Bill Parker on his last, pathetic run was breathe. The scent of the dying man was like a guiding light in the dark.

It came to him, approaching slowly, toying with the man or just observing, I'm not sure which. Even after all these years, I'm not sure how that thing feels about anything, or if after so many years of being around the human race, it's come to perhaps mimic some of our little behavioral traits. That's something for me to think on the next time I have nothing else to do.

The beast circled around him, around the tree, growling. Bill Parker shifted in the dirt, and murmured prayers he hadn't thought about in years in a high-pitched squeal under his breath. He got most of the words right. The beast came back around and paced before him like a man not sure what to do. The beast swiveled its shoulders as if loosening a knot; then it crouched down and brought its face up close to Bill's, sucked in the fear that leaked from the man's pores like vapor. Bill thought the thing smelled like a wet dog. The beast thought Bill smelled like barbecue.

Bill Parker tried to talk. I wonder what it was he would've said if he'd been able to get the words out. Would he have asked what it was, or *why* it was, or *who* it was? Would he have asked if he was going to hell? Would he have asked for forgiveness, or would he have launched off a final round of expletives like all the tough guys in the movies do?

The beast watched Bill struggle for a moment, at first with a curious air, then with something that could've passed for amusement. It smiled the most horrible smile that Bill Parker could ever have imagined. Drool dripped from its fangs, and a blast of stinking air rushed up from the beast's chest and hit Bill in the face like fumes.

Bill raised his one good arm, but before he could level the gun at his target, the beast grabbed him by his wrists with its two big, hairy hands and sank its teeth into the soft meat of Bill's neck. A blood-arch pissed itself from the wound like a stream, and before the blood hit the ground, Bill Parker was dead and gone. The beast drew back and tore a chunk of flesh away from the throat. It chewed, swallowed, and roared. Then it went back for seconds.

In the night, the life that inhabited those woods kept its distance and left that unnatural creature to its own devices. Its only company was the wind, carrying a trace of every single body in the world, and death. The moon watched like a quiet God, a beacon, a partner. But make no mistake. I was the wolf's keeper, its warden, and I called the shots.

The name I was born with was Marlowe Higgins. Due to some rather extraordinary life circumstances, I haven't always gone by that name, but I'm going to tell you a story, so I suppose I ought as well give you some facts to work with.

I'm a white male with long brown hair and a mustache that just won't quit. I have a little scar under my right eye left over from a childhood injury that came about during a rather heated game of Wiffle ball. If not for that mark, I could have been anybody, anywhere, but still, I had little trouble making anonymity my greatest ally.

Where I'm from doesn't matter, because it could have been right in your own hometown or a thousand miles away from you, and whether or not I got laid on prom night doesn't have a whole hell of a lot to do with anything either. There's only so much you need to know and even less I care to talk about, but the one thing that should be said, I suppose, is that I'm a werewolf, and I have been for the better part of my life.

What I'm about to tell you happened back in the spring of 1993. Sit back, and let the pain and the suffering begin. It seems to be what I'm good at.

ONE

I am a man who is apt to have bad dreams. In my dreams I am not falling, or drowning, or even being roasted on a spit or some such thing by the Vietcong, who, at the time of the war, were rumored to do piss-awful things like that to the boys they caught.

My dreams are a little more fucked than that. I have no soul, and the godforsaken beast that had replaced it does more than take lives. It takes their spirits. So when I plop myself down on my lumpy mattress at night and go to sleep, I don't dream like normal people do. Instead, I experience the memories of people who aren't around anymore to remember their own histories. What makes a dream bad isn't reliving how they died; it's remembering how much my victims loved the men, women, and children they left behind in this world. In my dreams I miss these widows and children as if I knew them. I have been responsible for the deaths of over three hundred people over the years. Consequently my nightmares are legion.

On the morning of May 1, I awoke from one of my bad dreams because the radio alarm clock went off by my head like a gunshot. I was cold but sweating, and that wasn't unusual. I looked around the room to get my bearings. It took a second to remember where I was, what year it was. I soon came to recognize my bedroom, and a razor slice of a grin appeared on my face because Led Zeppelin's "Immigrant Song" was playing on KBTO, but, aside from that one saving grace, it was another day in the life that no one in their right mind would ask for.

A thin sliver of sunlight came in through the curtains and

burned on the floor like the glowing edge of a heated knife. There were two windows in the bedroom. One was facing east, the other south. I had nailed the both of them shut when I moved in. The air smelled like old and rotting books. A combination of water damage and a few hundred old newspapers stacked up in the guest room helped create this scent, which was far preferable to how the house used to smell. I pulled back the damp sheets and stumbled across the creaking floorboards to the bedroom door. The door was closed, and I had a quarter balanced on the doorknob and a glass ashtray on the floor below it, so if anyone jiggled the handle at night, I'd know it by the noise of the coin dropping into the ashtray. I palmed the quarter, stuffed it into the pocket of the shorts I wore to bed, and moved the ashtray aside with my foot. Then I went down the short hallway to the bathroom.

I had a quarter resting on the bathroom doorknob as well, just in case anyone snuck in through the bathroom window. The bathroom window was the only one in the entire house that wasn't permanently sealed, because I liked opening it when I did my business. It helped more than you could ever imagine. If I ever crap on a plane, all those funny little masks would probably drop down in the aisles.

I jumped in and out of the shower to wash away the sweat, and when I got out I combed my long, awesome hair, which at the time came down to the middle of my back. Looking at my face up close in the mirror, I decided to do a little tidy-up work on my handlebar mustache. I saw a couple of gray hairs in there that I didn't believe should be so eager to come to fruition. I was forty years old, but a history of longevity ran in my nasty blood— despite the two packs I smoked a day—and grays in the face seemed to me to be redundant little creatures that hadn't earned their place yet.

My little house on King Street was down on the southwestern edge of town, constructed at the very end of a cul-de-sac. The houses were spaced far enough away from each other that I had never felt obligated to say hello to the poor fools who had the misfortune of living to my left and to my right. My house was what they call ranch-style, and it was made of wood so gnarled by time that it looked like it was made of boards that fell off other houses. All the glass in the windows was rippled. Out front was a little driveway—no garage—and a few bushes I never trimmed. They looked like afros in the wind. Out back I had a dead tree that my neighbors always bitched about because they were worried it would fall down in a bad storm, but I liked my dead tree. You could always see the birds crapping from its limbs with that blank look in their eyes, and the squirrels running all around its girth as they played their daredevil games. Further, I liked it because it would be impossible for a sniper to hide in it.

The woman who used to live in the house had been very old before she died. Or maybe it would be better to say that she was very goddamn old by the time she kicked off, but the point of it all is that she'd had cats. A lot of fucking cats. I'm told that when she died in that house, those cats went to work on her after a few days of having no other source of food. Sometimes I swore that I could still smell her deep in the fabric of the couch.

Her son, who lived over in Edenburgh, decided to rent the place instead of selling it outright, and when I moved in about three years prior, it took me a long time to keep those cats from coming around all the time. There were holes in the walls and in the floor where they'd sneak in, but I eventually found all those holes and sealed them up. I didn't want any cats in my house, especially cats that had supped on human flesh. Even though it had been years since I'd gotten them all out, it was as if their phantoms lived on, because whenever I turned my head, the furniture would be covered with clumps of orange hair. It was unbelievable. I always wondered if there was a hole somewhere that I didn't know about, or if those ornery little bastards had a set of keys for the front door.

After checking all the windows, I put on a pair of jeans and slipped my skull-and-crossbones belt through the loops. I put on a Sabbath shirt, a flannel over that, and then I laced up my construction boots. I grabbed my keys, locked the four locks on my front door, and got in the truck—a blue 1983 Chevy flatbed. There were so many rusted-out holes in it that it looked like some hunters had mistaken the truck for an elephant and emptied their scatterguns into it.

I turned the key and cursed. Doing these two things at the same time was almost like a prayer in and of itself, because God came down every morning to help make the piece of shit move. The engine groaned like it had arthritis, and I headed out.

I drove to the corner and took Picket Street east—a quiet, tree-lined street of one-story homes and the occasional nursery or doctor's office. There wasn't another car on the road as far as I could see. It was very early, and anyone who was up at the time was probably at church, where, as I understood it, they gave people free coffee.

I wasn't quite awake yet. I was picking at this piece of sleepy-sand in the corner of my eye that didn't want to go. I was picking at it so much that it began to irritate me like a sonofabitch. It just got worse and worse. I shut my eyes real tight, and when I opened them up again, I saw that damn Indian in the middle of the road up ahead with that damn plastic bag slumped over his shoulder, full of all the cans he had picked up off the streets, like a bum.

That woke me up real quick.

I hit the brakes and jerked the wheel left. I missed him by a foot, if that, though I don't know why I was so merciful. I stopped the truck and gave him the evil eye through the open passenger window. He was in a dirty black suit that he must have taken from a dead body. On his feet was a pair of cowboy boots.

He wasn't a young man. He seemed practically ancient, but his age was anyone's guess. His white hair was as long as mine, and in a ponytail. He looked back at me like he thought the whole thing was a fucking joke. It wasn't the first time this had happened, me almost hitting him with the truck.

"Hey, you old bastard," I yelled out the window, "what the fuck are you doing?"

My general distrust and hostility toward the natives was genetic in origin in the sense that my singular disorder evidently stems from a deranged red man whose vicious streak lives on through me. More presently, I had never had a good encounter with a native. Wherever I went, I felt as if they could smell the curse I carried inside of me, almost as if they saw me in a way that no one else could, could observe the inhumanity lurking beneath my flesh, and they hated me for not only what I was but why I was as well. Or at least that's how it felt.

In his halted way of speaking, the Indian responded, "What . . . does it look like?"

"Looks like you have a death wish," I replied. "Stay off the road. Next time, I won't swerve to miss you."

He pointed his sawed-off broomstick with the nail hammered through one end at me like it was a baton and said, "You have more important things to worry about . . . than me, paleface."

"What the fuck is that supposed to mean? I ain't too tired to take you to town, old man." I felt like getting out of the truck to clobber the sonofabitch. "You looking for trouble?"

"No, no," he said. "Trouble . . . is yours to find. Not mine."

I didn't know what to say.

"Arright, you cryptic bastard," I mumbled. "You want to talk like that, fine. Just stay off the fucking road."

He smiled. I flipped him the bird and took off.

I drove north on Hamilton Road to this little newsstand just off Main Street. I said hi to Gus, the old fellow who owned the place, and picked up copies of Evelyn's two daily papers—the *Harbinger* and the *Post*—and also a copy of *USA Today*. From there I went east on Main till I got to Grant. There was another little newsstand over there where I picked up a few more newspapers, but not local ones. These papers were from other cities, and some were from other states. I didn't like buying all my papers at one place. I wouldn't want someone wondering why I read so goddamn much.

I stacked all the papers on the passenger seat and kept going east on Main till I got to the restaurant, which was almost at the edge of town. The restaurant was set far back on the sidewalk so cars could turn off the road and park up front of the place. Since the restaurant wasn't open yet, all the spots should have been empty, but that wasn't the case. There was a puke-green Toyota parked there, and I could recognize that puke-green car from a mile away.

I pulled up next to it, killed the engine, and got out. The burly man sitting in the Toyota got out too, followed by a wall of cheap cigar smoke. He was wearing a pair of khaki pants that accentuated his heavy ass and a golf shirt that was the same color as the car.

I shielded my eyes from the bright morning sun and said, "Howdy, Frank."

"You're late," Frank said.

Frank owned the restaurant. It had been his father's, and his father's before that. I had never met Frank's father, and to be honest I never wanted to because Frank was a prick. If I had to meet a second one just like him I would have lost my mind.

I looked at my watch. It was five past the hour.

"Hardly," I responded. "Besides, it's Sunday. The place is gonna be dead."

"That's not the point," said Frank. "I pay you to be here at a certain time, and that's when I expect you to be here."

"C'mon, man, do you give anyone else a hard time when they're late?"

"That's not the point," Frank grunted.

Frank and I never got along, if you couldn't tell already.

"I think it is," I said, as shock invaded his face. "I think this is sexual harassment."

I had heard the expression once on the television. I thought it sounded cute.

"Shut up," he said, disgusted. "Just open the fucking restaurant."

"That's what I'm trying to do."

"Aren't you even going to apologize for being late?"

I looked at him with pity for a second, like he was a street urchin, a latchkey kid, and then said, "Frank, I never volunteered to work the morning shift, okay? If you don't like it, have me switch shifts with Carlos or something."

Frank got back in the car and slammed the door. He rolled down the window and said, "The thought of you working here at night scares me, Marlowe. Just get here on time. And tell Abe that he's a fucking asshole too."

"Will do," I said.

Frank pulled out of the spot, and I watched as he headed west on Main Street. Main ran from one end of town to the other, and right down the middle of the street was an old set of railroad tracks that carried about a half dozen freight trains through the town per day. Those trains, for all intents and purposes, were Evelyn's sole connection to the outside world.

Main Street met up with Old Sherman Road at both ends of it. Farther east of Old Sherman, Main cut through several miles of deep woods as a country road. The tall trees bent over the road, forming a canopy, and in the fall, when the red-copper colors of autumn came out in startling abundance, it was beautiful. The road and the train tracks went on still and led to Campbell's Bridge, which was an ancient thing of rusted metal and molded planks. The trains went over a separate bridge just to the south, and this one was just as old. Flowing underneath the bridges were the clear waters of the Ivy River.

Much farther south, the Ivy River connected to the St. Michael River, which ran in a southeastern direction along the western border of Evelyn, and made a hook along the southern end, thus encasing Evelyn on three sides with water. Many miles of dense forest served as a buffer between the rivers and this quaint little town, which rested, like a spider in a vast web, just outside the Tennessee border.

Up to the north beyond Old Sherman there were many, many miles of labyrinthine wilderness before you could come upon so much as a bottle half-buried in the dirt to remind you that you were still in the world.

I opened the passenger door of the truck, reached in, and pulled out my stack of papers. Then I climbed the three stairs to the front door, unlocked it, and entered the restaurant. A tiny, little bell jangled overhead as I entered. I flipped on all the lights, which, because of the sun, was hardly necessary. The restaurant had a fifties-era ambience, and the sun glinted off all the chrome along the tables and chairs. I took those hot, glowing chairs down from the tabletops and sat them all on the floor. After that, I turned the little radio behind the counter to KBTO. They were playing "Peace Frog" by The Doors.

I got the grill and the oven going in the kitchen, and just as I finished making that first precious pot of coffee, Abraham decided to show up.

Abraham Davis had worked at the restaurant about twice as long as me, about six years. He was a people person, very suave, which was why he worked the counter and dealt with the patrons, and why he never got fired for being consistently late. I, not even remotely being a people person, worked in the kitchen. Abraham wasn't a young man anymore—he was nearing fifty—but he seemed to live to go out and drink and dip his wick in whatever was around.

While I was off in the war, he was back Stateside getting his ass gnawed off by police-trained German shepherds. He'd been married twice, divorced twice, and to hear him tell it, the time that he spent "shackled" to women who, after getting to know him, didn't really care if he lived or died consumed about ten years of a precious life that would've been better spent chasing tail and having "experiences"—or getting into trouble, more like—that enriched the spirit and the mind.

Horseshit.

According to Abraham, he was making up for lost time by acting like a college boy on spring break, as if lost time could truly be returned to someone, like a deposit in a bank. As if anyone got a second chance to be happy in this world. It was foolish of him to think that way, and I think he knew it. But the hell of it was that it was hard to ever see the man without a smile on his face, which made it hard to vilify him for acting like a young man when he damn well knew he wasn't.

When Abraham staggered into the restaurant, I could tell immediately that he was half in the bag from a Saturday night of drinking that turned into a Sunday morning of wondering not only where he'd woken up but where the hell his pants were.

"Sorry I'm late," he whispered.

"Frank told me to tell you you're a fucking asshole."

"Great," he said. "I'm an asshole."

"A *fucking* asshole."

I put my apron on as Abraham seemed to slither past the counter and into the bathroom. A moment later, I heard him through the door losing what sounded like a hundred dollars' worth of used booze the hard way.

When he came out of the bathroom, he wiped his eyes with his fists and said, "Jesus Christ, man, I'm making up for sins from a past life this morning, you know what I mean?"

"Me too," I said. "I'm working with you."

"Cold motherfucker," he groaned. "That's what you are. You mind if I crash in the kitchen awhile? Just to rest my eyes. I can barely see."

"Moonshine does that."

"C'mon, man . . ."

"There's no fucking way I'm working that counter, Abe. I did it once and nearly killed a man. I'm not doing it again. I don't care how bad you feel."

"It's Sunday morning, man. I'll be golden before anyone comes in, I swear."

I thought for a second, then nodded. I was too nice sometimes. "In light of the mercy I'm showing, you still think I'm a cold motherfucker?"

"Man, you're like a turd in the snow."

Abraham took a chair from one of the tables and dragged it back into the kitchen through the double doors. He made some noises one would expect to hear coming from a circus tent, and then he fell asleep. I poured him a cup of coffee and set it down by his foot. I then went and made a cup for myself as well.

It might have been unwise to leave the restaurant unattended, but I didn't care. I wasn't paid to stand behind that counter. If anyone came in I'd know it because there was a long window looking out into the restaurant, and I'd wake Abe up by any means necessary. Until then, I took my stack of newspapers into the kitchen and got to reading. Behind me, Abraham didn't so much snore as labor for each inflammable breath.

Reading the papers was a daily ritual of mine. Information was a crucial thing for me. There was a very specific kind of article I was looking for in all those different papers. Big-city politics didn't mean a whole hell of a lot to me, nor did world affairs. I realized back in 'Nam that nothing was ever going to change, that the same mistakes were going to be made over and over and over again for the rest of time because that's just how people are made, I guess. You can have all the revolutions and protests you want, I don't care. They say history repeats itself, and I suppose that's just as true as anything else ever said, so I paid these articles no mind. I read the same ones when I was young, and I'd read them again when I was old and silver-haired.

What interested me were the smaller atrocities, the everyday miseries. Who was it—Lenin, I think—who said a million deaths is a statistic, but a single death is a tragedy? It's *true*, man. The murders are what I read the papers for. The deaths. More specifically, I always kept an eye out for unsolved murders.

I didn't get off on the stuff—I'll swear on a stack of Bibles to that fact—but it was more like I had made misery my business. After all, I was the wrath of God.

Wrath of God. Pleased to meet you.

I had begun reading as many daily papers as I could get my hands on around the time my mother died in 1981. I inherited this slightly creepy habit from one of my victims. You see, the wolf doesn't just kill, it *claims*. It's not just that the memories of the deceased become my memories; their traits become mine as well. I guess it's like when people get some kind of organ transplant and they develop a taste for a certain kind of food they never liked before. All of a sudden they're addicted to fish or chocolate because the person whose liver or kidney or heart they had couldn't get enough of the stuff.

There was a time in my life when this was very hard for me, inheriting other people's wants, their needs. This was back when I used to feel guilty about being what I am, when I felt as if I was losing my own identity every time someone got killed. One of the wolf's many victims had been a paranoid, reading all the papers every fucking day, but unlike so many other idiosyncrasies, I've allowed myself to keep the newspaper routine up all these years because all I have to do is find one unsolved crime in the paper, and then I have someone to send the beast after when it comes around to that time of the month. You see, I can't ever stop it from killing, but I can at least keep it from killing people who don't have it coming. That right there is turning two negatives into a positive.

I always started off the paper sessions with the *Harbinger* and the *Post*. After that, I went through the different newspapers for all the different towns based on how far they were from Evelyn. On this day the front pages of the two local papers were dedicated to what was dubbed "the Horror at the Mill." Some poor slob got his hand taken off by a saw over at the lumber mill all the way out west of town. That's what headlines consisted of in a town like Evelyn, and I could live with that, too.

Out in the restaurant, I heard the bell above the door jangle.

I kicked Abraham's foot, and he stirred.

"There's a guy out there," I said. "Get to it."

"Take care of him, man. Please."

"Fuck you," I whispered.

"Howdy, Marlowe," called the man in the restaurant.

I turned and recognized the tall, lanky blond man in the suit and tie as one of the regulars, a guy named Brian. He worked over at the life insurance place around the corner.

"Howdy, Brian," I said.

"You're open, right?"

"Yeah, pretty much. What do you need?"

"Just a coffee to go."

"Would you mind getting it yourself?"

"Are you serious?"

I nodded.

Brian went behind the counter with baby steps, as if he were a cat burglar. I hated the interruption, but he was at least funny to watch through the long window in the wall. He poured himself a cup of coffee without getting burned, and then he dropped a pair of quarters on the counter.

"You don't have to do that," I said.

"Sure I do," said Brian. He held up the cup of coffee in a salute, then went back out the door.

"He's a good guy," said Abraham.

I lit a cigarette and blew smoke in his face.

"If I have to talk to one more person today because of you, I'm going to burn you with this cigarette."

Buried in the back pages of the *Harbinger* was a short article about Crazy Bob. Crazy Bob was a trucker who lived not far from me. He must have been a big fan of getting arrested, because he did, a lot. When I first came to town he had just stolen an eighteen-wheeler and driven it into the river. He figured if he stole enough trucks, he'd be able to make a dam and flood the town. I guess that was around the time he lost one of his jobs. The article in front of me stated that he'd gotten picked up again, for breaking all the windows at a hardware store. He apparently had anger-management issues. What sparked this latest incident off was the fact that they had given him a Canadian penny.

When I finished the two local papers, I placed them in a new pile on the floor. I picked up the *Edenburgh Gazette*—the major paper for our closest neighboring town—and dropped it on the counter in front of me. At this point, Abraham got up off the chair, but instead of going to work, he went to the bathroom and didn't come back.

I put my hair back in a ponytail with a rubberband, ran my fingers through my handlebar, and got myself good and hunched over the pale counter.

Edenburgh was the kind of town where they wrote about the cats stuck in the trees, and if the cat happened to have some unusual talent, or if it had one good eye or something, then it was front page news over there, but on this day there was something just a touch more interesting: A local church had been broken into. The poor box was stuffed and intact. Nothing had been taken, and nothing had been vandalized.

A few pages after that, there was an even more interesting article. A seventeen-year-old girl had disappeared.

That, I thought, could be something.

A flash of light from outside the restaurant caught my eyes. I craned my neck through the space in the wall and saw a dusty black 1973 Mach 1 drive slowly past the restaurant, heading west. It then made an illegal U-turn and pulled up into one of the parking spots outside. The black car could have kept on going, but it didn't. The engine revved up once, and then was shut down. I didn't know it at the time, but things would never be the same again.

TWO

The black car rested in a space between my truck and Abraham's gold-colored Buick. I'd never seen the Mach 1 before. Evelyn was the kind of place where if you stuck around long enough you got to notice these kinds of things. I knew right then that this guy wasn't a local. He'd probably even want to see a fucking menu.

The driver got out, alone. He was a youngish kid, late twenties. He was of average height, and maybe a little more wiry than the typical underwear model. He was wearing Italian boots with squared-off tips and a pair of those jeans they sell at the high-end places that are a little fucked up and worn out already. An Italian *corno* hung from his neck, dangling from a thin gold chain. He had on a white T-shirt that looked slept-in, with one greasy fingerprint smeared across its front, and over that was a light leather jacket, the kind with lapels and such. It was the kind of jacket that cost just about as much as a month's rent in a nice neighborhood, but it looked like it would disintegrate in the rain. The leather jacket I had back at the house was the *real* kind, with zippers and studs all over the fucking thing, the kind that would still look good if you fell off a motorcycle and slid down the road on it.

The kid had on aviator shades, and five-o'clock shadow framed his chiseled, prettyboy face. His dark hair was neatly trimmed and slicked back across his head with oil. Hanging down over his forehead like a vine was a single lock from his bangs. He was wearing a ring on his left pinky. It flashed in the light, and then I saw what it was: a birthstone. Opal. I couldn't even smell the guy yet, but I already wanted to hit him. He reached into the car and took out a fancy camera, which he slung around his neck by the strap. He raised the camera to his eye and snapped off a pair of shots of the outside of the restaurant. Up along the top of the building was an old neon sign that read LONG JOHN'S.

He slammed the car door, looked into the backseat through the dusty window, then climbed the three stairs outside the restaurant. The door opened. The little bell jangled. He stepped in.

If Abe wasn't in the bathroom, I would have thrown his drunken ass through those double doors to avoid dealing with this prettyboy.

The kid stood near the door, the sun beaming in behind him, and he was perhaps a little hesitant to venture any farther. After all, there wasn't anyone in the place as far as he could tell. After a long minute he turned his eyes my way and saw me staring at him through the long window in the wall. He seemed to let out a sigh of relief. I breathed deep, made no motion to draw shut the paper, made no attempt at disguising the fact that I was trying to read his life with my eyes—a nervous habit of mine ever since I came back from overseas. I think I might have even given him the evil eye.

He got the hint and took off his shades, folded them up, and stuck them in the collar of his shirt.

Roy Orbison's "Mean Woman Blues" was playing on the radio.

"Are you open?" he asked in an even voice.

With that smirk on his face, I felt like throwing the pot of hot coffee at him, but I never did like the sound of a man crying.

"Yup," I replied.

He stepped across the black-and-white tiled floor and took a seat at one of the stools in front of the counter. Once there, he took the camera from around his neck, sat it next to his elbow, and gave the restaurant a good looking-over. There was a clock above the counter similar to the large, bland industrial-type ones that some might remember from grade school. Along the walls were a handful of framed pictures of horses.

After another long minute of silence, he became fidgety, seeing as how no one was coming to help him. He began to pick at a hangnail, and once he discovered that doing that didn't exactly get his goat going, he reached into the pocket of his fancy leather jacket and pulled out a pack of cigarettes and a book of matches. He wedged a cigarette in between his puckered lips and then looked at me again with raised eyebrows.

My nonfriendly expression had not changed, nor would it until Abraham decided to get out the bathroom and do his fucking job.

"Can I smoke in here?" the kid asked.

My reply: "I don't know. Can you?"

He looked down at his own hands, his wiggling fingers, as if trying to solve an equation. "Can you?"

I reached into my pocket and pulled out another smoke. Lit it. "I can smoke wherever the hell I want," I said.

"I see," he said. "*May* I smoke in here?"

"You can smoke wherever the hell you want, kid."

"Sorry," he said. "Sometimes, you go into a little place like this and the smoking or no smoking depends entirely on the, uh, the proprietor of the place. On personal tastes, you know? I mean, I've been in little diners like this . . ."

"This ain't a diner," I said loudly. "This here's an honest-to-God restaurant, arright? The kitchen is second to none."

"Sure," he said, looking away again and lighting up. "It's just that back where I come from there aren't a whole lot of honest-to-God restaurants called Long John's."

"Yeah? And where would that be?"

"What's that?"

"Where are you from?"

He said, "New Jersey."

"Well, in that case, mind your own business."

This was not turning out to be a good day for me.

"Jesus, guy, whatever happened to Southern hospitality?"

"I don't know. It died with the Duke, I guess."

He laughed. "What about you? Where are you from?"

"Nowhere," I said.

"Why's this place called Long John's?"

"Does it matter?"

"No."

"What's *your* story, kid?"

"No story. Just making conversation."

"The guy that opened this place up back in the thirties was named John. Used to be called just John's, but back when this place opened it was the warmest place to be when the cold months set in. Because of the big oven back here. Because of that, he changed the name, like an inside joke. Being in here was like having on an extra pair of thermals. Simple as that."

"That's nice," said the kid. "The outside is very retro. Very nice."

"Yeah," I replied. "It makes my fucking heart melt."

"So with that kind of long-term rep, with this place being reputable, seeing as how it's been here so long, where is everybody?"

"Where else?" I said. "Church."

"That's nice too."

"Yeah, that *really* makes my heart melt."

"Mine too," he said, chuckling.

"Whatever, kid. Listen, what's the story?"

Something about the kid—him being so friendly—rubbed me the wrong way. Like sand in a condom, maybe. Or steel wool.

"What? No story, just . . ."

"You trying to pick me up or something?"

"God, no."

"You ask an awful lot of questions for someone who just wants a coffee and a scrambled egg, or am I just presuming? You here to use the commode?"

"What? No, I'm parched, actually. I'd love a cup of coffee. And an ashtray."

I stood silently for a spell to see if I could hear Abraham in the bathroom, but I heard nothing. I angrily barged through the double doors, reached under the counter, and grabbed an ashtray for the kid from the stack on a low shelf. I slammed it in front of him.

I poured him a cup of coffee and slammed that in front of him too.

He said, "Thanks."

I said, "Thank me by telling me the story."

"What makes you think there's a story?" he replied.

"Are you saying there isn't?"

"No."

"Then let's hear it," I said.

"Why? Why the curiosity?"

"You're the curious one, pal. Asking about one thing, then the other. Besides, everyone's got a story."

"I don't know. It's not that interesting."

"Try me. You'd be surprised what passes for interesting in a small town like this."

"Okay, well . . ."

"You a nancy?"

"What? No, I, I, I . . ." he stuttered. "I'm a photographer."

"What kind? Flowers and shit?"

"Models. As in people. Women, mostly. And I'm kind of driving cross-country, all around and about and so on, and, you know, going from coast to coast. I started in New York, and, uh, I got the idea on a flight a couple years ago. Do you fly often?"

"No."

I had not been on a plane in many years. Last time I was it was with a fake name.

"Well," he continued, "when you fly over this country, you see these huge gaps of land between cities, and hidden in all the nature down there are all these little towns in the middle of nowhere, so I got the idea to go through all this *nature,* all these little roads, and see what's down there. Down *here,* in what they call 'the flyover states.' So that's what I'm doing."

"I have no idea what you just said."

He sighed. "I'm driving to the Pacific Ocean. I'm photographing my road trip. I'm taking pictures. Writing essays. I hope to make a book of it. A coffee table book. Big color prints."

"Is that right."

"Yes it is."

"Well, isn't that nice."

"Yes it is," he said, glowing. "Anthony Mannuzza."

He held out his hand for me to shake.

I gave it a look like it had his love juice on it. "Whatever. This ain't a fucking AA meeting over here."

He put his hand back on the counter.

"Okay, Mr. Happy, what's *your* name?"

"My name's none of your business," I said.

"You from around here?"

I said, "No."

"Here long?"

"Long enough," I said.

He took his cup of coffee and took a seat at one of the tables by the window.

I saw the unmarked police car pull up outside the restaurant through the window. It was a beige Ford that was already a handful of years old, but the way they built those cop engines, they could practically travel through space if you put the right gas in them.

The engine purred itself to sleep, and out the driver's-side door came my old buddy Pearce. Danny Pearce was a cop, a detective, actually, and if you want to know what irony is, he was the closest thing I'd had to a friend since I went off to war. He was a good man, a barrel-chested man with a good heart and a desire to do good deeds.

When I blew into Evelyn one night a few years earlier, I was still hitting the sauce pretty hard. I initially drank because it made it easier to deal with being what I had become, but there came a point when I kind of accepted that part of myself, or at least became very stoic in a Marcus Aurelius kind of way. Still, I drank heavily when the mood struck me, and that mood usually urged me to go into a watering hole and pick a fight with somebody. I had a very wild hair growing in a very itchy place, and, to me, bars were made for two very distinct purposes: for fisticuffs and to pick up broads.

My first night in Evelyn, I had wandered into some dive called the Cowboy's Cabin. I'd seen a million places just like it sprinkled across the world. The jukebox played either Hank Williams or Willie Nelson, and the women were either too young or too old. There was sawdust on the floor, and a pull handle on the crapper in the back. There were the serious drunks minding their own business in the corners, and making all the noise around the bar and the pool tables were the college boys and weekend partiers who wanted to hit somebody almost as much as they wanted to get laid.

I sauntered up to this one particular group of clowns who had claimed one of the pool tables and started staring at them really hard with this big, shit-eating grin on my face. They began to get uncomfortable and whisper among themselves. Finally, one of them summoned up the courage to ask me what in the blue hell I was looking at.

I said, "I've never seen anyone as ugly as you before."

It was on.

In hindsight I guess it wasn't so much a fight as it was a small-scale riot. The ordeal began with me and those three men at the pool table, a trio whom I will refer to as Larry, Curly, and Moe, because that's what they looked like. As they came at me and I knocked them back, the other patrons became embroiled one by one. The fight kept getting bigger and bigger, like a plant (albeit a very violent plant), until the whole place was swinging, even the staff.

Shit was flying all around the place—tables, bottles, and chairs. It might have been the alcohol I'd consumed, but I think I even saw a guy hit another guy with a fake leg. That was a hell of a thing, let me tell you.

By the time the responding officers showed up, the mirror behind the bar had been replaced with an unconscious male, and a small fire was burning in the corner of the room.

One cop came in and was immediately confronted by one of the drunks. The drunk suffered a kick to the sac and crumpled up in a fetal position on the bloody floor. The cop doing the kicking was Danny Pearce. He didn't bat an eye about what he'd done. He just moved on to the next fellow who needed some calming down.

The other cop, Danny's partner, started blinding people with pepper spray the second he walked in. Bodies fell, caught in the pain and the seizure-like grip of freaking out because you think you're never going to be able to see again. Everyone started screaming.

The screaming distracted me, and in that one instant, the guy I was duking it out with picked up a bottle and smashed it over the handsome side of my face. Some would say that's the side of my face that doesn't actually exist, but they would be wrong. I could feel the cold beer sink into my clothes, and the hot rush of salty blood running along the line of my jaw. I went down, merely because I could feel a piece of glass in my eye, and it made me a little weak in the knees. I couldn't see. Pearce ran over to defend me as this fucking guy started dropping kicks into my ribs, with cowboy boots, no less.

Pearce clocked him good, brought him down with one punch.

"You okay?" Pearce shouted over the commotion.

"Good enough," I said.

He helped me to my feet.

With my one good eye, I saw this other guy running up behind Pearce with a pool stick. I hollered something foul, grabbed Pearce by the shoulder, and pushed him out of the way. The stick hit me square on top of the head and broke, but there was no stopping me. I tackled the guy and went crazy on his face with a flurry of short punches.

Pearce pulled me off, but the poor bastard was already sleeping the sleep of the lost and swollen.

Afterward, I didn't want medical treatment. I only wanted them to get the piece of glass out of my eye, but they wouldn't listen.

They put me in the back of the ambulance, and just before it took off, Pearce got in and thanked me for saving his ass back there.

"Don't mention it," I said. "You'd have done the same for me."

"I did," he said. "You should be thanking me too."

"I know, but I won't."

He laughed.

The friendship grew from there.

Considering the magnitude of that fight, he urged me not to go out drinking anymore. Up until that point, I hadn't considered staying any longer than I already had. Before moving into that house on King Street, I had lived in a trailer that I carried around on the back of my truck. There was an army cot back there, and a hot plate. Previous to having come upon that trailer, I had lived in motel rooms and train stations for the better part of a dozen years.

It surprised me that my short reign of mayhem hadn't caused this cop to run me out of town like a dozen other lawmen had done before him. Pearce was a deeply religious man, and I guess it was the inherent kindness that can come from that that allowed him to view me as an actual human being as opposed to a burnt-out vet with an ugly truck. That kind of kindness had never been my experience in all the towns I'd ever been.

I liked Evelyn. I liked the way the wind smelled. It carried on it a dozen different natural perfumes—earth smells. I liked that it was quiet (except for me), and I guess it was because of this kind of camaraderie that had blossomed almost out of nowhere that I promised him I wouldn't raise hell anymore.

What amazed me then was that the promise actually meant something. I stopped going out, and before long, I stopped drinking altogether. I wouldn't have done that if I hadn't earned that man's camaraderie.

Once I cleaned myself up, he vouched for me and helped me get my job at Long John's. It wasn't just that I was a good cook—no one makes a burger the way I do—it's just that without his personal okay, Frank wouldn't have hired a bum like me.

I hadn't had a real job since high school, but when I was taken on at Long John's I had to use my true name. It had been a very long time since I had last used it, but since I had flown under the radar for so many years with many an alias, my record was virtually spotless. That's why the people in town knew who I actually was.

I'm sure my gleaming record surprised Pearce. To look at me, you'd have to presume there was a slew of felonies behind me, but on paper, there wasn't. Pearce knew I wasn't a stranger to the wrong side of the tracks, but I seemed to be reformed. That, coupled with my inherited urge to read every single newspaper I could get my hands on, eventually made him feel comfortable talking over his cases with me, figuring I'd have some genius insight into the minds of criminals. For him, he got a hooligan's perspective on crime and an excuse to check up on me every so often. For me, I got information I would not have otherwise had, and any cases it seemed the Evelyn PD couldn't solve became my problem—though neither he nor anyone else would ever know that.

Danny Pearce slammed the door to the cop car. He was wearing a pair of jeans, a button-down shirt, and a sports jacket. His shield hung on his belt. He was clean-shaven, but his blond hair was getting longer than you would think would be appropriate for a guy with his kind of job. But he had a kid on the way, and I guess his hair was the last thing on his mind.

He hopped up the stairs outside and entered the restaurant. The bell jangled. I could make out the silhouette of another human being back in the unmarked car. It was his partner, Clancy Van Buren. Van Buren and I didn't get along. I guess you could say he hated my guts for some reason.

Danny was smiling, exposing a perfect row of glowing white teeth. He was excited about something, I didn't know what. We exchanged nods as he came up to the counter and took a seat. I poured Pearce a cup of coffee, put the mandatory two packets of Equal in there, and set it in front of him.

"Mr. Trouble," he said softly.

"How are you this lovely morning?" I asked.

"Why did he call you Mr. Trouble?" Anthony asked from across the room.

"Shut up," I said.

"I got news," Danny said, then shot a curious glance at the kid.

"He's a photographer," I said. "I thought he was a fruit too, but he takes pictures instead."

Pearce snorted. The kid turned red in the cheeks.

"Yeah," I continued, "I think he said his name was Ansel Adams."

"Anthony," he said to Pearce's back as he lit another cigarette. "The name's Anthony."

Pearce grimaced at the sound of the match being struck, fished around in his jacket pocket, and came up with a piece of nicotine gum. He tore at the wrapping with a knife he picked up off the counter and popped the tan-colored lump into his mouth. He chewed on the gum like it was a tough piece of steak, or a rubber band wrapped tight around a human testicle.

"How's that going?" I asked, pointing at his mouth.

"Jesus Christ, Marley, I'm dying over here," said Pearce as he banged his fist on the counter three times.

"It's for the best, man. You got a kid now."

"I know, but Jesus," said Pearce, and he shot the kid another look.

I shot the kid a look too, and to this he put out the cigarette and put the pack back in his pocket.

Pearce said, "Thanks. Sorry about that."

"Don't be," said the kid, going back to work on the hangnail.

"So what's the word? You look wound up, Danny."

"We found Bill Parker," he said. "At least what was left of him. Out in the woods."

"What does that mean? Like, he was all chopped up, or animals got to him?"

"I don't know," said Pearce. "I mean, yeah, the animals had to have gotten to him. He's been missing for two fucking weeks. Of course they got to him. But this is all . . . very interesting."

"What's interesting?" I asked. "I mean, obviously the circumstances of his disappearance were very peculiar, you know, considering the abandoned car out on Old Sherman and all . . ."

"See, that's the thing right there," Pearce said. "'Abandoned' ain't a good word. That car was full of blood, Marley, and not just one kind. Our lab guy can't figure out where the blood came from, though he thinks it might be from a dog. But the lab has no clue, and we don't have the kind of resources to send a sample out . . ."

"That's strange."

"Very," Pearce said, flashing those teeth.

He'd gotten them cleaned when he stopped smoking.

"Maybe it was a yeti," I said.

"Don't joke about that," Pearce said. "And not only that, we got shell casings. Shots fired. We got blood in the car, on the car, and out on the road. We got a trail of blood going into the woods, but for weeks we've had guys scouring those woods, and they didn't find anything."

"Was Bill in the same vicinity as the gun you found last week?"

"No. I mean, who knows, man? The thing with bodies in nature is . . ." Pearce stopped and looked at the kid, then asked, "You got a sensitive stomach at all?"

"Me? No, no, no . . ." Anthony stuttered. "Please, continue."

Anthony got up and came back to the counter.

"Okay," said Pearce, "the thing with bodies in nature is that as a body gets ripped apart, gets lighter, the parts get scattered. Some animals will carry body parts to where they're comfortable eating, and because of that it gets hard to figure out where a person actually, well, dropped down. A good dog could help with that, or . . ."

Pearce trailed off, thinking. No one said anything. After maybe a full minute, he continued.

"These two kids found his skull out there in the woods. They had gone out to mess around without their parents finding out. What luck, huh?"

"I guess it killed the mood," I said. "But that's all they found? Just a skull?"

"Yup. Well, a couple hairs. That's how we know it's Bill. We got claw marks, maybe bite marks, all over the fucking thing. They don't look like any kind of marks I've ever seen. . . ."

"You know, Danny, I don't know if you're looking at a murder here," I said.

"I know, but this ain't right."

"Could have been a bear for all we know."

"I know, but . . . *shit*."

"Let me get this straight," said the kid, interjecting himself, "and stop me if I'm wrong about anything. From what it sounds like, some guy got in a shoot-out with a wild animal, got dragged into the woods and chewed up. Is that right?"

"No," said Pearce.

"What's *wrong* with the story?" I asked.

"C'mon," said Pearce, "it's not like King Kong lives in a little house in the woods. There's no such thing as a shoot-out with an animal."

"I don't know. It sounds good to me," I said.

"Aside from the shoot-out part," said Anthony.

Pearce said, "I know it sounds good, but . . ."

"But what?" asked Anthony.

"There was only one trail of blood going into those woods. Whatever happened out by that car . . . I don't know. It almost feels like what happened at the car was a separate incident. If Parker encountered some kind of animal on the road, where was the body? Why did Parker go in the woods if he was injured? Why wouldn't he go to a house? Why did he take the gun with him?"

Evelyn wasn't a place known for its high mortality rate. Hell, it wasn't known for anything, but Pearce, being the fresh detective that he was, wasn't exactly Columbo when it came to crime-solving.

"You don't know he took it with him," I said.

"True, and with that, it makes this whole thing even a little more fucked up."

"It could have been wolves," I said.

"Wolves," repeated Pearce.

"Wolves," shouted Anthony. "I'm going cross-country, and I step into the fucking animal kingdom over here. What kind of town is this?"

No one said anything.

"I guess this passes for interesting in a small town, right?" he asked me. "I swear, I was planning on passing through here by the end of the day, but seeing how things go around here, I think I'll stick around awhile. See how this plays out."

"What're you? Fucking Angela Lansbury?" said Pearce.

"Priceless," said Anthony. "This is going in the book, I swear. You guys have got to let me take your pictures."

Anthony went back to his table and picked up his camera.

"Don't," I said. "You're not taking pictures of anybody."

"Yes I am," he said. "Don't you want to be famous?"

"What's the story with this guy?" asked Pearce.

"He's making a coffee table book about his fucking road trip."

"What is he, Kerouac? I don't want my fucking picture taken."

"Maybe you should arrest him."

"For what? Being a pain in the ass?"

"He's from Jersey. That alone's a good excuse."

"I can't do that."

"He tried to put his finger in my ass before you got here. How about that?"

"I'd arrest him for that if it were anyone but you." Then: "You know what this reminds me of? The Bill Parker thing? Remember when that guy disappeared a couple years ago? Carter? It was the same thing with him. Found a piece of him in the park after he'd been gone a month. Same damn thing as this."

"We *are* in the middle of nowhere, Danny. This doesn't have to be a mystery. Shit like this happens more often than you think."

"Do your twenty newspapers a day tell you that?"

"Please," interrupted the kid. "Look at the camera. I'm gonna start snapping with or without your permission, guys."

Pearce and I looked at each other, smiled, and then we both flipped the bird at the camera. The flash went off three times in rapid succession.

"Speaks volumes," said the kid. "I swear, this place is amazing. I'm here for an hour and I'm already caught up in a horror story."

I looked at Pearce.

Bill Parker's ghost haunted the corners of his brain, crying out for answers. Pearce chewed his nicotine gum, thought of his baby, his town, and what—or who—had devoured our upstanding townsman, Bill Parker.

"You have no idea," I said.

THREE

It happened overseas. The fact is that Marlowe Higgins died in 'Nam. He never made it. On that night when the beast entered me, when I *became*, the Marlowe Higgins that had dreams of making it back Stateside, the Marlowe Higgins that loved baseball and motorcycles and had a girl named Doris waiting back home for him, ceased to exist. In his place was a shell, a husk, a host for the ungodly thing that had invaded him. Indeed, one can't truly have a life when what lurks on the inside feasts on death.

I found that out the hard way.

Once I realized what I had become, I started drifting, going from place to place, town to town. I was a stranger on every street and in every city, and that's the way I wanted it. The name I was born with was a worthless thing to me, and wherever I went I left a trail of blood and grated bones in my wake.

I was never able to go fast enough to escape the horror in my head, the truth of what I carried soul-deep. I alone was hell on earth, and knowing that I was responsible for the gruesome murders of so many innocent people was often too much for me to bear. Even in combat I'd never had the nerve or the desire to kill another human being. It disgusted me that the monster forced me to do what I'd thought I would never be capable of. What made it worse were the dreams I told you about. I started drinking out of necessity, and in my weakest moments, when the liquor wore off long enough for me to find the keys, I'd get on my motorcycle and see just how fast I could go.

I woke up in hospitals a lot those first few cursed years on the road. They chalked up my suicidal tendencies to combat shock, or whatever the hell the term was they were using at the time, but they never took it too seriously because I never got hurt that bad. I was lucky, they said. What it really was, and this bothered me immensely, was that it had just become harder for me to die.

My "accidents" on the black-veined roads of America began to get a little more elaborate. One time I hot-wired a semi and drove it through a gas station in Cheyenne, Wyoming. I woke up burned like a motherfucker, handcuffed to a hospital bed. I was so burned up there was no way they could identify me. When the next full moon came, the handcuffs didn't mean much to the beast, and it got us out of there, but not before butchering a handful of nurses and an eye specialist.

I woke up the next day in the cellar of a local antique shop, naked, as usual, and the burns that had covered a healthy portion of my body were gone. I woke up in immaculate physical condition, just like I always do the day after. I haven't gotten so much as a cold in the last twenty years.

The blood on my hands made me a monster by proxy, an accomplice to the supernatural genocide machine that had affixed itself to my being. I couldn't take it, so once I found my way out of Wyoming, I got myself a rifle. A Remington. With a little bit of liquid courage I strolled up to a pawn shop and threw a garbage can through the window. I made off with the first weapon I saw. I figured a nice, concentrated attack on my skull would be the ample dose to keep me down for good, and in doing that, I'd be putting the beast down too.

I drove this pretty '63 Monterey I'd wired out into the wilderness and found a spot on a hill that overlooked a stream. I was surrounded by trees, the pink-orange rays of the day's dying sun. Brown leaves hugged the ground like a blanket, holding in its moisture so it could turn to ice in the coming frozen months, and the clear, chill water in the stream sent cool air up over the hill that passed through me like a prayer.

As night came on I loaded my rifle. I pressed the butt of it into the grass and rested my chin at the business end. I took a few deep breaths, then a few more, and just as the cold of night set in, I cursed myself for not having the stones to do what needed to be done.

I drove off to the next town.

That was the first time I ever put a gun to my head, but it wasn't the last.

And so it went like that—going from town to town, stealing, working odd jobs, sleeping in dives or hot cars, drinking and fighting, trying to forget, being responsible for the slaughter of yet another poor soul because I was too yellow to take myself out, waking up, then doing it all over again.

It took the unfortunate death of my mother at the hands of a junkie in 1981 to change my life, and with it, the very nature of the beast itself.

I called her every so often from wherever I was. I guess she was the only person who really understood the fate that had befallen me, and she knew why I could never go back home. Sometimes I'd call and hang up. Other times I'd be crying by the time she picked up. Sometimes when I was crying, she'd hang up because she just couldn't take it. Sometimes I'd call her with a fierce drunk on, and I'd scream.

One morning I called and a cop answered the phone. He asked who I was, and when I stated that I was the son of the woman whose house he was in, he told me she'd been attacked. He didn't tell me she was dead, not over the phone. I thought there was still a chance for me to see her. I drove at a hundred miles an hour and got there by nightfall. That's when they broke the news to me.

She had been coming home from work. She put the key in the front door, and the scumbag, or "the perpetrator," as they called him, pushed himself in behind her, knocked her down. What it was supposed to have been was a simple robbery. A street thug intimidating an old lady bad enough that she'd give up where the cash was in the house and that would be the end of it. But things didn't go down that way. He either thought she was lying when she said that was all there was, or maybe he just felt like doing what he did. Maybe he saw it as a perfect opportunity to say "fuck you" to the world. I didn't know, and I still don't. In the end, it doesn't matter. What he did to her claimed her life before her heart stopped beating anyway.

They had his fingerprints, some stains left behind, as if he were a dog marking his territory. But that was all. He was just another faceless criminal. Another tragic tale of America's youth gone awry.

I wanted to take the world itself and throttle it like a baby. I was sick with anger. Not even in combat had I ever felt a feeling akin to the pure, unadulterated fury that coursed through me in the weeks following her death. I harbored the hope that the next time the beast came out, he'd wipe out the whole fucking city in one fell swoop, mark it on the maps as a red zone the way they would with Chernobyl a few years later.

On the night of the full moon, I was in the car I had at the time, parked on a dark road. I was naked. Clothes would get destroyed in the change—the beast maintained a human shape, but was so much bigger than I was—and I didn't like to waste them. Outfits cost money, and I was consistently in the position of barely being able to feed myself, much less buy anything.

For the first time in my life I welcomed the beast. I looked forward to the lashing out that was about to happen. As night fell, the pain in my body grew stronger and stronger, just like it always did, but it didn't bother me, not that night. It was just more fuel for the fire.

When the beast took over, I had no idea what was happening. I had no control over it, and I did not live the experience as it happened. I remembered what the beast did after a few days, or a week, or even longer, but I was just happy with (or at least resigned to) the fact that someone was going to get it bad. Someone certainly deserved it. Someone, perhaps, who had done something as bad as I had done.

When I woke up the next day, I was still in my car. Usually, I woke up in an unfamiliar place, so this was an oddity. I knew the beast had gone to work because the inside of the car was filthy, and I was covered in dried blood. I dressed in the clothes I had in the backseat, and then drove to the motel I was staying at.

The phone rang a couple of days later. I picked it up, and it was the police. They said they had to have some words with me. I figured they found out I was driving around in a stolen car. I didn't care. I drove over anyway.

They sat me down and explained to me that a man, a boy, really, had been "attacked" by what must have been rabid dogs in the park. When they said that, my hairs stood up.

The detective said, "These dogs, whatever they were, they tore this boy to shreds. There isn't a whole lot left, but his head and his hands were found intact. Some of the officers at the scene recognized the victim as a known burglar. For the hell of it, we checked his prints, and they matched the prints lifted from your mother's residence."

I said, "Well, knock me down."

I couldn't understand why the beast—which without fail had always struck as ruthlessly and randomly as a tornado—singled out the one motherfucker I wanted dead more than anybody else in the world. The more I thought about it, though, I realized what did it, and that was the desire. The want. The absolute and utter need that I felt in my heart and soul to make this filthy little devil pay. That was the spark.

Whereas every other time the full moon had rolled around I prayed for the beast not to hurt anybody, this was the one time I had called upon it with my prayers. This was the one time that I gave it a mission. A purpose. A target. With that, the beast had a goal, and with that, the quality of my life, as doomed as it was, got a whole hell of a lot better.

How it was able to fulfill its end of this operation became apparent rather quickly. Whatever it was—some ferocious demon or wrathful demigod—it had the physical properties and abilities of an animal. It worked on scent, on taste, on sound. The piece of shit that killed my mother left a scent. On that night when the beast struck back, it found his scent. From there, it was a simple matter of catching the boy on the wind.

My life is a black streak on a calendar, a sentence that has no end in sight. I go to bed every night knowing that when the reaper finally *does* point his rusty sickle at me, I'm going to spend the rest of time melting in my sins, but ever since that bloody night in my hometown, I have at least been able to live with myself. I wouldn't call it apathy, and I wouldn't call it peace, but at least I can sleep at night.

As for the dearly departed Bill Parker, he did something he shouldn't have done. On one of his late-night drives, he sideswiped an old lady who came out in the road in pursuit of her cat Sprinkles. Bill was speeding, as he was prone to do, and didn't notice her in time. If she had been in her prime, she probably would have survived, but the trauma was too much for her little body. She left behind two daughters and three grandchildren. It was a goddamn shame what happened.

The police had no suspects. The article in the paper urged the driver to come forward. Bill Parker never did, so the wolf and I went to work. I may be a monster, but as long as I'm the only one in town, I can live with that.

FOUR

As Pearce went to work on his second cup of coffee, Van Buren stepped out of the unmarked police car and climbed the stairs. Through the glass, he looked like a vampire in his dark suit and pale skin. He rapped on the glass door with his ringed finger, beckoned Pearce out with a wave, then turned silently.

"Guess I better head out," Pearce said.

"How's Mr. Happy?"

"I don't know why you two don't get along."

"Don't worry about it. Tell him I said hi."

"I won't," Pearce said, and he walked out without paying. He was good at that. By my calculations he owed the restaurant somewhere in the neighborhood of half a million dollars.

"He doesn't seem like a cop," said Anthony after the man left.

"I know," I said. "That's how I put up with him."

Anthony laughed and threw down a ten-dollar bill.

He said, "I'm off. You have a very nice restaurant here. And a lovely town."

"Whatever," I said. "Take a picture."

"I plan to. See you around."

He walked out. The bell jangled. When he got to the car, he took off his jacket and tossed it onto the passenger seat. He pulled out, heading west on Main. A minute later, Abe came out of the bathroom, seemingly as refreshed as he'd ever been.

"Perfect timing, you scoundrel. I had to deal with that prick the whole time he was here. I'm keeping this tip all to myself," I said, waving the ten.

"Fine," said Abraham. "I was waiting for that damn kid to get out of here."

"You were up the whole time?"

"No. Not the whole time. Just . . . some of it." He smiled.

"Cold motherfucker," I said.

After the church crowd filtered in for lunch and ice cream, I sat down in the kitchen and went to work on this story about the missing girl.

Her name was Judith Myers. She was seventeen years old, blond, blue-eyed, and pretty as all sin. I knew that by the picture above the caption that read, "If you have seen this person . . ."

She was last seen the previous night. She left her home around seven to go to her girlfriend's house. The girlfriend stated that Judith left to go back home sometime in the neighborhood of nine-fifteen. The walk between their houses was five blocks of beautiful, upscale suburban houses. No suspicious characters were seen by anyone living in between the two residences, and no other suspicious activity was recorded that night, save the fruitless intrusion at the church. The two incidents seemed entirely unrelated.

Yes, I thought, *this could definitely be something.*

When Mandy and Carlos showed up in the afternoon to take the place over, Abraham and I skipped out. Mandy was twice divorced, like Abraham, but with a girl from each marriage, and it was by that deep and blazing fire that rages in every woman that she was able to raise a family on her own with such a meager income.

Carlos was a Mexican in his early twenties. His arms were emblazoned with tattoos, none of which, he said, meant a damn thing. Most he'd done himself with a hot needle and the ink from a ballpoint pen. If you looked closely, you could see the rows of carefully placed blue-black dots that formed these rich tapestries of fire, dragons, and wizards. He and I were talking once and he told me that he had killed a guy. I asked him why, and he said the guy had messed with his little sister. He didn't say how, but he didn't have to. He didn't want to go to jail, so he ran, and Evelyn was where he ended up.

Ever since that day, I liked him. He was also a very good cook.

Abraham climbed into his Buick and turned on the radio. Marvin Gaye was playing, as he was apt to do in Abraham's car.

"Are you going to go home and take it easy tonight?" I asked.

"I can't," Abe said. "I'm supposed to meet some of my people for dinner tonight."

"But it's Sunday, man. Don't you give it a rest?"

"I don't got time for rest. I'm a firm believer in spreading my seed, man."

"You're gonna end up in a fuckin' wheelchair," I said.

"Only if I do it right."

"How do you do it?" I asked. I couldn't imagine living the way he did at his age if I had to deal with the consequences.

"I do it like I do it," he said. "The key is not to save anything for tomorrow. Tomorrow may never come, Marley. Every night may be your last, know what I mean?"

"Yeah, I hear you," I said. "I'll see you tomorrow, brother."

I got in my beat-up, piece-of-shit truck and went grocery shopping.

I drove over to the big Elroy's supermarket down on Grove Street. I quickly loaded up the cart with the essentials—coffee, hot dogs, tuna, and milk. I kept my diet very basic because it was cheap to do so.

I found myself in the bread aisle with the purpose of buying some hot-dog buns, but before I even knew what was going on, I saw that my hand had grabbed a loaf of rye bread off the shelf and was about to drop it in my shopping cart. It wasn't me loading up on rye bread; it was one of the dead ones.

I broke the spell that my hand was under and dropped the loaf of bread on the floor. As I bent down to pick it up I noticed that there was a little Asian girl with her mother a little farther down the aisle. The little girl was looking at me like I was crazy. There was some fucked-up part of my mind that immediately thought that she and her mother were VC. It scared the shit out of me, so I turned the cart around without getting any bread at all and flew down the next aisle.

I soon found myself in the produce section, and it was there that I saw Alice. She was wearing a pair of blue jeans and some beat-up sneakers. A thin, formfitting sweater showed off her natural curves, and her silky blond hair was hidden under a baseball cap. There were earplugs in her ears, attached to a Walkman on her belt. I wondered what she was listening to.

She had a cart full of fruits and vegetables. Near the bottom was a container of orange juice and a steak, or maybe a piece of fish, I couldn't tell. I was always curious about what she ate at home. I wondered if she was good in the kitchen.

I wanted to come up behind her and put my arms around her. I wanted to say, "Guess who," and upon hearing my voice, I wanted her to smile. I wanted her to like it. I wanted her to be happy running into me in the supermarket of all places, and then maybe we could go cook something together, some family recipe that only she knew. But that's not the way it was. It wasn't the time, and it certainly wasn't the place.

I knew she wouldn't appreciate my going up to her, maybe even if it was just to say hello, so I got on line without having picked something out for dinner, paid, and went out to the parking lot.

I saw her Honda, almost as certainly as she would've noticed my truck. I thought about putting a note under the windshield wiper, but decided against it. It wouldn't be right. That's what she'd say. And I would rather have lived with the fantasy than the reality of hearing her upset, or . . . I don't know. Embarrassed. So I got in the truck and went home.

It had been a long time coming at that point, but as I drove, I felt so low that I thought about drinking. I felt very low indeed.

·   ·   ·

That night I called Pearce.

I sat down in my living room, which was still furnished with all of the dead lady's stuff. I took a seat in the dead lady's recliner, which was crinkled and cracked with age. Still, it was comfortable enough to fall asleep in, even if it smelled like a hundred mating cats.

I finished with my cigarette, that way he wouldn't have to hear me smoking on the phone, and put it out in my naked-lady ashtray, which was in the shape of a swimming pool and had a topless broad sprawled out at the rim. Only a sick man would put a cigarette out on the actual porcelain girl.

Anyway, his wife picked up the phone and said, "Pearce residence."

"Hey, Martha, what's shaking?" I said kindly.

Martha was seven months' pregnant and wasn't a big fan of mine. She didn't like it that her upstanding citizen of a husband associated with a wretch like me.

"I'll get Danny," she said, and she slammed the phone down hard enough to make it sound like a gunshot. A second later, he got on the line.

"Pearce."

"Danny, how are you?"

"Christ," he said, "I'm freaking out, Marley. I need a cigarette."

"No you don't. You can't be smokin' around the, uh, embryo and all that, you know what I mean?"

"It's not an embryo, Marley. *She* is a fucking *baby*."

"Sorry."

"Is this why you called? To torture me?"

"I just wanted to say hi."

"Hi."

"There's a girl that disappeared in Edenburgh the other night."

"Do you want to confess?"

"It was in the papers today. Did you hear about it?"

"No. You got a funny feeling about it?"

"Yeah."

"Your funny feelings scare me, Marley."

"On that note, I was also thinking about the Bill Parker thing. How are you feeling about the Bill Parker thing?"

"How am I feeling about the Bill Parker thing? I don't know how I'm feeling about the Bill Parker thing. It pisses me off that things have to be so damn complicated sometimes."

"I know. It makes your head hurt, doesn't it?"

"Maybe yours, but not mine."

"Well, I was just thinking that you shouldn't be making a mountain out of a molehill. I mean, let's say he hit a coyote, or a bear, or some fucking thing, and he shot it. Let's say he was in shock and unknowingly wandered into the woods where he died. Maybe he was eaten, I don't know. But that sounds good, doesn't it?"

"Yeah, Marley. It sounds like Beethoven."

"I'm serious."

"I know what you're saying. I'm not worried about it. We'll see what the lab comes up with, if anything. If we were in a big city we'd have the money to play with all kinds of equipment, but we got jack. Regardless, there was no damage to the front of the car. He didn't hit a damn thing that night."

"I hear you," I said. Then: "I was also thinking about something else."

"And what would that be?"

"You remember that old lady that got run over a little while back?"

"Yeah," Pearce said hesitantly.

"Well, I remember you telling me she was hit by a white car. You could tell because of the paint chips on her . . . whatever you call it. A muumuu . . ."

"Housedress, Marley. Normal people call it a housedress."

"Bill Parker had a white car. Since you have his car, you ought to test it, you know what I mean?"

"Yeah, Marley, I'll do that first thing in the morning."

"C'mon, man . . ."

"This isn't some sprawling metropolis we're living in here. We don't have the money to have every little thing tested and analyzed because we feel like it. Listen, I gotta go. I'll see you at the diner."

"It's not a . . ."

He had already hung up.

I put the phone back in its cradle and lit another cigarette now that I was off the phone. I had at least tried to tie the old lady's death to the man who had killed her, but I wasn't about to ruffle any feathers about it.

I did have a funny feeling about the missing girl over in Edenburgh, and it wasn't just because I hadn't come up with a target for the wolf to go after the next time the full moon came around. I still had time.

I cut the article about her out of the paper and taped it up on the wall in my bedroom. Doing this with certain articles was not unusual. It didn't bother me, because I knew no one would ever see it. I never invited anyone into the house, and anyone who tried to gain entry would be met with certain resistance.

FIVE

I went over to Mama Snow's place on Carpenter

Street the following night. Ever since I had run into Alice at the supermarket the previous day, I couldn't get her out of my head. While she would have said it was inappropriate to approach her at the store, seeing her at Mama Snow's was always fine. It was where she worked.

She was a prostitute. And she meant a lot to me.

I was not a man who had ever frequented prostitutes, that is, until I met Alice. A lot of men enjoyed the company of prostitutes back in Vietnam, but I didn't. In a way, I was too scared to, but more than that was the fact that I couldn't possibly betray Doris. Doris was my great love, my soul mate, and she was back Stateside waiting for me to come home in one piece so we could live the rest of our lives together. I didn't want to pick up the clap and bring that back to Doris as some kind of fucked-up gift.

The men in my company used to make fun of me for remaining celibate while we were in Vietnam, but joking around too much meant you weren't paying attention, and if you weren't paying attention, you died, just like that cat Krueger did.

It was my introduction to bloodshed, two weeks into my tour. This was in 1971. We were going north along this lightly worn path, and the tall trees were forming a double canopy. This blocked a lot of sunlight from hitting the path, but it also obscured the vision of our lieutenant colonel, who was monitoring us from the C&C ship. Slimy water was dripping from the leaves onto all of us, and this foreign liquid coating just made things worse—it was like it did the job of trapping all the heat in our bodies, like it wasn't hot enough in that fucking country without getting rained on during a hot, cloudless day. Sometimes the humidity was all you could think about.

Some guys were strung-out. I came to understand that the number of addicted soldiers had grown exponentially since the late sixties. I couldn't blame them—they called that place "the green hell" for a reason. Some guys were doing the dozens and talking shit in hushed tones, snickering about whores and children and knives, about blowing up livestock for no good reason, about getting action from each other's mothers. Some guys were making fun of me for being what they called a "boy scout."

Some guys—just a few—wore armbands and spoke out against what we were doing over there every step of the way. It was commonplace. More so than you would ever read about in the history books. But not a lot of guys were happy to be there, that much is fact, and there was only so much the sergeant could say about this thing with the armbands, and the "passive resistance" that some guys would offer up when they were asked to do something just a little bit above and beyond walking, and hell, there was maybe only so much he would've wanted to say as well.

We all kind of knew that if the shit hit the fan we'd protect each other, we'd be there. Just because some guys didn't go along with things as much as other guys did didn't mean they harbored hopes of seeing their brothers die. That's what the fear of war did for most of us—it forged a bond between some of the men that can only be described as brotherhood.

Some guys were too wide-eyed and scared to join in on the verbal jab-fights, like me. What I was doing was watching the guys who didn't say shit, the ones who just kept their eyes open and walked methodically, as if they'd dreamed about walking through that green nightmare all their lives, preparing for it, and they wanted to do it right. I figured if I kept my eyes on them, I'd have a warning a split second before danger reared its ugly head in the form of a half-buried claymore, a poorly disguised tripwire, a trapdoor. These careful men would at least see it coming, not like the lunatics who couldn't shut up.

Krueger was one of those lunatics.

Krueger seemed like the kind of guy who was born for combat, the kind of guy who was no doubt a bully from his first day of school on, and now that he was older and had an M16 (and an AK-47 strapped to his shoulder, taken from the burnt, dead hands of an NLF guerrilla), he had a whole nation of mostly un-armed people to fuck with. He was buff, and he shaved his head more often than his face. He had a big, white circle painted on the front of his helmet, and in the middle of that white circle was a red dot about the size of a quarter. He put that red dot there by rubbing in the blood of a farmer he'd killed just days before I met him. It was like he was asking for it.

Before long, that red spot turned brown, but the discoloration, the spot of human rust that decorated his head, just served to an-nounce more clearly what it was, and what kind of man he was.

A scar decorated the left side of his neck, but it wasn't from a firefight. The story he told was that a shoe-shine boy had set off a bomb in a nightclub one night during his first tour and killed a bunch of people. He was the only one to walk away, his only in-jury being a scrape from a piece of flying shrapnel that just missed his carotid artery.

"That's the closest this goddamn yellow country ever got to me, and that's only cuz I was drunk and getting handwork under my table."

The whore had died, he said, her last act on this earth being the performance of a handjob on this lunatic Krueger. If you got him in the mood, he'd talk about the quality of it—the handjob—and how when he realized what had happened, that half his mates were dead and the little girl next to him was dead, he'd tried to loosen her grip on him but couldn't.

He'd say, "I couldn't get her to let go, but it didn't bother me none. It was like even in death, she couldn't get enough of me. To this day, her ghost goes crazy down there. And that, comrades, is why I'm always in such a pleasant goddamn mood," and he'd laugh that crazy laugh of his.

Krueger was always on point. He had good ears, so if he heard someone talking smack behind his back, he'd turn around and give everyone shit.

I was a few heads back behind the crazy bastard, sandwiched between two of the quiet guys. One of them was our sergeant— Hooper was his name—and I just kept one eye on the sergeant and one on my feet.

Hooper was always deadpan. He never smiled, and even when the sun was at its most devastating, he'd never wrinkle his brow. He'd just squint like he was John Wayne. His movements were slow, deliberate, and his orders were quick and precise. He was able to tell who you were by the sound of your footsteps. I trusted him with my life.

I saw him flinch, like a cat hearing some noise you didn't even know had happened, and I froze. Up ahead, a Bouncing Betty went off. Krueger's upper half somersaulted through the air and came to rest in the mud. His legs and some of his torso all stayed attached, and it all got blown back a couple of feet. When that huge part of him came down it was feet-first, as if he had jumped backward, but then it crumpled down lifelessly, shattering any of the illusions we might have had that it was still possessed of spirit. We were covered in red like someone had set off a paint bomb. Two other men had been peppered with shrapnel—screws, bolts, bits of aluminum cans—and were groaning in the dirt.

Four men got mad and started firing into the green. The sergeant ordered a stop to that. Some guys didn't do shit, just looked. Some guys cried. The sergeant walked up to a tree, crouched, and peered out into the jungle like he was a hawk. If anyone was out there, he would've seen them. He didn't say a word.

I watched the sergeant and I cried. And I thought of Doris.

She and I were the big item in high school. I remember I would fidget to a higher and higher degree until three o'clock, when I finally got to see her. Doris and I always met out front of the school, and it was the same every day, the explosion of an almost spiritual happiness when her warm face would press up to mine, and we kissed. In my old age, I can see that the wait for her, that daily anticipation for the quitting bell, was almost as pleasurable as finally holding her, because it was the expectation of seeing her that always made for such a glorious payoff. We were going to get married when I came back.

But that's not a story I talk about.

The place on Carpenter Street was a three-story home—very well kept—and every room therein was a little bit different from the other. Some were soft rooms that had nice walls, pretty paintings, and silk sheets. Fluffy pillows. They were made to look like you could live there.

Some rooms were hard.

The hard rooms were painted black, or red, and had chains up on the walls and closets full of gadgets like handcuffs and whips, and God knows what. Vibrators, and all that crazy shit they use in the dirty movies. One room had a birthing table, with the things for someone's legs and everything. Stirrups. I didn't like that stuff. I didn't like any of it. Neither did Alice. That's why she had no scars to speak of.

Alice was twenty-eight. At least that's what she'd told me, and I had no reason to doubt her. She was a natural blonde, maybe a little shorter than the average woman, and she had a simple, petite body. She never had any plastic surgery done on her, but none of the girls there at Mama Snow's had work done on them either, I think, because Evelyn wasn't that kind of town, and Alice was a native.

I'd been seeing her for three years. Usually it was the day after I got paid, but that wasn't a hard-and-fast rule.

I liked her, and I like to think I got to grow on her too, not that I ever hoped anything would come of it, or that I had any fantasies of saving her from "the life." It was nothing like that. More than anything, I think we just got used to each other. I liked her body and her personality. I liked it that we talked, now that we knew each other, and I liked it that once we got to grow on each other, she was comfortable enough with me to let her guard down and fall asleep on me afterward. It got so whenever I went to Carpenter Street, I paid for the night, not the hour.

What I was paying for was the time with Alice when she slept, not the sex, because that was . . . I'm not smart enough to know a good word for it, but the sex wasn't the object of my desire. What was important to me was being in a soft, good-smelling bed with a beautiful woman who smelled good. What I paid for was the time when I felt like a normal man. An ordinary man who had a girl. I paid for the illusion, because the fact is that after Doris, I had no heart for another woman.

Once Alice picked up my routine, that I was there to see her approximately every six to ten days, she knew what to expect from me. She knew she wasn't going to get hurt, and she knew *it* wasn't going to hurt. She knew my rhythms. She knew she had a freedom with me she didn't have with strangers. She knew me as much as anyone could.

Sometimes I saw her at the gas station or something like that. If there was eye contact, she would smile and wave. I'd ask her how everything was going. I got warm on the inside when she actually told me about her real life, the one far away from Carpenter Street. I would tell her what was up with me, not that anything ever was, and I would ask her if she felt like getting a coffee with me, or a milkshake, because at this point I had stopped drinking, and my understanding was that she was a diehard nondrinker because of her mother. Alice would point out the line in the sand and say no. She always did. Not in a hard way, but in a way that made it sound like it just wouldn't be appropriate. She had compartmentalized me.

I had my reasons for never having a girl in my life, and somewhere deep down and private, I guess she had her reasons for never having a man. Regardless, I always walked away sad.

Mama Snow was concerned that she had a stalker on her hands

when I kept coming by and asking for Alice. There were typically four but never more than five girls working in the house on any given night, and I only ever asked for the one. The business was small but lucrative because the location was secure and the girls were clean. Mama Snow was a Haitian woman, probably in her fifties, though it was hard to tell. She was a big woman, but she had the kind of body that a boxer gets once he lets himself go. Soft, but no less dangerous.

Relics and artifacts of a quasi-religious nature decorated the front room of the house. Homemade candles with leaves and twigs buried in the wax burned twenty-four hours a day.

At first, Mama Snow came off like some voodoo queen and tried to give me a warning with her one good eye. Normal men would've been bothered by it, I'm sure, but I didn't give a shit. I couldn't be any more cursed than I already was, and there was only so much her goon—Leon—could've done to me on any given day, him being the weird creature of the night that he was. Sure, he was bigger than me, and tougher, but I was harder to take out than a goddamn cockroach, and I had a right hook that could knock walls down.

When Mama Snow warned me about asking for Alice, all I did was give her a look. Maybe in some crazy, voodoo way, she saw what was inside me, and from that day on, she was more than ac-commodating whenever I made an appearance.

I parked my truck down the block, walked up to the front door, and rang the bell. It sounded inside the house. After a full minute's wait, the heavy, wood door opened, and the monster known as Leon blocked my path. Leon was from the Philippines. He had the build of a sumo wrestler, and his head was shaved bald. He sported a Fu Manchu mustache. His hands were so big he could've choked the life from a bull if he was pissed-off enough. He was wearing a black suit that would have been a tent on any other man.

"Leon," I said, by way of hello.

He squinted.

"Alice around?"

He nodded.

"Nice talking to you," I said. Then, as a joke: "I'll see you at the beach."

He grunted.

I stepped into the parlor, which looked like a legitimate parlor with wood furniture, pretty prints on the walls, and the forever-burning candles. I went up the stairs and down the hall. I opened the third door I passed, and inside was an old-fashioned bed with bedposts, drapery across the top. White sheets covered the bed, along with a feather-stuffed comforter. The walls were covered with wallpaper with a simple floral design, and three Cezanne prints in heavy glass frames decorated the walls. Soft light poured forth from an antique-looking lamp, and a candelabrum burned brightly on the dresser. There was a coatrack.

I took off my Stooges T-shirt and hung that up, then lit two cigarettes.

Alice came in a minute later, wearing slippers and a night-gown. For other men she dressed up some, I think, but she knew I didn't need anything like that, any kind of show.

I gave her the other cigarette and said hello.

"Hi," she said, smiling, and we kissed.

I put my arms around her and lifted her off the ground, sat her on the edge of the bed. Her slippers fell off in the process. I buried my nose in her hair and told her she smelled good. She said thank you.

"I saw you yesterday at the Elroy's, Alice."

"Did you?"

"Yes."

"You should've said something."

It was probably a lie, but it was exactly what I wanted to hear, and she knew it.

"What's new, girl?"

"Nothing much," she said. "Saw my mom a couple days ago."

"How'd that go?"

She blew smoke, looked down. "Nothing changes. I'm worried about her."

Her mother must've been loaded.

I ran my fingers through Alice's hair and said, "I'm sorry."

"You don't need to be sorry."

"I am, though. It's a shame things . . ."

"What?"

"It's a shame the woman never saw what an angel she had."

She smiled.

"And it's a shame that family has to hurt," I continued.

She took my hand and pressed it to her face, kissed my fingers. My rod shot up like the lighter end of a seesaw.

"Is she healthy?"

"She's never been healthy," Alice said, "but she's been with this guy lately who . . . I don't know. He is not a good influence."

"What's his name?" I asked.

"I don't know," she said, lying. "But let's not talk about that now."

"Sure," I said. "Later."

"How was your day?"

"Oh, you know. Same shit, different day. No surprise there."

I put my hand around the back of her neck and caressed her. She purred.

"I'm not the most terribly interesting man in the world."

"You don't have to be."

I took her cigarette and put it out in the green glass ashtray. Mine too. I put my hands on her face and felt her, felt the warmth come off her.

She bent forward and undid my pants. She took it in her mouth. I exhaled.

After a few seconds of getting lost in my head, I gently pulled her head back by the hair and pushed her down on the bed. I bent over and pushed the nightgown up to her navel. I kissed her knees, and then ran kisses up her smooth thighs. Her head went back into the soft bed, and she scraped her fingers through my hair.

"Alice," I said between kisses.

"Marley," she said.

I couldn't say what I wanted to say.

I parted her legs and licked her until she quivered, and the taste of her became heavy in my mouth, inside me. I got on top of her, kissed her like there was no tomorrow, and placed myself inside her.

In the morning, we awoke as the sun struggled to make a new day happen. We smoked a couple of cigarettes and talked. She talked about what kind of shopping she had to do. That was all I could get out of her that was real, but it would have to do.

I dressed. She watched from the bed as I slipped a stack of bills under the ashtray. It embarrassed me, paying for her like she was a tool, a product, anything other than the beauty she was. I tried to smile, and she told me not to worry. That was something she had to tell me often. I kissed her good-bye, and then went to work.

It felt like I was leaving home for good. It always did.

SIX

I took a quick look in the Evelyn white pages to see where Alice's mother lived. It sounded to me like the woman needed a visit from the tooth fairy.

It would be proper for me to tell you here that there once was a time in which I happened to see Alice's Honda on the road late at night. At the time, I doubt she knew what my truck looked like—seeing my truck once would brand it in your brain like a picture of a dead body—so I decided to follow her home. Just to make sure she got home safe.

She went about as far north as you could get in this town, to this house that was almost as small as mine, but much nicer. She parked in the driveway, and I passed her and parked on the corner. She got out of the car, set the alarm, and went in through her front door.

About an hour later, she turned off the bedroom light. That's when I got out of the truck and went back to see her name on the mailbox.

Halliday.

So that's how I knew her last name.

I checked the white pages, and there was Alice, over on Perry Street, and the only other Halliday in the book, I presumed, was her mother, Rebecca.

Rebecca seemed to live over on the east side, about a mile north of my restaurant. Now that I knew that, I knew what I'd be doing once the sun went down.

When I got home from work I ate a dinner that consisted of two boiled hot dogs sliced up like a banana into a can of tuna. I polished it off with a half a pot of coffee and a dozen crackers. Everything a growing boy needs.

Once I did my dishes—or should I say my *bowl*—I went into the living room and opened the big steamer trunk, which doubled as a coffee table.

I stored a bunch of odds and ends in there that I didn't want out in plain sight. Not that anything was incriminating, and not that I had ever let anyone through my front door, but I just did not believe in leaving stuff out for people to see or know about.

I rummaged about for a few minutes and finally came out with an old pair of sunglasses and a Redskins cap.

From my bedroom closet I took out a beige sports jacket I had never worn but had found at a thrift shop once for a dollar. You never knew when you'd need such a thing, and now I needed it.

I put my hair back in a ponytail and then wound it up under my cap so it looked like I had short hair. Then I put on the jacket, put the sunglasses in my pocket, and got in the truck.

I drove to the east side, stopped at a Laundromat I'd never been to before, and picked up a roll of quarters. Given the proper life circumstances, a roll of quarters could be a man's best friend.

Rebecca Halliday lived in a shit-ass apartment complex on a bad block. Two doors down was a no-tell motel, and on the northern corner were a pair of drug dealers who whispered slang names for drugs (trees, chronic, crazy train) to the pedestrians as they walked by. Most didn't respond. Those who did shook hands quickly with the dealers and then took off like bolts of lightning. There was a kid on a bicycle going up and down the block who I suppose was the lookout for the police.

I parked the truck two blocks south, put the sunglasses on, and then walked back the rest of the way to the apartment building. When I got to her building, I saw that the front door was locked. There were buzzers up on the wall, one for each apartment, but I didn't want anyone to know I was there. I looked over my shoulders to make sure no one was watching me, then I pushed the door hard, and the cheap lock gave.

I went up to 3G—Rebecca Halliday's apartment—and put my ear against the door. I heard a woman crying, and the deep voice of a man telling her to shut up. I knocked.

I heard footsteps coming closer. I stepped to the side so I couldn't be seen through the peephole, and I slipped the roll of quarters into my palm and squeezed it tight. I didn't know what to expect.

"Who the fuck is it?" shouted the man behind the locked door.

"Tacos," I said. It was the first thing to come to mind.

"Tacos?"

I heard him take the chain off the door, and then I heard him unlock the one lock. It swung open, and I let loose.

His hair was dark with strips of white above the ears. His gnarly mustache was nothing compared with mine. Either he or the entire apartment reeked of alcohol. The man was over six feet tall and weighed somewhere in the mid-two-hundreds, but it didn't matter. His face exploded in a tidal wave of blood and splintered bone as my fist bent his nose to one side of his face. He fell back into the apartment with a wet scream, holding his face like it was a crying baby. I stepped in and slammed the door behind me.

The apartment was poorly lit and filthy. All the light came from one scrawny lamp with a torn shade, and there on the couch was the woman who I presumed had a beautiful daughter. What I saw before me was a shell of a woman. She was horribly thin, with bleached blond hair, a fat lip, and a row of bruises the size of the man's fingertips running up both of her arms. She wasn't wearing anything other than a stained bra and a pair of Daisy Dukes. She sat there with a shocked look on her face, but didn't make a sound.

A half-eaten slice of pizza rested on the table next to a hunting knife—the kind that had a serrated edge to gut something. It even came with its own leather sheath. Right next to that were the keys to a big rig.

The man wore a mask of red. He roared and tried to get off

the floor, but I made short work of him with a kick to the ear. He went back down, howling.

"Are you Halliday?" I asked the woman.

She nodded.

"I understand this ain't the greatest guy in the world. Mind if I take him out for you?"

She nodded again, which I couldn't help but laugh at. I reached over and took the knife and stuffed it in the back of my jeans. I also grabbed the keys. Then I turned to the man.

"Let's go, tough guy."

I grabbed him by the collar.

"Get the fuck off me," he mumbled.

"Shut up."

I dragged him into the hallway and kicked him down both flights of stairs. When we got to the lobby, I pushed him onto the street and made sure the door with the cheap lock closed behind me. As I did this he took a wild swing, but his eyesight must have been shit-awful because he didn't connect. I threw a kick into his knee, then hit him with the right hook from hell. Like a bag of wet towels, he hit the street hard and didn't get up.

"If I find out you've been in that apartment again, I'll be back," I said, tossing the set of keys onto his soft gut.

The dealers on the corner turned. With that, I walked away. I must tell you, it's a mighty fine feeling knowing there's only so much damage a human being could do to me. Break my bones, I'll be fine with the next full moon. Same thing if you were to take away one of my hands or legs. Personal safety isn't some-thing I think about, and after kicking that goon's ass, I felt happy to be alive.

The Redskins cap and jacket were left in the first garbage can I saw.

My good deed for the day never made the papers.

The next night, I went back to the house on Carpenter Street. I didn't have the money to play with to go see Alice as often as I wanted to, but I wanted to know what happened with her mother. I couldn't very well call Alice up on the phone and say something roundabout like, "Hey, Alice, by any chance has some mysterious hero in disguise recently beat seven shades of shit out of the man your mother was shacking up with?"

That wouldn't be discreet.

Aside from being curious about the effects of my intervention, I just plain wanted to see her again.

I met her in the same room, and we did what we always did.

After, she told me that her mother had called. Some hooligan had dragged her man out of the house, and she hadn't seen him since. The mother presumed he owed someone money, and he might be dead.

The mother was upset because she didn't know if she had witnessed a kidnapping or not. Alice had told her to leave the police out of it, and to be happy that the guy was gone.

Alice didn't want her mother mixed up in anything as bad as murder, but I asked her if she was at least happy that the guy was out of the picture.

"Of course," she said, settling her head on my chest.

I smiled.

SEVEN

"The Rose Killer Strikes Again."

This was the screaming front-page headline of the *Edenburgh Gazette* that smacked me in the face the next morning.

At first I didn't connect it to the girl that had gone missing. My first thought, considering that Edenburgh was just about the sleepiest place in the known world, was that some deranged housewife had thrown a fit and went to work on a neighbor's garden with a pair of shears. I was very wrong.

Judith Myers's body was found in the backyard of someone's home. The house was surrounded by a lot of land at the end of a cul-de-sac. Out back of the house was a deck, and past that was a large swimming pool. Past that, the yard merged into an orchard that stretched on for quite a ways. There were a few beach chairs set up in front of the pool in the backyard, facing the pool, but, according to the residents of the house, it was still pretty early in the year for swimming, so they never went near the pool. This means it took them six days to realize there was the dead body of a missing seventeen-year-old girl propped up in one of their beach chairs.

Judith Myers had been very pretty, but not anymore.

Her father was the local locksmith, and the Myers family were all churchgoing people. Judith sang in the choir. The *Gazette* painted the Myers family as the kind of people who would water a neighbor's plants and collect their mail for them if they went away.

Judith had last been seen alive by her girlfriend who lived just a few blocks away from the Myerses' house. Judith's body was found over two miles to the east.

I thought about the church break-in. This shit was getting interesting. The two incidents seemed entirely unrelated, but if I had to put them together to make a picture, I would have presumed that some young assholes went out to paint the town red when they happened upon a young girl alone.

But, of course, they *were* unrelated, because the murder was the doing of someone called the Rose Killer.

The Rose Killer, as the papers had named him, was not a local phenomenon, which explained why I had never heard of him. He used to be someone else's problem. As far as the reporters knew—because law enforcement sure as hell didn't divulge everything they knew—his reign of terror began almost two years before in California with the discovery of a paid escort's body just outside of Los Angeles.

He was a one-man plague of locusts, traveling haphazardly east, leaving every place he visited mourning and bitter. He did six in California, two in Idaho, three in Colorado, then two in Arizona, one in New Mexico, four in Texas, and two in Missouri. He had killed twenty women, or maybe it would be more accurate to say that they had found and identified twenty bodies that he had cut the life from. They knew they were his because there were roses in their heads where their eyes used to be.

Judith Myers was the twenty-first woman to meet this grisly ending.

I vowed that the killer would never again be allowed to claim another life, because right then and there, as I sat in the kitchen at Long John's, I decided that this motherfucking Rose Killer had made my to-do list from hell, and when the next full moon came around, I was going to take his sorry ass out.

I hate psychopaths. I'd dealt with a serial killer a few years before—this was in a place called Peoria, in Illinois—and I must admit that it was one of the high points in my career as a boogeyman. The difference was he was a local monster who was pretty habitual, dumping people in the river every so often. He wasn't a ramblin' man like this bastard seemed to be. The Rose Killer had proven to be highly elusive, not married to a specific type of victim, like Bundy was, nor was he uncomfortable with being in a dozen different places. He was adaptable to his surroundings, whatever they were. He blended well, or was at least a master when it came to blending into the shadows. In a bad way, a way that made me grit my teeth for a moment, this Rose Killer reminded me of me in the way he went from place to place, leaving blood and blues in his wake.

I didn't know what to make of that connection. I'd been in Evelyn for years, but there was a time when I didn't stay in one place too long. I didn't want to be around when my targets were found, and I didn't want people remembering my face or the fake name I lived under. The road was my home, and there was a strange kind of solace in that.

I remember when I came up with my fake name—the persona I would live under for many years. I was starving, and I went into this little family-owned deli and asked if there was anything I could do around the store to help feed myself. I had never looked for handouts before, and it was humiliating. I once had a home, a girl, a side job I'd worked when I was in school at a local burger joint, but at the same time, I was the walking embodiment of bloodshed, so who was I to complain? Without thinking about it beforehand, I had used a Southern accent when addressing this deli owner. I was the only guy in my company who had been born above the Mason-Dixon Line, and the Southern accent was one I had become accustomed to. What compelled me to use an accent at the time was beyond me. But it did serve as an excellent disguise, and continued to in Evelyn.

The deli owner eyed me up and down and asked my name. The first thing that came to mind, for whatever reason, was Captain America, from the *Avengers* comics, so I gave his name.

"Steve Rogers," I said.

The old man gave me a broom, and I went to work.

After a couple of days of doing the floors and the windows, he gave me a clipboard full of papers and had me take inventory of the whole store—every can, every bottle, every pack of gum. As the inventory was coming to a close, I knew the hospitality would run out quickly, so once I palmed the money for that last day, I took off again on the bike, and I lived under the name of Steve Rogers till I almost forgot my real one.

I guess I always felt like I was running from something, something that was always at my heel. I had no destination because there was no escaping it, but I was always running, and I had to wonder how much of that applied to this traveling Rose Killer. Was he running away from something, or was there a destination for him? And if there was, what in God's name would happen when he got there? What were the chances that Evelyn was the end of that journey?

Whatever this guy was doing, it obviously threw all the investigators way off. There's no such thing as an immaculate crime scene, I know that much. And with the fact that several state agencies let this guy slip through their fingers, I had little faith that our minuscule police force could accomplish what those people couldn't. I wasn't a fucking sleuth, and I wasn't a goddamn defender of the public, but I knew this was something I'd have to talk to Pearce about.

There are many things the papers can't mention about crime scenes. These are the bits of information the cops hold back, the ones that only the killer could know about. And in regards to serial killers, which this sick fuck definitely was, they do all kinds of crazy, fucked-up shit at crime scenes. Pearce, being who *he* was, had access to that information, and if I could squeeze any of it out of him it would only help me take this sonofabitch down when the time came.

I folded the Edenburgh newspaper and dropped it on the floor next to my stool. I was sweating, and I felt this throbbing at my temples that I knew wouldn't go away until the next morning. I opened up my copy of the *Evelyn Post* and leafed through the pages, just to calm myself down.

It didn't work.

The *Post* informed me that there had been a church break-in the night before, the lock on the back door jimmied open with a crowbar, in all likelihood. Nothing was taken, nothing broken. And a woman who lived about ten blocks away from me had been reported missing. I would definitely have to call Pearce.

"I told you I had a funny feeling," I told Pearce on the phone that night.

"And I told you your funny feelings scare the shit out of me."

"I try."

"Either you're psychic or you're the world's most evil man."

"A little of both. Have the Edenburgh cops contacted you guys, or vice versa?"

"They put out a description when the girl went missing, just in case she came thisaways, but that was pretty much it."

"Listen, man, you gotta figure out what they know. I only know what I read in the papers, but that's not everything. They may have a suspect, a description, a car, anything. Anything to help with this lady missing here."

The missing woman was a drinking woman, in the sense that whoever bought her a drink got to take her home. She was single, with a little boy at home. The kid was the one who reported her missing. A good Christian family had taken him in until his mother decided to show up again, but my gut instinct told me that was something beyond her to decide. Her name was Gloria Shaw.

"So far, she's just missing, Marley, and that's it."

"But you can't deny the coincidence."

"No," Pearce said solemnly. "I guess I can't."

When we got off the phone, I immediately lit a precious cigarette, then cut the new articles out of the papers and put them up on the wall.

EIGHT

Abraham stuck his head in through the long window in the wall. "I need a Louisiana Burger with cheese fries. Hold the slaw."

"I need a new truck," I said.

"Don't start," he said, and he rushed back behind the counter.

The lunch crowd was just beginning to filter in. There were maybe five or six people in the restaurant, but that number would quadruple within half an hour.

The investigation into Judith Myers's murder over in Edenburgh was going horribly, which was expected. Their police were even more useless than ours.

The *Gazette* wasn't reporting anything about any new leads or any such thing, but what they did print was an extended history and hit sheet about the traveling scumbag, a time line of his reign of terror going all the way back to the beginning. The information was good for me—I mean, none hurt—and the handful of pages voicing the population's outrage over the crime only added fuel to the fire. I wasn't worried about what would happen when that full moon came around.

Out in the restaurant, I heard someone ask for me by name. I couldn't place the voice, but it didn't sound like a lawman. Abraham said I wasn't around, just like I always told him to just in case anyone ever came around for me, but I couldn't help myself from peeking through the window to see who was out there.

It was Anthony Mannuzza, the kid from back East, all duded up in a pair of blue slacks and a silk button-down shirt with flared sleeves. His hair was slicked back. I could smell his cologne all the way from the kitchen. The fruit looked like a backup singer for the fucking Bee Gees.

I poked my head out the window and said, "Hey, kid, you're still hanging around?"

"Yeah," he said, smiling. "I've got to see how all this plays out, don't I?"

"What do you mean?"

"This thing with the dead guy," he replied.

I lit a smoke and pushed my way through the double doors. He took a step back.

"That's kind of morbid, isn't it? Putting your sexy little life on the back burner for some small-town antics?"

"To hell with that. Like I said, this is great material."

"I don't know about that," I said. "Things pretty much went down the way you said. Animals and all."

"Is that the word from the cop guy that was in here?"

"You mean your most glamorous model?"

"Yeah."

"That's affirmative."

"Huh. In a way, that's too bad."

"Why's that?"

"Oh, I don't know," he said. "It just sounded too weird to be true. I mean, how many animals eat people?"

"All of 'em, you give 'em the chance."

"Yeah, I guess that's true," he said.

"You going to be on your merry way, then?"

He gave me a look like he wanted to hit me, but something in his eyes let me know that he knew it would be the most foolish thing he ever did.

He'd finally made me smile.

"I don't know. Maybe. I got a room over on Lincoln already . . ."

Lincoln was over on the east side, in the rough part of town.

"A regular Charles Kuralt," I mumbled.

"Who?"

"Forget it," I said. "Anyway, I got shit to do. Is that what you came for? To hear about the monsters out in the woods?"

"Well, yeah, actually."

"Well, there you go," I said. "Go back to Jersey."

"You sound like a New Yorker when you say that," he said. "You ever been there?"

"Nope," I lied.

"Ever been to Jersey?"

"Nope." Another lie.

"It's not that bad," he said.

"I'll take your word for it."

"Well, tell me something about Evelyn. Something for the book. You must have a million funny stories."

"You're at my fucking job, man. I got work to do."

"How often do you get asked to do an interview?"

Just then the phone rang. I was actually kind of peeved about that, because I had a good insult all lined up and ready for the kid.

Abe picked it up, said, "John's," listened, then handed it over to me.

"Yeah," I said into the receiver.

"Pearce."

"Hold on," I said as I put my cigarette out. "Arright, go ahead. What's up?"

"I hate to say it, Marley, I really do."

The hairs on me stood up. I sucked in a great, big breath and let it out fast.

"Have I told you how much your funny feelings scare the shit out of me?"

"Tell me," I said.

"You were right. Gloria Shaw's body was found up on the Crowley property early this morning."

"Is it the same guy? The one from the papers?"

"Oh, God, yeah."

I didn't know what to say. He continued.

"We got a big crew over here working on this. I just want you to know that. They have it organized. This is beyond anything . . ."

"We need to talk," I said.

"I know. Put your thinking cap on."

He hung up. I lit another smoke and watched the flame on the match dance for me. Another kind of hell had come to Evelyn. There wasn't room for two.

"What was that?" asked Anthony.

"That was our detective friend," I said, blowing out the flame.

"Oh yeah? Any news?"

"Yeah. A murder."

"Wow," he let out with glee, and ran his fingers through his wet hair. "This place just gets better and better, doesn't it?"

I gave him a look. He swallowed hard and walked out.

The Crowley property was up on the northern edge of Evelyn, about a mile past the circle of Old Sherman Road. The property consisted of a big old farmhouse the descendants of the once-opulent Crowley family lived in, a few dozen apple trees, and a vast stretch of tall-grassed land surrounded by a short white wooden fence. It was accessible only by a dirt and gravel path because there were no paved roads north of Old Sherman. Even though the town's richest people lived there, I guess they liked feeling cut off from the plain folk that lived in town. Maybe it made them feel safe.

Maybe they wouldn't feel safe anymore.

The man who ran the bank owned one of those houses up north, surrounded by acres and acres of blessed land. Some retired actor who went down in flames and had his livelihood ruined because of that rat bastard McCarthy lived in another house up there. He pretty much kept to himself. Only a few people in town knew what he actually looked like now, and most of those who did were the delivery boys from the local shops. The rest of the homes were held by the old families of Evelyn, handed down from generation to generation ever since the close of the Civil War. Familes like the Crowleys.

It all would've been perfect land to do a little bit of farming on—the dirt seemed rich and heavy, and the ground was flat—but there was something almost sinister about the land that Evelyn rested on that made seeds die.

And now blood had been shed on that land.

Gloria Shaw was thirty-eight, but she would be remembered as "twenty-two," because she was the Rose Killer's twenty-second victim. Her little boy, Luther, was nine years old. The father's identity was a complete mystery. He could have been dead for all anyone knew. If he was, the boy could have very well been an orphan and no one would have known it.

The papers seemed to suggest that on the night she didn't come home, Gloria Shaw went over to that little watering hole called the Cowboy's Cabin—God, I missed that place sometimes—and had a few drinks by herself before getting into an argument with a big, burly guy that no one had ever seen around before. He had offered to buy her a drink, but I guess she had some set of standards because she didn't want anything to do with him. He eventually walked out, and she left alone about an hour later with a noticeable drunken swagger, which placed the last time she was seen alive at about eleven in the evening.

The burly man was being called a "person of interest." He was described as being between six-two and six-five, forty to fifty years old, white, and he had a broken nose.

Three days came and went before I heard from Danny Pearce again. They say the first forty-eight hours of an investigation are the most crucial, but I guess this investigation was just a little more special, hence the extra twenty-four hours before he was able to pull himself away.

It was night. I was sitting at the edge of my bed, looking at all the sad articles that I had taped up on the wall, all connected. A collage of sin. Through the curtains I could see the curved sliver of moon up in the sky, like a crooked grin. Like it knew something I didn't know.

The phone rang, and I ran into the living room and picked it up.

"Pearce," he said.

I heard him blowing smoke as he said it. I held my tongue about that. Having to see what he saw . . .

"Talk to me," I said.

"I'll be there in five minutes," he said, and hung up.

I got nervous. The man had never set foot in my house before. I had never let *anyone* in before. I didn't want anyone invading my personal space, but he didn't exactly give me a lot of options on the phone.

I ran through the house quickly, hiding anything that could look odd at all, like the articles on the bedroom wall, which I tore down and stuffed under my lumpy mattress, and the old rifle I had perched against my nightstand, should anyone ever be unlucky enough to think they could sneak in at night and get away with it. The rifle went under the bed.

I ran into my kitchen, where I had that scumbag's hunting knife on the counter. I hid it under the sink, where I had a collection of cobwebs that would make Dracula blush.

In the living room I had a book out that I was reading at the time. I quickly stuffed it under the couch cushions, and, as far as I could see, that covered all the bases. I closed all the doors in the house so he wouldn't be able to look around without being extremely rude. I thought about what would happen if I had to knock his block off for snooping around my house, and just then, the doorbell rang.

The doorbell used to play "O Come All Ye Faithful," but after years of inactivity, it sounded like a dying robot. I swung the door open, and there he stood.

He had a thin beard and wore clothes that smelled like sweat and wet earth. His hair was slicked back with what smelled like dirty water, and dark rings circled his eyes like hungry sharks. His hands were shaking.

I led him into the living room and helped him sit in my recliner. He sank into it like it was his bed at home.

"I haven't slept in two days," he said as he smiled nervously, perhaps in a vain attempt to bolster his clearly fractured manhood. "There's a lot of work getting done."

He took full advantage of my naked-lady ashtray and lit a smoke. I lit one too, and hurried into the kitchen for a glass of water for the man. I didn't want to give him caffeine. He looked dehydrated. When I came back with it, he sucked the glass down in one hungry gulp, and then burped.

"I don't want the wife seeing me like this," he said, looking at his shaking hands.

"Don't worry. I'll tell her you're here."

"You don't mind?"

"Of course not," I lied.

"Thanks. I had to get out of there, you know . . ."

"I know."

"I know you do. Seeing that . . . it was the worst thing I ever . . ."

"Tell me what you know," I said. I knew I had a small window of opportunity to ruthlessly pick his brain, having caught him in a highly weakened state. I needed everything he had.

"It was horrible," he mumbled, settling further into the soft chair.

"Don't pass out on me. Sleep will come, but you need to talk to me."

"Oh, Marley, always digging for information. You're like Nancy fucking Drew."

"Yeah, that's right," I said. "Make me happy, man."

"It was horrible. He ripped her up, man, like when you gut a fish. He just opened her up . . ."

"Were the others like that?"

"Yeah. Most of them."

"They told you this?"

"Pictures. They have pictures of all of 'em."

"Do *you* have the pictures?"

"Marley . . ."

"Are they in your car?"

He nodded.

"You got anything else in the car?"

"Just my files."

Once he passed out, I'd snatch his keys and do a little research of my own.

"And it was the same thing this time as all the others? Flowers in the eyes?"

"Yeah," he said.

"White?"

"Red."

"Red? They were white for Judith Myers, there were white roses. Was this the only time they were red?"

"No. It's always some color or other. Like, whatever he could find, what was around. Or whatever struck him. That's what they said."

"Who's *they*?"

"The feds."

"The feds are here? Do they have a suspect?"

"They have what they called a 'profile.' They have a basic idea of what kind of person this killer is, but they don't know who. They don't have a suspect."

"What the fuck is the *profile*?"

"It's complicated."

"But they don't have a suspect? Is that what they said, or is that what you know?"

"No, I know it. They said the same. You should've been a cop."

"Not with my track record," I joked. "Were any of these girls drugged at all?"

"No. Some are known to have a drink now and then, like Gloria Shaw, but it doesn't seem to be relevant to anything."

"Any religious articles left around the body?"

"No. Why?"

"In Edenburgh a church was busted into the same night that Myers got it. Same thing happened here. Just an idea. Do the feds see any religious connection at all?"

"No. They see a sick fuck. Like you do."

"How else was she hurt?"

"No bruising, really. Just some about the head, the mouth, like he'd grabbed her, but she was bound."

"How?"

"Hands, mouth, feet."

"With what? Cords? Ropes? Socks? What?"

"It seems to be twine," he said. "It cut into her. Tape on the mouth."

"Any fingerprints on the tape?"

"No tape left behind. Just the sticky residue. I guess he took the tape with him. *And* the bindings."

"And they're all like that?"

"Yeah, most of 'em."

"Was there a weapon left behind? Anywhere?"

"No."

"What happened to the eyes?" I asked.

He swallowed and said, "No one knows."

"What's he doing the cutting with?"

"Something sharp, Marley, I don't fucking know. Talk to a fucking metallurgist."

"Same injuries every time?"

"No."

"What's changed?"

"Jesus, it's gotten so much worse," he said, his eyes as sad as they've ever been.

"It always does," I said. "Was anything left behind? Anything at all?"

"No. Well . . ."

"What?"

"There was an empty film box on the dirt road that runs along the edge of the property."

"Like what? Like, for a video? A tape?"

"Film. For pictures. Color. Polaroids."

"Pictures," I said.

Polaroids: a scumbag's best friend. Any lowlife in the world with a few extra dollars can pick one of those cameras up and document whatever heinous act he could possibly think of, and no one would ever know it.

"There was a spent cartridge, and the cardboard box for a new cartridge, like he had used one up and had to load another."

"Was the box new? Like, it rained last week, so . . . was it rained-on? Was it moist at all?"

"No," he said, "the box is in as good a condition as it could get."

"But the little black screen that shoots out of a Polaroid when you put the thing in the cartridge . . . that wasn't around?"

He didn't answer me. I looked over at him, and his hands weren't shaking anymore. He was out cold. I put my hand on his and squeezed. He was a fucking saint.

"Arright, Detective. Enjoy the hospitality," I whispered. "I'll call the wife."

His cigarette still burned in the ashtray. I put it out and drew shut the curtains. After that, I worked my nerves up a bit and called Martha from the kitchen.

"Pearce residence," she said in her squeaky, little voice.

The man had married a mouse.

"Hey, Martha, it's me," I said softly.

She didn't say anything right away. She didn't have my voice memorized unless I said something vulgar.

"It's Marlowe," I said.

"He's not here," she said briskly.

"That's why I'm calling. Just to let you know that your man's passed out on my recliner over here on King Street."

"Why?" she asked accusingly, as if to say, "What did you do to my man?"

"He's in a bad way here because of the case, and he told me to tell you that he doesn't want you seeing him this way."

"Is he hurt?"

"No, but he looks like shit, Martha. I kid you not."

"Oh, my baby . . ." she said, referring to her husband.

I couldn't help but smile.

"But how's the tyke?" I asked. "Coming along well?"

"Quite," she said.

"You guys pick a name yet?"

"No."

"You're running out of time, Martha. How about 'Marley'?"

"No, I don't think so," she said. "We're expecting a lady. . . ."

"Arright. At least I tried. I'll have him call when he wakes up, okay? Take care."

"Yes, you too," she said, not meaning it.

"Good night," I sang.

She hung up, obviously disgusted.

It comforted me to know that I could still have that effect on women.

I checked to make sure Pearce was still in sleepy land. He was. I could have wrapped him in Christmas lights if I wanted to. I went through his pockets till I found his car keys. Then I went over to the window and peeled back the dusty curtain. His car was halfway up my driveway, blocking in my truck.

I went out. The night was dark and cool. The wind carried in its waves the smell of cooked food from somewhere close by. I peeked in through the windows of Pearce's car and saw nothing. I opened the trunk.

There, between the extra tire and the first-aid kit, was a cardboard accordion folder stuffed to the gills with papers. It was held shut with one of those giant rubber bands that only mailmen seem to have access to. I lifted the folder out and was surprised at the weight of it.

The night was still and quiet. I heard the beating of wings, and a lone cricket singing, but the sounds of men were nowhere to be found. Then, off in the near distance, somewhere behind me, I heard a noise like a twig snapping. I was immediately brought to attention—a leftover symptom of being in war—and couldn't help but think that I was being watched, that someone had misplaced a step. That a gun was pointed at me.

I slammed the trunk, crouched, and hustled backward into the house, scanning the horizon the whole way. I saw nothing, but I locked all four locks on the front door.

I went through the documents in the bedroom with the door locked. I wasn't one for technical information. I mean, I wasn't a goddamn sleuth, but I was able to piece together enough from the pictures. They say a thousand words, don't they?

The first murders were in California.

Those early murders were the ones he learned from, the ones that gave him the lesson that he could do whatever he wanted to and get away with it, that given enough time he could do whatever his sick mind came up with.

The first two victims looked different from the others. The girls were escorts, which, considering this was California we were talking about, probably meant they were struggling actresses. They were strangled, beaten, bludgeoned. Roses were incorporated, but in that first kill, which occurred in a motel room, a rose from a nearby dozen was singled out and placed atop her corpse, almost as if it were a decoration. The star at the top of the Christmas tree. Or a sick gift.

For that second girl, the stem of the rose was pushed up inside her.

The first two were the only two that weren't marked with semen. With the third, traces of semen were found just feet away from the dead girl's body. He couldn't take it anymore.

After that, the sky was the limit, and like Pearce said, things had just gotten worse. That's the weird thing about serial killers: the more they do it, the more sophisticated they get, yet at the same time, they become more animalistic, more savage, as time goes on.

The rest of the crime-scene photos, when viewed chronologically, seemed like a virtual flip-book showing how the female body could be mutilated to greater and greater degrees. The roses became his calling card, placed in the sockets where a pair of eyes should have been. The question was, did he do it because he thought it was important, or did he do it just to let people know that he was the guilty party?

They didn't seem to have any hair or blood from the killer, but if they had semen, that meant he left a scent, and if he left a scent, I had the utmost confidence that the wolf—all teeth and nails and bad intentions—would hunt the man down without even breaking a sweat.

I put everything back in the folder and went back out to the living room. Pearce was still sleeping in the chair. I peeked out through the curtain, and even though I spent an extra minute looking around out there, I saw nothing. I had to presume that the sound of the snapping twig was caused by a cat, or a dog. I unlocked the door, ran to the car, put the folder back, and zipped back into the house.

I put the keys back in Pearce's pocket, along with a handwritten note I hoped his wife would find. She didn't like me for any particular reason. I figured I ought as well give her one. The note read:

Danny—
You know I have been with a lot of men, but no one has
ever given me better cock than you. I love your cock inside
me. It fills me up like I'm a balloon. I know you still love
your wife, but if I could feel you cum inside me every day
of the week, I would die a happy transvestite.
                                        Love—
                                        Tommy Candy

I threw a moth-bitten blanket over him that probably smelled like phantom cats, turned out the lights in the living room, and locked myself in the bedroom. It was two-thirty in the morning. I had to be at the restaurant at seven. I would have liked to have slept a few hours, but Pearce snored.

NINE

More people than I had ever known showed up

to pay their last respects to Judith Myers. Pearce was there, at least in spirit, because his mind was fried. I think the only respite he'd had since Gloria Shaw's body was found was when he dozed off at my place. Since then, all he did was work. I was there in a cheap brown suit I had gotten at a thrift shop for fifteen dollars. It was shiny at the elbows, and was probably last worn by the man who had died in it back in the mid-seventies. It fit like a glove. I was also sporting a pair of black shoes I had to pay a little more for—men don't part with nice black shoes until they are destroyed—and the sunglasses I wore when I kicked that guy's ass a handful of days before.

There were a lot of church people at the funeral, as well as students and friends of the dead girl. Everyone else was media, and if not that, then *federales* in disguise, which meant, as far as I knew, that they weren't wearing their earpieces with their black suits and ties. I guess for a funeral they were dressed as inconspicuously as they could be. In a black Chrysler off a ways, and also out by a willow tree, were a couple of lawman-photographers taking pictures of all the people who showed up. Sickies apparently had the bad habit of showing up at the funerals of their prey. I had to presume that they would later compare their new pictures to the photos taken at the funerals in the other states, see if anyone matched up.

As the priest went on with his shtick about eternal life coming down to the little town princess, I started thinking about all the people I'd put down over the years. I wondered if any of them got any kind of burial service. As far as I know, there just wasn't a whole hell of a lot left of them to bury—and that kind of got me all maudlin. There were a handful I'd have liked to have seen off, if for no other reason than I'd know where to go back to if I ever felt like pissing on someone's grave.

It wasn't often that I felt completely justified sending the wolf after a particular person. Sometimes I had to settle for someone who didn't really deserve to die. But I had zero sympathy for my new target. In regards to pissing on someone's grave, I figured if things worked out right, I could start off with this fucking Rose Killer, once I got my mitts on him.

TEN

I woke up on the day of the full moon in a great mood, and why wouldn't I have? The world was just hours away from having a creep known as the Rose Killer wiped from existence. Yeah, I felt pretty chipper indeed.

When I got to work my usual five minutes late, Anthony Mannuzza's Mach 1 was parked out front, and he was leaning against the side of it with a cigarette in one hand and a handful of loose papers in the other.

I pulled up next to him and got out of the truck. I put my keys in my left hand just in case I had to put the right one to work.

He smiled. "I've been waiting for coffee."

"Keep waiting," I said, and I brushed past him to climb the stairs.

"Aren't you even curious why I'm here?"

"I know why," I said. "You're a glutton for punishment."

He smiled again and sidled up next to me. He showed me what the papers were—black-and-white photographs. The picture on top was an eight-by-ten shot of me in my suit and sunglasses.

He had been at the funeral.

"How the fuck did you take this without me seeing you?"

"Telescopic lens," he said. "I have all kinds of equipment in the car."

"I thought you were full of shit about being a picture man."

"I wasn't."

"It's a good picture," I said honestly. "But if I'd have seen you, I would have broken your camera for taking it."

"I know."

I unlocked the door to the restaurant, and Anthony followed me in. Once I took all the chairs down and got the gear in the kitchen going, I made a pot of coffee. Outside, I saw Abe's Buick pull into a spot, but he didn't get out, the prick.

"Who develops these?" I asked. "I wouldn't think the local pharmacy would do a nice job like this."

"I do it myself."

"What, like in a darkroom?"

"I do it in the hotel room. Turn out all the lights and so on. All the equipment fits in the car. I wouldn't trust some small-town rummy with my negatives."

"Not bad."

"Of course," he said. "I'm a fucking great artist."

He showed me another shot of a woman and her baby, sitting near the big fountain in Applegate Park.

"Nice," I said.

He showed me another.

This one was of a tree.

"Is this in the park?"

"No," said Anthony.

The tree was massive, but lightning had cleaved it clean in half some time between now and who knows when. As it stood, it was a ten-foot-tall pillar of wood, probably about five feet across.

He asked, "Do you know this tree?"

I looked at him like he had farted in an elevator.

"How the fuck am I supposed to know every goddamn tree in the world?"

He didn't respond. He handed me another shot. This one was a close-up of the same tree. A crest was apparent in the wood. It was an elaborately carved heart with two crossed arrows darting through it at angles. In the center were the names Johnny and June, and even the names were carved elaborately.

"Damn," I said.

"You like that? Those carvings go into the wood about a quarter of an inch. Whoever did that spent a lot of time working on it."

"Never seen it."

"It's south. In the woods. That's my cover shot for the book." Anthony glowed as he inspected his own work.

"You can keep those," he said.

"Fabulous."

I folded the pictures and stuffed them in my back pocket, which made him flinch visibly. I smiled.

"Any word on the guy that was eaten in the woods?" he asked.

"Nope."

"That's too bad. You think there's any way I could get a shot of the guy's car?"

"I doubt it," I said. "Either his wife got it back, or it's been impounded. I have no idea, and I don't think anyone would go to the trouble of finding out for you."

"What about with this dead woman? Any news on her? Or I guess it's not just the one, the way the papers are talking. . . ."

"I know what you know."

"I find that hard to believe."

"What's that supposed to mean?"

"Hey, man, no offense. I only mean to say it's like you seem to have your finger on the pulse, you know what I mean? You know what goes on around here."

"What do you care? It's not like you live here. . . ."

"I don't want to sound shallow, but this is great material. I mean, here I am driving through the middle of nowhere, and all of a sudden the bodies start piling up. I couldn't write this stuff if I wanted to, but I could still make a book about it, since that's what I'm doing anyway. If they think this Rose Killer guy has moved on, then there's no point in me sticking around any longer than I have to."

"You don't strike me as an intrepid reporter," I said.

"Never planned to be," he replied.

"Well, like I said, Jersey boy, I know what you know. However, I will say this: It's only a matter of time before this sick fuck goes down hard. I guarantee it."

"How do you know? Do they have a lead?"

"Fuck leads, Liberace. We got monsters in the woods, remember?"

What bothered me more than anything was watching Pearce run himself into the ground, just like he did every time something went down in this town. It didn't matter that the *federales* were in town, or that they went so far as to manipulate the newspapers and the words that were coming out of the mouths of the talking heads on the local news shows. It didn't matter that they had all the technology and headshrinkers in the world, not to Pearce. Day in and day out, he pored over his evidence, his thoughts, the section of land he was charged to protect. When the time came, he wanted it to be none other than him slapping the meat hooks on this guy. So he went to the Crowley property every damn day and just walked around. Walked around and thought. Maybe, he thought, he would get lucky and find a business card.

I spoke to him on the phone that evening.

"What are you up to?" I asked.

"Going back up to the property," he said. "Just stopped at home to get some grub. Martha made some meat loaf. Enough for a battalion, actually. I'm loading up my Tupperware with it. If this fucking town was willing to pay more overtime, I wouldn't have to do this surveillance crap myself. . . ."

"You'd do it anyway."

"But I'd be getting paid."

"You're hiding out in the bushes on your own time?"

"Of course," he said, as if I had just asked the stupidest question of all time. "The feds are going to be trying some proactive stuff soon. They're going to be pulling together some kind of press conference on the TV, but it's going to be more like some kind of subversive attack on this guy, to try to draw him out of hiding. But these bastards come back to the scene of the crime,

Marley. The feds have honest-to-God proof of that, so, hey. You never know. I could get lucky."

"You got lucky with the Polaroid stuff," I said. "Before that, those goons didn't even know he took pictures."

"It's not enough," he said. "It won't be till I have him in my holding cell. The feds ain't Danny Pearce."

"Good one."

"Thanks," he said, "but not as good as leaving a note in my jacket, right?"

"Oh, you found the note, eh?"

"No, asshole, the wife did."

On the inside, I laughed. On the outside, I said, "Well, isn't that a shame. I hope she took it well, you cheatin' on her with such a chesty girl and all."

He said, "Marley, I've never met anyone in my life who pushes their luck like you do. Balls like a gorilla."

"You'd know," I said.

"I know more than you think. Like how you went through my files the other night."

"Shit, man, how the hell did you know that?"

"I'm a detective. It goes with the job. And I know *you* more than you think."

I had nothing to say.

"Nothing to say for once? It's about fucking time," he said, and he laughed. "Now I can die happy." I laughed too, nervously, because I didn't know what the hell he was talking about, or if he was just fucking with me.

"Keep smoking, and it'll happen sooner than you think."

"I only fell off the wagon the one day, Marley. Martha saw to that."

"Good. That's why she's your better half."

"Don't I know it." He paused. Then: "I got a good feeling about this case. I'll see you in a few days."

"Take it easy, Danny. Get some sleep."

"A few days, I'll sleep. Now, not so much."

He hung up.

That ended up being the last time I ever spoke to the man.

It was just before midnight. Night had settled upon the sky like a calm black sea. Up high, forcing itself through the darkness, was the full moon. I could feel that moonlight tug at my skin like a baby's fingers, but I held it at bay on the other side of the curtains that hung from every window and were each drawn tight.

For me to change from my usual, happy-go-lucky self to a plain old creature of the night, I actually have to come in physical contact with the moonlight. The transformation never happens automatically, so until I was good, ready, and confident that most of the population was at home and sleeping, I sat around the house with a book.

I was reading *The Captive and the Fugitive*. Proust. In French.

I had once killed a Frenchman. It wasn't something I was proud of (just kidding), but the hell of it is that from that day on, if I heard two guys talking in French (not likely in the deep South) I knew what they were saying. And I could read Proust without its being translated. What a world.

I also knew Greek, Mandarin, and Spanish, apparently.

I haunted the used bookshop over on Markson Street from time to time, but all the books I had in the house were thoroughly hidden behind heavy boxes in the bedroom closet. In case anyone ever came in, like Pearce did, I didn't want anyone to ever think I was someone who could read. The less people knew about me, the better. It was bad enough that half the town knew my real name.

The pain of the transformation from the world's greatest chef to a being that eats only raw meat is almost indescribable. When people actually come apart from the inside, they usually don't live long enough to have a sit-down with somebody and verbalize what the experience was like. If I had to put it into words, I'd have to say that it's like feeling each and every one of my bones shift and rotate inside me, and then shatter into dozens of pieces, all throughout my body. After that, it's like feeling those sharp little pieces try to pass through all my pores like kidney stones. That would pretty much do it.

It isn't a pleasant feeling, but I used to experience a pain far worse, back before the beast and I came to work together, and that was the pain that would come with the evening of the full moon and grow stronger and more unbearable as the hours passed. It was like the most hellish of chemical withdrawal symptoms—the running shits, the pukes, and the twitchies—and the only way to relieve that pain was to let the light of the moon touch me. However, seeing as how I didn't used to want to change, this was a real catch-22. Coming in contact with the moonlight meant I had to break down and give up. It meant I had to allow myself to change into a life-snatching monster. Psychologically, this didn't do me any favors. With the withdrawal pains gone, the pain of changing wouldn't feel that bad, because I at least knew it was temporary.

If not for this pain—this torture—that attacked me like a mob and compelled me, sooner or later, to touch the moonlight, I would've locked myself up somewhere, and I never would've let the beast do what it did to all those innocent people all those years ago. Because of the pain, though, I had no choice.

I was never man enough to conquer that pain, to shrug it off and wait for a new morning to come, and it was so amazingly internal, so undying, so beyond any other pain I had ever felt, that I am quite sure there has never been a man alive who had the nerves and the stamina to endure it. I never could, and a lot of people aren't here anymore because of that.

One night, I tried. This was back in '75. I was twenty-two years old.

I was already on the road at that point, and I was as close to insanity then as I've ever been. For the better part of the seventies, I was on a righteous quest to find a cure for what I had become. My mission led me from one end of the country to the other, but all my leads—the rumors of witch doctors, of magicians, of all-powerful Indian shamans—either turned into dead ends or turned out to be frauds. There were a couple of people I encountered—one a medicine man in New Hampshire, and the other an unbelievably ancient German man, a hundred and thirty years old, who was kept in the basement of a nondescript apartment building in San Diego. He wielded powers and abilities not of this earth, but even they were unable to help me, and I realized then that I was beyond all hope. My chances of saving my soul fell away like sand through my fingers, and I was lost.

Then there was Maine. I encountered a group of people up in Maine that I thought might be the answer to my prayers, back when I thought my prayers would be answered. But it turned out to not be so, and I don't ever talk about what happened in Maine.

Anyway, back in '75, I was up in Saratoga Springs for a while. It had been raining all day, so it was hard for me to tell when true night was coming. I was drinking whiskey in the park they have up there, with all those nasty, sulfurous springs all over the place, when all of a sudden, the pain hit my guts. I heaved the half of the bottle I had inside me back into the bushes and ran. I had to get away from the sky.

I broke into a two-story home a few blocks away. I figured I could hide in the darkness for a while, but before long the family came home, and I ducked out the back way. It was better to find another cover than to be around children.

I soon found myself back on Broadway, and at this point, I could barely walk straight. My depth perception was starting to get funny, and I knew I really had to get inside somewhere. I figured I ought as well try to get myself arrested. They could lock me in a cell, then I'd have no choice but to deal with the pain, and in the morning, if I made it, there would be one less dead body on my hands. I went into a clothing store and started knocking racks over and cursing at the women.

This kid that worked there came up to me and said, "Sir, I'm going to have to ask you to leave the store."

I feel bad for that poor kid nowadays. He had terrible acne, and probably weighed a buck fifty soaking wet. I hit him with such a mean shot, his tooth was stuck in between my knuckles.

The cops came, and there I was in aisle five, surrounded by all the black, liquid crap that had slithered from my bowels. Instead of taking me to the jail, they put me in an ambulance. It took eight men to tie me down, and then they loaded me into the ambulance.

On the ride to wherever they were taking me to—either the hospital or the madhouse—I caught the light of the full moon through the window.

I changed.

The last thing I remember was the men screaming and the ambulance flipping onto its side and bursting into flames.

The next day, I woke up naked in a ditch far away.

I had to go back to Saratoga to gather up my stuff. Everything I had was in a shitty little motel room, but all my clothes and my keys were gone. I broke into a house and stole a pair of pants and a shirt.

Up in the motel room, I collected my few possessions into a bag and dressed myself in my only other set of clothes—blue jeans, a Beatles shirt, cowboy boots, and my leather jacket.

Downstairs in the lot was my motorcycle, the one I'd had for years, but it was worthless now without the keys. I did not yet know how to hotwire a vehicle. I walked it out of town, and when I came to a little pond hidden behind some trees on the side of the road, I rolled it in. The air was cold and sweet. The sky was gray. I felt like I'd lost the only friend I'd had anymore, the only thing that kept me free and human.

When I got back on the road, I stuck out a thumb. After a few minutes, a red truck stopped.

The driver asked, "Where are you going?"

I said, "I was going to ask you the same thing."

"Canada," he said.

"Sounds good to me."

Since the beast and I joined forces back in the early eighties, the pain that blossomed throughout the evening didn't hurt so much anymore. I've often wondered how much of it was psychosomatic, and how much was supernatural. It became a kind of buzzing feeling, like having to go to the bathroom, and as the years went on, I got to savor the feeling for the buildup that it was—the foreplay to a night of brutality and mayhem. And I always waited long enough to change for there to be a minimal amount of people out on the streets. The pain of changing has remained just as horrible over the years, but it can hardly be argued that I don't deserve it, and maybe a little bit more.

I sat in my recliner. An old lamp rested on a desk against the far wall of the living room, illuminating just a quarter of the space. There were electric lights that ran across the ceiling, but they hadn't worked for months, and I was always too distracted to get around to fixing them.

On the trunk in front of the recliner was my naked-lady ashtray, and the remote control for a television that picked up three or four stations, depending on the weather and the time of day.

The beating of my blood was like getting punched from somewhere deep inside. The heart pounded so furiously, so continuously, I almost felt like I was vibrating. I smoked my cigarette, and the carbon monoxide that those fuckers pack in there only made the pounding in my ears that much stronger. Someone could've gone at my door with a battering ram, but I wouldn't have heard it over my own frantic heart. It was time.

I put the cigarette out in the naked-lady ashtray and went over to my front door. I unlocked the four locks. After that, I checked all the windows. Then I went to the bedroom.

I rolled up the old piss-colored rug that covered the floor and dragged it into the corner. From one of the dresser drawers, I took out a plastic tarp and laid it out on the floor. I pushed my bed into the corner, and had forgotten that I had put the gun under the bed when Pearce came over. I slid the gun back under the bed with my foot. I was, after all, Mr. Safety.

I took off my nasty white T-shirt and threw it onto the stack of dirty clothes I had in the corner. I unfastened my brown leather belt with the silver skull-and-crossbones buckle and rested it on a chair. I took off my jeans and put those on the bed. They weren't dirty enough to warrant getting put in the wash. My socks and undies, however, had earned their place in the laundry bin.

There was a night-light with a clown's face plugged into the outlet in the corner. I flipped the small switch on it, and the night-light came to life. It glowed just above the floorboards. The clown had a white face, which was made a sickly yellow with age. It had black makeup around the eyes which made it look like it was sad, even though the mouth was frozen in a maniacal grin. The hair was orange, the nose was red, and the lips were red. It had on a green hat with a black band. There was a little yellow flower sticking out of the band.

That night-light meant more to me than anything else I had. It once belonged to Doris. She'd had it since she was a little girl, because no matter how old she got, there was something about the dark that scared her. I used to tease her that it was a wonder she was never afraid of clowns, but she loved clowns. For some reason, *I* was her clown.

The night-light had the job of guarding the house while no one was home.

I took the rubber band from my hair, and ran my fingers through my mane. I looked at myself in the mirror. Every once in a while, it was hard for me to believe I was forty fucking years old.

Up on the wall, the numerous articles I had put back glowed in the faint yellow light the clown gave off. Each was a cry from the public, a plea from the world at large for restitution; only the law wasn't going to be the one dishing out the justice. Not that night.

Standing at the bedroom window, the moon yearning on the other side of the curtains, I felt that buried pain roll up my nerves, felt it lick my ribs. I breathed in deeply through my nose with my eyes closed, and then I opened the curtain.

Hard white light hit the glass and came through silver, bathing me. A spasm flared through my body from my ankles, up my spine, to the back of my neck. My head shot back, and the veins in my throat became engorged, thick blue, with burning blood. I hit the floor hard just as the milky, white froth began to bubble up from my insides. I forced myself to crawl over to the tarp.

Tears leaked from my eyes from the pain, and snot ran down my face in a rivulet. In a moment's time, my body would no longer belong to me at all. It would be the vessel of a ghastlier, more terrible entity.

Lying on my side on the plastic sheet, I saw the nails fall off my fingertips, replaced by thick, cedar-colored talons. Black hair oozed out from every pore. New muscles bulged and flexed under tearing skin, and where I ripped, smoke billowed and blood spurted out like children spitting up food.

I thought of the Rose Killer. Through the pain, I smiled.

It was the last act of the evening I would be able to will my body to make, because from that point on, my mind was on the back burner. Marlowe Higgins was going someplace farther than sleep, a place that was too deep for even the sandman to tread lightly. As I fell away, I heard my scream turn into a howl, and then I was gone.

ELEVEN

I woke up on the bedroom floor the next morning,

right in the same spot where I had blacked out the night before. A lot of the blood on the tarp had dried black, and it was as sticky as sin. It felt like there were a million grains of sand mixed into the slush that had been my body, but it wasn't sand. It was pulverized bone. I stretched and spit the thick muck that lined the walls of my mouth out onto the tarp.

It was a workday, and the alarm clock was going off. "Magic Carpet Ride" blared from KBTO. I could hear birds chirping outside, just like everything was hunky-dory according to them.

I would always set the clock a little earlier than usual the morning after—that way I'd have the chance to do some tidying up before heading in. I hated leaving the place looking like an abattoir while I was off whipping up Louisiana Burgers for the general public.

I was naked, of course, and covered in a thick layer of dried blood. As I wiped the sleep from my eyes and began to rise, the dried blood flaked off of me like flower petals and fell to the hardwood floor. All about me were hairs, sinews, and short lengths of muscle—some of them mine, some of them not mine. A row of teeth rested by my foot, attached to a brittle piece of jawbone. A handful of fragments of my victim's skin rested in a constellation all about the floor, and drips of blood dotted themselves all along the floors of my house.

I'd pull the piss-colored rug back later, once I cleaned.

I limped to the living room—still not comfortable in my own skin—and lit myself a smoke. My lungs felt new and clean.

Everything was as I'd left it. All in all, I felt fine, maybe even a little happy. I felt like I'd done someone a really big favor when I didn't have to. Like I was a Good Samaritan. That kind of feeling.

After a brief inspection of the house to make sure I still had all my windows and there wasn't anything horrible out in front—some eviscerated remnant of a human being, a stack of dead bodies, claw marks along the outside of the house—I made a pot of coffee. As that was going, I took the all-important shower.

It never ceased to amaze me how much effort it took to get all the blood out from around my fingernails. It was always a pain in the ass. That, and my hair. On skin, I'd often resort to using steel wool on myself, like I did that day. It hurt, but it worked, and any cuts I received would be gone by the end of the day. On hair, like the hair on my chest and around my happy place, I used one of those back-scrubber brushes. It worked well enough, but there were always little bits of blood I'd have to pick off hairs with my fingertips.

I shampooed twice, then conditioned twice. As the second bout of conditioner went to work, I got out of the shower and went over to the cabinet above the sink. I pulled out my razor, my comb, and some shaving cream, then went back in the shower. I shaved in there with the use of a small mirror fixed into the wall, and combed the dried blood flakes out that had eluded the washings. The water going down the drain was pink.

That was twenty minutes of my life right there, but I was once again the most handsome sonofabitch who'd ever lived, mustache and all.

Before I dressed, I turned the radio up, hoping to hear some good news. I listened as I went around with my bucket of soapy water, cleaning up the bloody floors with a few rags. I figured it wouldn't hurt to have a go at the doorknobs too, so I started cleaning those. A special report came over about another body found up by the Crowley property, but details were nonexistent. I smiled. I even laughed. It was just like those crazy motherfuckers, going back to the scene of the crime.

"Probably to get himself off," I said out loud. "Good riddance."

In the bedroom, I rolled up the stinking tarp and put it in a black Hefty bag. After I scrubbed the floor, I pulled the rug into place and got dressed in my blue jeans and an old Motorhead shirt. I put my belt on, my boots, got the keys to the truck, and headed out. The day was proving to be very sunny. It matched my mood.

I turned the key in the truck, and the engine coughed.

"C'mon, you fucking worm! Fucking work!"

God came down, and the truck came back to life.

"Thank you, Jesus."

I went to work. In four weeks, there'd be another full moon, and another chance to make someone pay. Before that, I'd have to pick another target and do the same thing all over again.

The radio in the truck didn't work. Nor did the air-conditioning, but that's why I had been able to afford the thing. I wasn't worried, though. I'd get the full report from Pearce by the end of the week.

Actually, I'm lying. I *was* worried just a little bit about killing someone within the confines of Evelyn two months in a row. That was something I never wanted to do, for hysteria's sake, and that's why I got the newspapers from so many neighboring places—so I could spread the love around. This time, it was unavoidable. The Rose Killer had forced me to make an executive decision, and I didn't regret it. The killer was an abomination who had to be stopped.

I drove through town and stopped at my newsstands just like I always did.

A few minutes later, I pulled up outside the restaurant and saw I was the first one there that day. I thought it was strange and kind of off-putting that I had somehow become the responsible one at that place. I was still late, but not as late as Abraham, and he *liked* his job.

I unlocked the door and turned the lights on. I put my stack of newspapers on the stool in the kitchen and fired up the grill. By the time I started taking the chairs down off the tables, Abraham showed up.

I was happy to be the first one that day. The day after—and it has never stopped, this feeling—I always struggle to act as normal as possible, because I'm a fucking paranoid. I missed having my motorcycle. The urge to take off was sometimes overwhelming. I missed the road. The wind. I've always had this useless worry that someone would come after me, as if the beast and I had some kind of passing resemblance. As if someone would be fortunate enough to live after seeing the goddamn thing and say "Hey, that animal that just tore apart old man Burns looks a hell of a lot like that guy from the restaurant!"

In my calmer moments I believe this will never happen, but when you grow up on G-man movies, you can't help but think you come off like a suspect no matter what.

"Hey, brother," I said.

"You're one cold motherfucker, starting in with the 'brother' shit on a morning like this."

"What the fuck do you mean?" I asked, trying to sound as nonchalant as possible.

"You don't know?"

"What?" I said, giving a great performance of being genuinely pissed.

"I don't know how to say this, but don't you have a television? Contact with the outside world at all?"

"I get smoke signals, but they've been on the fritz lately."

Abe took off his cap and stared at the floor.

"Your man Pearce bought it, man."

My heart sunk somewhere below my bowels, and the taste of a dinner I couldn't remember having came up into my mouth. My legs turned to spaghetti.

The word "What?" came up out of my mouth.

"I'm sorry to be the one to tell you. He got attacked last night, this morning. Some kind of animal or something like that, like that shit you dudes was talking about a while back. It's all over the fucking news, man."

I sank onto a stool at the counter.

I couldn't think of anything to say. Me, Marlowe Higgins, the man of a thousand four-letter words, was speechless. And I couldn't think of anything to feel. Nothing felt appropriate. Nothing felt true. I rested my head in my hands. I couldn't do anything else.

Abraham came over and put a hand on my shoulder the way men do. I let out a groan from somewhere deep. An old place I didn't like to visit.

"I'm sorry," he said.

"I can't fucking believe it," I said. "I don't know what to say."

"You want a moment?"

"God, I don't know. I don't know. I think . . . I think I gotta get outta here."

"You want I should call Carlos to take over for you?"

"Yeah," I said. "Yeah, I think you're gonna have to."

"Done," he said, and he went and got on the horn.

As he was talking on the phone, I oozed off the stool and headed toward the door. Crossing the black-and-white tiles made me dizzy. It was as if my sense of equilibrium had been destroyed, and everything appeared as if through a kaleidoscope.

I reached for the doorknob like a lifeline and made it out into the warm air. The bell jangled, and then I was outside in the blaring sun. I felt blinded, on display, ashamed. It was a feeling I hadn't known so closely in many years.

I got to the truck, took out my keys, and then stopped myself. I went back to the restaurant, got my papers from the stool in the kitchen, and slithered back out, not saying a word to Abraham. He didn't say anything to me either.

I started the truck up and backed out of the space slowly, not being quite too sure of my movements, and how true they would be. My hands were shaking.

I started driving toward the center of town, toward the build-
ings and the radios and the police and the people, but I couldn't
do it. I made a left and went down to Old Sherman Road, driving
slowly.

I took Old Sherman west, and then it curved around and
started going north. After a few minutes of driving, I passed my
block and just kept going. I made the full loop around town, just
like Bill Parker used to do before he was killed. It was then that I
realized that some part of that man that I had killed had become
a part of me, because here I was doing my worrying on that long
and winding road.

I pulled over on the shoulder.

As if everything prior had been shock, I realized, as in it truly
hit me, that Pearce had been wiped out, butchered, ripped apart,
maimed unrecognizable, and that it had been me that had done it
to him. I felt the parts of his body that were still in my stomach
react to the coffee I'd drunk, and it twisted me up inside.

"Martha," I said out loud without thinking to.

I squeezed my eyes shut and bit my hand.

"Martha, are you okay?"

I was being invaded by a memory of his.

I saw it all through his eyes. Rushing into the living room from
the office, and there she was on the couch, holding her belly. She
had that one wrinkle on her forehead—a deep crease that only
existed when she was hurting. The sunlight was pouring in through
the windows.

"She kicked," Martha said.

I sat next to her and placed my hand on her belly. I felt my
baby's power as it shifted an arm or a leg, as it kicked out. *My
baby's getting ready to hatch,* Pearce thought. I rested my head
on her stomach. I heard my wife's heart, and I think, somewhere
down deep, I heard my baby's.

In the truck, I screamed out loud.

Tears spilled down my face. I couldn't hold them back. Everything I had built for myself, this whole cardboard life that—even

though I didn't know it until that moment—meant everything to me, had been pulverized with one man's death. I didn't know how it had happened, but there wasn't a solution, no magic words to turn back the cruel hands of time. The wolf had betrayed me. I had killed an innocent man. I had killed my one friend.

TWELVE

On the way home I passed a liquor store. I hadn't
been in the place in years, but before I had the house it was like a
home for me, just like the bars were. I was messed up. All I could
think about was having a drink or two or twenty to dull the pain I
felt inside. The stuff was poison, but God had never made a more
effective salve for people like me.

I stopped the truck outside the liquor store, knowing damn
well what Pearce would say about this if he were still alive.

I didn't go in.

I came home and locked the door behind me. Checked all the
windows. The sun was pouring in through all my curtains, it was
that powerful. It was like God was shining the floodlights on me,
saying, "There he is."

I turned on my little black-and-white television, and all that
came through was a garbled wall of static, alien shapes moving
through the rough snow. I twirled the rabbit ears around in a circle
and finally found a position for them in which I was at least able
to receive the audio clearly.

I guess there was a news conference in progress. I didn't know
if it was the one Pearce had mentioned—the one the feds had
been orchestrating in some kind of attempt to set a trap for the
Rose Killer.

It wasn't.

I saw a wall of reporters outside of the police station on the
other side of town. On the bottom of the screen was a scrolling
message: OFFICER KILLED.

"This is Linda Roth reporting from outside the Evelyn Police

Department," the lady with the microphone said. "Details about the death of Detective Daniel Pearce are scarce, but to reiterate what we already know, we take you back to the studio."

A man appeared in a newsroom.

"Detective Daniel Casey Pearce," the man said, "was one of Evelyn's finest. Born in 1964 to Carol and Herbert Pearce, he attended school here in Evelyn, graduating as valedictorian from Stephen Bailey High School in 1982. Upon receiving his diploma, he entered the United States Air Force. He came back home to Evelyn in 1985."

I reached for my side. It felt like it was on fire.

"He immediately joined the Evelyn Police Department, and through years of hard work and a strong work ethic, quickly became one of the force's most decorated officers," the man continued. "In the fall of 1991, he earned his gold shield after his involvement in what has become known as the Starling Street Hostage Crisis."

Two men had gone into the jewelry store to rob it. Someone tripped the silent alarm, and it quickly became a hostage situation. Pearce was the responding officer. He put both men down before his backup arrived. Not a single hostage was injured in the short gun battle.

"Daniel Pearce is survived by a sister, his wife, and his unborn baby girl. He was twenty-nine years old."

These were the bare facts about the man who saved me. The man I killed. I felt like the careful balance between life and hell that I had worked so hard to keep up over the last few years had crumbled just like that and just so quickly that I didn't even know where the pieces went. I didn't know what to think.

They cut back to the intrepid news lady on the street.

"At sunrise this morning, Daniel Pearce's body was discovered on what is known as the Crowley property here in Evelyn, about a mile north of Old Sherman Road. As we have reported, this is the same site where, just a short time ago, the body of Gloria Shaw was found murdered at the hands of the serial murderer known only as the Rose Killer. Detective Pearce, in a joint effort with the Federal Bureau of Investigation, was conducting surveillance at the scene of this brutal crime. Now it seems that tragedy has struck twice here in Evelyn, and we can only hope that these two deaths are unrelated. We take you now to the PD conference room. Bill?"

They cut to a crowded room in the precinct.

"Bill Hagmeier here, where Captain Louis Thorpe is about to read a brief statement, and answer a few questions about this tragedy."

A man with a shock of white hair climbed the steps to the podium at the far side of the room. He was decked out in his dress uniform with about twenty-five pounds of medals pinned to his chest.

"Ladies and gentlemen of Evelyn," he said in a deep voice, reading from a sheet, "and members of the press, at approximately five-forty-five this morning, the body of Detective Daniel Casey Pearce was discovered on the property of the Frederick Crowley family on the north side of Evelyn."

"Who found him?" someone shouted.

"A resident on the property, and that is as specific as I am going to get at this time. The authorities were notified forthwith and . . ."

"How was he identified?" someone else shouted.

Someone else yelled, "Is it true that the body was dismembered?"

More shouts rose.

The captain silenced them all with a sharp bang on his pedestal, a closed fist raining down on the board the microphones were attached to.

"He was identified by his shield. The investigation is in its earliest phase, and . . . Detective Pearce was . . . he . . ." and then he broke down, right up there in front of the world. The press jumped on him like vultures.

"Was it true his body was found beheaded?" they asked. "Is it true that it was a bear? Is it true that shots were fired? Was it a suicide-by-shotgun? Was he involved in any illegal activities that the department is aware of? Was this a crime of revenge? Is there any connection to the Rose Killer?"

The captain responded to the questions with yes or no answers, and finally got fed up enough that he walked off the stage. The sounds of the camera flashes were almost as loud as the shouts.

Someone else stepped up to the mike, a sergeant, I think, and warned the public to be aware of any dogs roaming around that weren't tagged at all. This set off another maelstrom of questions from the press, but the sergeant promptly exited stage left.

I went into the bathroom and threw up.

They said it was a tragedy. A hundred times I heard them use that word. It *was* a tragedy.

In the kitchen I untwisted the twisty-tie that held shut the big black Hefty bag the bloody tarp was in. I opened the bag, and right there, resting atop the thing like a candle on a birthday cake, was the piece of the jawbone I had presumed belonged to the Rose Killer. It was about the size of a pack of cigarettes, and was crowned with two sterling, white teeth. Danny's clean teeth.

Dear God, I thought. I wanted to reach down and touch it, to express how sorry I was, but that fragment wasn't Pearce anymore. It was an item that proved to me what a curse I was to the world. It was evidence, and it had to be destroyed. I was sorry to have to think about it. I closed the bag.

I went into the bedroom and closed the door behind me. Up on the wall were all the articles about the Rose Killer and his victims. The Rose Killer was supposed to be dead, not the man who had believed in me, had trusted me, and had been my friend. Something had gone horribly wrong.

I briefly came upon the thought that if the wolf had known what it was doing, that if it had gone out with a mission last night and had killed Pearce, then he must have been guilty of something, if not the Rose killings, then maybe he . . . I don't know. Left his seed on the bodies of those dead girls, perhaps. But I knew this was impossible. Pearce couldn't have been involved in the murders or anything as filthy as I was thinking. First off, he was a normal guy. He had a wife and a baby on the way, and further, those murders went back for years and had occurred all over the country. There was no way that Pearce, while being a family man and a cop, would have the time to travel all over the United States to carve up a couple of dozen women.

But no one knew who the Rose Killer was. So maybe Pearce was a copycat killer.

Maybe he freaked out. Maybe he couldn't find a cigarette, and he snapped. Maybe he snapped, and to cover up his ghastly crime, he made it look like all those murders out West?

No fucking way, I thought. But why was he dead when he wasn't the one I'd sent the wolf after?

Could he have left his seed on one, or both, of those girls? *Could* he have been a deviated pervert like that? He *was* awfully dirty when he came over to my place that evening not so long ago. . . .

No fucking way, I thought. There was only one logical explanation for the tragedy that had occurred. I just didn't want to admit it to myself.

I went over to my lumpy bed, which was still in the corner because I had forgotten to move it back that morning, and got on my knees to reach under it. I slid out my Remington. It was always oiled and loaded, ready to go.

I sat on the bed and leaned forward. The butt rested against the floor, and the long barrel came up to me like the stem of a flower. I put the business end in my mouth and hooked my thumb around the trigger.

The bottom line was that after so long, so very long, the beast had gone mad. In killing Pearce, it went against my orders and did the one thing it was never supposed to do, and that was to kill an innocent person.

The beast had gone rabid. The beast had fucked our little arrangement right in its pearly little ass. It could not be trusted anymore with the responsibilities I'd bestowed upon it, and because it couldn't be trusted, *I* couldn't be trusted.

There was no way in hell I was going to let myself go on anymore after that. I wasn't about to go back to living the kind of life I lived before I learned how to control the fucking thing, when every single day was an exercise in torment and every moon was a study in damnation. There was no way I could live with myself, not after having it so good for so many years. I wasn't going to go backward. I couldn't be responsible for the death of another child, I just couldn't, and the knowledge of having killed Pearce burned an acid hole in my stomach.

I glimpsed one of his memories again behind my eyes.

He proposed to her in an Italian restaurant, all cheesy-like, by putting the ring in a glass of champagne. She cried, and it bowled her over. Everyone in the place clapped.

"You're the best thing that ever happened to me," he told her.

"Get out of my head!" I screamed to no one in particular.

Knowing that this kind of tragedy (there's that magic word again) could happen again to some other poor soul so easily made me absolutely sick, hence the gun to my head.

No more blood. No more tears. No more running. *Sick* of running. I would never again look in a mirror to see my face with that blank, shell-shocked look plastered onto it like a death mask. *No more face*, I thought. *No more killing. No more head. It's over now.*

"You motherfucker," I gurgled. "We had a deal."

I could feel the snot and the tears and the spit running out of me, spilling down the barrel of the rifle. I didn't want to die. I truly didn't. Jesus, I didn't have much. I had a truck, an ashtray, a recliner. Doris's night-light. An old leather jacket with half its flairs missing and a twenty-year-old Led Zeppelin patch on the back. A stinky old eagle feather my mother gave me years ago, which, apparently, was my legacy.

That gun.

My thumb tightened. The trigger went back a hair's width at a time. I clenched my eyes, wondering if I'd hear the bang.

That fucking beast. How could it betray me?

When all the madness started, the beast would go after anybody—women, children, old folks, you name it. The thing had none of what a common thug would call "decency." Once I tightened the leash on it, though, it only went after bad guys—people I singled out for it to hunt, even if I didn't know who they were. I'd give it enough hints to do its job, and it never failed. You'd think that after so many years of routine, the thing would be reliable. I had more than enough information on this Rose Killer to give the beast a good lead, not only from the papers but from a goddamn detective too. And it took my friend down. No one in the world would ever be safe again. The beast was loose. I had to stop it the only way possible.

I would be leaving behind a ratty house with half of its contents hidden, like I was a paranoid old man. No one would ever know who I was, what I was, but because of the articles on the wall, people would be talking about me for years.

In the silence of my bedroom I heard the spring in the gun coil. It was the sound of death made real, and would have been the last thing I ever heard in this world, if not for the roar that erupted in my brain.

I opened my eyes, and I was in the woods.

No I wasn't. I was in a graveyard. The graveyard in Edenburgh.

The wolf was giving me one of its memories—a brief clip from its night on the town. A single piece of the puzzle.

The wolf was down in Judith Myers's grave, a great big wall of dirt piled up on one side of the desecrated hole. The full moon rained down silver light.

With one of its giant hands, the wolf angrily swept the dirt from the lid of her coffin, and then broke the locks on it as if they were made of plastic instead of steel. The stench of death wafted up into the monster's face, forcing a long bellow to echo out from between its frothy lips. The stench of chemicals was thick, of formaldehyde, and alcohol, of makeup for the little girl's corpse.

It reached behind her neck and lifted her head up. Her lips were red, her dress was a light violet, a draped and high-necked thing of silk. It covered the stitches in her chest. Her eyelids were sealed shut with glue. Behind them, balls of cotton rested where a pair of blue eyes used to be.

Her stiffened abdomen cracked like a knuckle when the wolf raised her up, bringing her up to its pulsing snout. This was something I had seen the beast do before—busting into graves to pick up the scent of its prey from the victim's body.

The wolf breathed in deep, hungrily searching to pick up the scent of he who it was sent after. Then the wolf cried, loosening its grip on the dead girl. Her head came back down on the fake pillow heavily, like a brick. The wolf screamed.

And then the spell was broken, and I was back in my bedroom with a rifle in my mouth.

The wolf couldn't speak the King's English, but it was clearly trying to communicate with me, perhaps in a simple effort to keep me from blowing a hole in my noggin. It was telling me that it had tried. It *hadn't* flipped its lid, and it hadn't gone after Pearce out of the crystal blue. Something had gone wrong. Something beyond the wolf's control. But my connection to the monster wasn't strong enough at that moment to get more than just a snapshot of what had happened the night before. The rest would come to me at some later date. I pulled the barrel out of my mouth. I never did have the balls for that dirty business.

Pearce was a victim. Maybe because he was in the wrong place at the wrong time, but he was a victim all the same. I had to find out why. On the one hand, the Rose Killer was still out there. All those dead women needed justice. Pearce needed avenging too. But just as important, I had to find out what had gone wrong. That way I could stop it from ever happening again.

"God have mercy on me," I said as I slipped the gun back under the bed. As I did so, my telephone began to ring in the living room.

I opened the door to the bedroom, walked over, and picked the phone up from its cradle. I cleared my throat.

"Hello?"

No response. Just breathing.

"Hello?" I said again.

The line went dead.

Evelyn had suffered two losses inside of a week. That should have been bad enough, but it wasn't. Things were about to get much worse.

THIRTEEN

Pearce—or at least what was left of him—was
buried several days later. I woke up real early that morning so I
could get dressed for his funeral without having to be in a hurry.
I put on my cheap brown suit—the same one I had worn to the
little girl's service—and put on the same black shoes. I would
have worn the suit to Gloria Shaw's funeral, which was two days
before Pearce's, but I didn't go. I wouldn't have felt comfortable
being there without him. I knew the *federales* would be there
with their cameras, and I didn't want to be the weirdo that stood
out. I combed my hair back and put it in a ponytail. After that I
sat down on the couch and watched the television with a cup of
coffee. The news station was doing a retrospective of the man's
life. Following that was yet another report of a local man putting
a bullet in a stray dog.

Because of that fucking sergeant at the botched press conference, dogs were becoming an endangered species in our little
town. Every once in a while I heard a shot in the distance. It was
like being overseas, hearing shots in the night, and I didn't like it.

The night before, the FBI had taken over the network and put
on an hourlong show about the Rose Killer. It had broadcast na-
tionally from right there in Evelyn, the middle of nowhere, to
every corner of the country. All during the show an 800 number
scrolled along the bottom of the screen. For anyone who had information, operators were standing by, eager to talk.

The program gave a time line of the events in the case going
all the way back to California, and all the victims got their fifteen

minutes of fame. I suppose this was a technique to humanize the girls, to try to inspire crippling guilt in the killer.

One of the agents read off a laundry list of evidence they had gathered from all the crime scenes: semen, which I knew about, a hair, and a fingerprint, which I *didn't* know about. I wondered if they were lying to make the killer think it was only a matter of time. I also had to wonder what they were holding back.

Halfway through the program, another agent described the FBI profile of the killer. He was supposed to be a white male. He wasn't supposed to have a regional accent, and if he did, it would be very faint. He was high school educated, but in all likelihood didn't graduate. They were presuming the lack of job opportunities that came along with a poor education would have made it easier for the killer to wander. Either that or he was a trucker.

I immediately thought of the goon who had been beating on Alice's mother. He had blown into town from God knows where, and clearly wasn't a people person. I had his knife in my kitchen. *Maybe,* I thought, *I should track the fucker down and see what he knows.*

According to the FBI, the killer had no *visible* scars, mutations, or defects. He was a normal-looking man, which was why he was always able to blend into his environments without being noticed. He was a chameleon. A guy with a peg leg and an eye patch would have stuck out. However, they did believe he either had a stutter or was missing toes or something. Something for the man to feel insecure about without it showing for all the world to see.

They believed the killer's mother was abusive, perhaps overly promiscuous, and the killer maybe even had an aunt or a sister who didn't do too good by him either. They believed that there was some cataclysmic event that touched off the murders in the first place, something like the killer losing his job, or finding out his old lady was cheating on him, or that she was pregnant. Something stressful to drive him over the edge. The FBI man explained that whatever it was, specifically, it would surely be something that they had come across before, and they understood. There were people out there who cared about the killer, and they knew he needed someone to talk to. It would be better for everyone involved—both the FBI and the killer—if he came to them before they dragged him out of whatever bed he was sleeping in, and whether it was tomorrow, next week, or next month, they would find him.

They said he should turn himself in. Even if the killer didn't think so, there were people out there who cared about him and didn't want to see him get hurt. This was something they had seen a thousand times. They said that once he was apprehended, the people who cared would pop up like flowers to comfort him. The reference to flowers was obvious, and was clearly another attempt to connect to the man.

I don't know if the FBI program was always scheduled to take place when it did, or if they bumped it up so there was a potential for good news on the day of a fellow lawman's funeral.

I was nervous about going to the funeral. More than anything I was dreading seeing Martha. I couldn't bear to see her in pain. There was a part of me that was now a home for Danny Pearce. Because of that, I knew her likes, her dislikes. I knew what she tasted like, what her bathroom habits were. I knew how much she loved him, and what she looked like naked. I could never make those images go away no matter how much I wanted to. They just happened.

The phone rang. I broke into a cold sweat and reached for it. "Hello?"

A shallow breath on the other end of the line.

"When I find out who this is . . ." I said, and then the line went dead.

I had been getting the hang-up calls since the day Pearce died. They were relentless. Somehow, whoever was behind it always knew when I was home, when I was awake. I didn't like it one bit. I had enough to worry about as it was—I didn't need a fucking stalker making me look over my shoulder. I felt like I was being targeted.

I polished off my cup of coffee and headed out the door.

Wild Oaks Cemetery was about a hundred and fifty years old. There was a large area of Civil War burials that took up a good quarter of the land space. Off to one side of the grounds was a narrow pond, like a cascading teardrop on the ground, and scattered about were mangled trees consumed by foot-high patches of ivy. Some of the older graves were buried by the stuff, and no one ever bothered to clear it away. That's how you knew the families of the deceased weren't around anymore—no one looked after the final resting places of the ancestors.

The feds' forensic team had retrieved all the information they could from the detective's body, but the question still remained: What had killed him?

No one knew. The scientists wanted to have the burial postponed as long as possible to do their tests, especially after word filtered through to them from local law enforcement regarding the slew of similarly disposed-of bodies in the area surrounding Evelyn over the last few years. However, the pressure was on to have the service, both from the wife and from Pearce's friends on the force.

"Shouldn't have to keep the man on ice like that," I heard some black-clad cop say before the service.

"Fuckin' A, man," said another.

"Unless it's a rape."

"Yeah, that's a different story," said the other.

I slipped on my sunglasses and kept on walking. In my brown suit I stuck out like a sore thumb caked in shit.

His wife was sitting up front, weeping, and I guess his closest friends were up there too, because he really didn't have any blood family left alive. I saw his partner, Van Buren, up there in the front row, and I pretended not to. Then there were a few rows of law-enforcement types, all wide in the shoulders, and behind them were some of the townsfolk who'd come out to pay their respects. I was mixed in with that crowd. No one back there was crying for the man, but I was, under my shades.

Off in the distance, behind some trees and shrubs and so on, was a small handful of chaps who were no doubt *federales,* taking pictures of the crowd with long-distance lenses. I thought I saw Anthony Mannuzza up on a hill. He was taking pictures, talking to some other guy in a suit. I figured if it was him, he *would* pull some shit like that, taking pictures of the dead man's service for his shitty little photo book. I made a mental note to kick his ass if I ever saw him again.

The priest went on and on, talking about goodness, service, care, the Lord, and finally, ashes and dust. The wife broke down twice. The second time, they had to hold her up because they were worried she'd fall in the hole with the coffin or some such thing, injure herself and the baby in her belly.

It occurred to me that Pearce was like a father figure to me. On the one hand that was ridiculous because I was older than him and he only thought he knew me. Instead of locking me up for chronic disorderly conduct, he gave me a chance to prove I was a decent man. But on the other hand, at the age of forty, I still wouldn't have had anything that resembled a normal life if it wasn't for him.

His casket was closed, but I pictured him. I know that his wife helped him tie his tie every morning because he hated doing it. I think she would have insisted on being the one to do it for him one last time when they were dressing the body. I now knew that was the kind of woman she was.

Anyway, being at Wild Oaks got me thinking about my own father, roasting in hell, as he must be.

My old man fought the Nazis in the Second World War. A few years after, my father settled down with a woman named Rosemary, and then I came along, as did my brother, Jeffrey. My little brother lived only a week and a day.

My childhood was fine and dandy because my mother was kind and my father was a war hero. My grandfather, Jacob Higgins, amazed me with more stories from the Great War than I could shake my tiny fist at. Everything was aces.

My grandfather died when I was eight years old. He was ninety-nine years old, but he looked great and still had a swagger to his step like Robert Mitchum. What had finally done him in was a car accident. A head-on collision with one of those fast and fancy foreign cars that had begun to spring up on the roads, like the kind James Dean had died in. After that, the mood around my childhood home changed. The folks got a lot quieter than they were known to be. The reason, of course, was that my father had assumed the mantle of the beast.

The curse of the wolf had started with my grandfather's father, a man who lived to be a hundred and fifty (or thereabouts), and had passed down the bloodstream, father to son, so when Jacob Higgins bit the bullet, my father became a werewolf. He knew it was coming. The curse had not been kept a secret from him like it had been with me. I had no idea that anything like this could happen outside of a Lon Chaney movie.

My father's secret didn't interfere with our home life too much, save for the silence and secrets I could almost taste, hanging in the air like dandelion spores, but once a month, my daddy would disappear, and I never knew where he went. He was a bus driver, but I never felt it would be good to ask why such a job required business trips on a regular basis. I think there was a part of me that believed, or at least wished, that he was a government agent, like in the Jimmy Cagney movies.

I was in high school as the whole situation in Vietnam was going down. A lot of older kids from my neighborhood were being sent back in caskets, and as a token of the nation's appreciation for the lives of the young, the grieving parents were given folded flags. My best friend Ben's brother got killed over there.

I had no intention of ever going to war with anybody. My

concept of war was hitting someone with a piece of metal I boosted from shop class and that was about it. Wars lasted as long as it took to hold a grudge and for a teacher to turn his head.

I wasn't politically active, which was kind of looked at as a sin by certain people, but everything that was going on in the world hardly seemed to me to be my problem. I mean, I wanted to play baseball. I'd picked up the passion for it from the television, then Little League. I was the best first baseman my high school had ever seen, and I had big dreams for myself, all of which included Doris, the greatest girl who's ever lived. The girl of my dreams.

Whatever I did, I wanted her with me. There was no way I was going to go overseas to some godforsaken country no one had ever heard of. There was no way I wasn't going to go pro and have Doris hanging off my arm like Marilyn Monroe, telling jokes and making the whole world wish they were me.

Doris was amazing. She was funny, smart, had silky brown hair done up like the hot wife from *The Dick Van Dyke Show,* and had legs that wouldn't quit. I mean, she was so much more to me. She was everything I could've ever hoped for. Just kissing her made me feel like there was nothing else in this life I could ever think to do beyond that moment. But then I got drafted.

I wanted to run. The prospect of being a deserter didn't mean anything to me, even if it meant I could never play baseball in the major leagues. My dream up to that point, as far-fetched as it was, was to win the World Series—and I wanted to be a goddamn Pittsburgh Pirate doing it.

However, if denying my part in the American War Machine would destroy the possibility of living that dream, then so be it. I wanted to pack a bag, pick Doris up on my bike, and hit the road. I didn't care, so long as I had her with me. That's how much our life together meant to me.

I talked with my father about it. He was the man I respected most, and I was proud to be his son. We went out back of the house where we had these flowering bushes, and a couple of trees. In one of those trees hung a tire from a rope. When I was a little kid, I was always on that thing. I even read on it. The course that life was steering me toward sucked—how one can be purely happy out back of the house and then be forced to dwell in a blood-drenched war zone. It hardly seemed like this was the way the world was supposed to be. It just didn't seem fair.

"Dad, I don't think I can go," I whispered.

I didn't feel good saying such a thing to my father. He had been a soldier raised by another soldier. It would've been so much easier to just take off with Doris and not tell anybody. That's what I should have done.

"I don't want to die. Ben's brother died, and I'm not about to end up like that."

"You sayin' you're better than that dead boy?" he said.

"Of course not, but no one deserves to die over there."

"Son," he said, "I ain't going to tell you what the government likes to say, because most of the time it's bunk, but there are times in life you gotta play by other people's rules, no matter how crazy they are, just to get by. It ain't fair, but that's the way it is."

"So I should throw my life away to play by someone else's stupid rules?"

"It may not be right, what's happening over there, but the fact that it's happening cannot be denied. Taking off may be what you want to do, but there would be real-world consequences you'd have to face after making the decision to run."

"I can live without baseball," I said bravely.

"A lot of people wouldn't want to hire a draft dodger. A lot of people wouldn't want to hire a woman who runs with a draft dodger. A lot of landlords may not want to rent to you. You could end up in jail, doing hard time. They got a unit out there in the FBI that hunts down little men like you who take off. There are kids out there getting two-year, five-year sentences for doing what you're talking about doing. How would being an ex-con affect the rest of your life? What would happen to Doris? Even if you never got picked up, what about the strain that could come between you from running?"

"That's impossible."

"Trust me, it's possible. Misery makes it very easy for love to feel like hate."

"So you think Doris and I would be miserable?"

"I wouldn't want to speculate," he said. "The decision is up to you."

Little did I know that he could've cared less about the happiness she and I created just by being around each other. He just wanted me to die before he did.

My brother, Jeffrey, had died as an infant. He wasn't even a distant memory to me. Jeffrey was something that made my parents uncomfortable when his name was mentioned. With no more children to carry on the bloodline, the curse would be broken, and he would be the last. Dad *wanted* to be the last one. That's why I never knew the family secret—about the evil that lived inside me, biding its time—until it was too late. He wanted me to die without being tainted by that secret, and the best way for that to happen would be to get myself killed in a rice paddy a million miles away with a belly full of lead and a stained picture of my love tucked inside my helmet, just like how my father had tried to die in combat, and his father before him.

So I went. I spent a few months in training, and just over four months in the shit before they shipped me back with discharge papers. They said I was certifiable. In 1971, mental breakdown was the reason for a full half of all the medical evacuations from Vietnam. I was nothing special.

Letters came from Doris regularly. I wrote to her once that she didn't have to write so often, but her letters never ceased. I never received a word from my father. I didn't know that I had been written off prematurely. That's the kind of guy he was, a fucking werewolf. All things being equal, he could have lived to be two hundred years old. But he didn't. He died under the wheels of a bus at the bus depot. A day later, I was shot by a sniper in the jungles of Vietnam. Had my father been standing in a different place, he would have gotten what he wanted. He would have been the last one. I would have died in combat, but instead I became the healthiest man alive.

When the service for Danny was over, it started to rain. Everyone got up to go to their cars, huddling in groups under large black umbrellas.

I went over to Pearce's wife. Martha had a big heavy cop in dress uniform on each side of her. They had her held up under her arms, like she was a drunk who couldn't go on anymore, and they were leading her to one of the long black cars.

When I approached, they gave me a look like I was a field mouse that had stumbled into their yard, and they were the big dogs. I didn't want to get in a situation with them, which was apt to happen, me having the face that I have, so I approached with a friendly wave.

"Mrs. Pearce," I said, extending my hand for her.

She didn't take it.

"I was wondering if I could have a word with you for a minute."

She looked away, said, "No, I can't talk," in a low, guttural voice, like any music that had existed inside her had died with her man, and the way she said it, I knew it was true. But I had no choice. She had to know how much he loved her, and I had to know where he was on the night that Judith Myers disappeared.

"I swear, Mrs. Pearce, I just . . ."

"Hey, guy," said one of the cops at her side, "did you hear what she said?"

"Yeah, but . . ."

"I don't want to hear it. Back off, her fucking husband died."

Mrs. Pearce wailed at the insensitivity.

"Ma'am," I said, "please."

"Leave me alone," she cried, "all of you."

She broke the grips of both men and hurried down the gravel road toward her waiting car. The two cops looked at each other, and then looked at me.

"Thanks, asshole. You see what you did?" said one of them.

"Yeah," said the other. "Why don't you go drop dead?"

They stormed off.

Under my breath, I said, "I'll give that a shot."

When I called Pearce's home number that evening, a cop answered, and I hung up. A moment later, my phone rang. I figured they had caller ID over there, and she was calling back to see who it was. I picked up the phone.

"Hello?"

Silence. Then a man's voice. Very soft.

"I know what you did."

"Who is this?"

A shallow breath, then the line went dead. I slammed the phone into the cradle.

My roots to the town were dead and buried, and I really had no reason to stay. In fact, staying would only make things worse, if not for me, then most certainly for someone else. But then, no matter where I went, someone would have to die. There was no alternative to that short of my own death, and suicide, obviously, was not in my repertoire. But if I left right away, I reckoned it would only bring about a suspicion surrounding my sudden disappearance, and I didn't need anyone looking for me. I had to do something.

The Rose Killer was still out there, whoever he was. He was the first person I had sent the wolf after who managed to make it through the night. I was concerned that the wolf was no longer under my control, but I was somewhat convinced that something had gone horribly wrong that allowed the target to live.

The only person who would know was the killer.

I didn't know what could possibly have gone wrong. Was it something internal in the beast, or something the killer could have done to throw the beast off? And if that was the case, was it intentional, or was it some cosmic snafu? I had to know his secret so I would never again kill an innocent man.

I was tempted to take the easy way out, to select another target for the next full moon. Someone easy, like some scumbag already in jail. But that would've been evading the issue of whether or not the beast could be as trustworthy as it once was, and further, I needed to know what its weakness was.

I came up with my plan of action.

I had to get the Rose Killer. I had to try again. Not only for myself, but for Pearce and all those girls who weren't around anymore.

Before the last full moon, I had been able to acquire a lot of information about the killer thanks to Pearce, but now I was on my own. Anything I hoped to learn from that point on would not be privileged information. It would be filtered through the media first before it got to concerned citizens such as myself. Real information would be scarce.

I needed to do some digging on my own. Just like Nancy Drew. I wasn't a sleuth, but to get to the bottom of all this, I had to put my neck out there a lot more than usual. I didn't like it, and try as I might, I couldn't get the wolf to relinquish any more of *its* memories from the night Pearce died.

If the police caught the killer, the wolf could've just busted into his cell and took him out, lickety-split. It would have no problem doing that. After all, it had gotten us out of one, once.

If, by the grace of God, *I* was the one to catch him, I would be tempted to kill him. For all my big talk *I* had never actually killed a man. Never wanted to. I would have to turn him over to the authorities, or kidnap him. Maybe question him myself. Tie him to a chair in my house so the next time the moon came up, he'd be right there. However that bastard evaded me would be known once I had his memories.

I decided that after the next full moon, Evelyn would no longer be my home. I knew that much for sure. I had outlived my welcome. Maybe I would be Steve Rogers again, somewhere a thousand miles away from that place. With the proliferation of background checks and all the fancy computer stuff that the *federales* were coming up with, I wasn't sure how hard it would be to reinvent myself again. A new identity, a new voice, a new home town. Maybe Steve Rogers wouldn't have been such a sweet idea at that point. He was probably on file somewhere. Jerk Jerkenson had a nice ring to it.

But all this was wishful thinking. It assumed that I would be successful in taking out the Rose Killer. If I sent the wolf after him again and it failed again, Evelyn would be the last place I ever lived, because I would be dead. I'd find the balls to do the world a favor.

So the way I figured it, I had three weeks' time to save my own life.

FOURTEEN

The following day I took the hunting knife that
belonged to the trucker out from under the sink and inspected it.
Since it had been in my possession I'd never closely inspected it.
I had no reason to, but I had such a bad feeling about the guy that
Alice's mother had been shacking up with—the kind of feeling
that used to mean something back when I could trust myself—I
wasn't sure if it had been a murder weapon or not.

I let the kitchen light shine off the knife's edge. I was looking
for blood, but didn't see any. I knew the cops, with their liquids
and fancy lighting, would be able to detect even the most minuscule speck of blood, but I didn't have these gadgets at my dis-
posal.

I washed the knife off, which might have been stupid if I was
worried about evidence, but my fingerprints were on it. I
couldn't have that. Holding it with a paper towel, I wrapped it in
a rag and dropped it in a manila envelope. With a marker, I wrote
out the address of the Evelyn Police Department and left the
space for a return address blank. After that I slapped on a bunch
of stamps. I would drop it in a mailbox on the way to work with a
note that stated I, a concerned citizen, had found the knife in Applegate Park. Hope it proves to be useful in your endeavors. With
love, Jerk Jerkenson.

I got in the truck, cursed it to life, and headed out. The knife
went into a mailbox three blocks south of where I bought my
morning papers.

When I got to the newsstand, there was a crowd gathered
around. *This,* I thought, *is not a good sign.* I pulled to the curb

and left the engine running. I had the exact change for the two local papers and a copy of *USA Today,* so I broke through the milling people, dropped my nickels and dimes on the counter, and ran out with the three newspapers.

Behind the steering wheel, I looked at the front page of the *Harbinger* and gritted my teeth. "Another Woman Missing," it read.

The sonofabitch was still close by.

I read the articles in the kitchen at work. Luckily, it had proved to be another slow and rainy day. It seemed to me that since Pearce died, the rains hadn't stopped, just took a break every now and then to get people's hopes up so they could be crushed again.

While the article in the *Harbinger* was quick to point out that this woman's disappearance and the fact that there was a killer loose was merely coincidental, it couldn't stop itself from sounding like she was already dead. Maybe if the missing woman hadn't been a prostitute, they wouldn't have been so quick to write her off.

The thing with hookers going missing is that it happens more often than anyone cares to realize. The law would be quick to state that hookers are not the kind of people who develop deep ties to their communities, that they don't have to worry about getting oodles of mail, and they usually don't have a million houseplants and pets to take care of. That they tend to be transient by nature, going where the work is. But it cannot be denied, a hooker is easy to commit the perfect crime against. And if not for the Rose Killer, the story of a missing prostitute wouldn't have even made the papers.

I could only thank my lucky stars that it wasn't Alice. I was frayed enough as it was. If I had lost her too, I think it would have sent me over the edge. This, though, was a small consolation. I recognized the woman, and she sure as shit worked out of Mama Snow's house. Her name was Josie Jones.

A "friend" of hers reported her missing the previous evening, though the last time she had been seen alive was the night of the twentieth. It occurred to me that the FBI show on the television aired the night of the twentieth.

Maybe the killer took her away in response to it. Maybe he was communicating by taking a hooker. Maybe he was saying something about his mother. Manson's mother was a hooker. Maybe he just took a hooker because she was easy to get to, and he wanted the lawmen to look bad. On another page was a short article about a church break-in the previous night. Nothing taken. Weren't they picking up on this? It had to mean something.

Abraham came through the double doors to steal some French fries. He must have seen me gritting my teeth over the paper.

"Are you okay?"

"Sure," I said.

"You haven't been the same lately. If you need to talk . . ."

"I feel like I need a drink, Abe." It was the truth. Just then, I realized that my hands were shaking.

He came over and hit me in the arm. "I don't want to hear it. Drinking is my deal, not yours. Besides, if you hit the sauce again it would be the excuse Frank has been waiting for to can your sorry ass. Don't give him the satisfaction." He hit me in the arm again. "Don't fuck up," he said.

"I won't."

"Because I love you."

"Fuck you."

"I don't want anything to happen to you."

"Get the fuck out of my kitchen," I said.

Most of the time, I hated the bastard, but every so often, Abraham knew how to make me feel better.

That night I put the new articles up on the wall. There were getting to be too many. It shouldn't have been that way. I was starting to feel that if another girl died, the blood would also be on my hands.

I went back to the living room and fiddled with the rabbit ears until I got a decent picture. Then I sat down with a can of tuna and watched the news late into the evening.

I was very much hoping for the joint task force to come through on their promise of catching the fucking guy. It would save me the trouble of doing it myself. After all, if they had him in custody, I would surely know who to kill when the time came. But what was still killing me was whether or not the wolf would still obey.

Another fucking question mark. The biggest one of the bunch.

I tried constantly to get the wolf to reveal any of its memories from the night Pearce died. If it did, I would at least know enough to come up with a theory as to what went wrong. I lit a cigarette, having forgotten that two were already burning in the naked-lady ashtray.

The phone rang at just about the stroke of midnight. I knew it was the prick who had been calling me lately. But it kind of worried me that I had been targeted for something at the same time all these other events were going on. It made me feel . . . involved, and I didn't want anyone to make me feel that way. I had to know who it was, and what they thought they knew about me.

I picked up the phone. "Yes," I said.

Silence. The sound of light traffic in the background.

"Mom?" I said.

"I know what you did," the man's voice said.

"What did I do?" I said softly.

"You know what you did, and I know too."

"Who is this?"

"It's Pearce," said the voice.

My blood ran cold in my veins. "Fuck you."

"Do you miss me?"

"You're a sick fuck."

I hung up the phone.

It began to ring again. I picked it up.

"Leave me the fuck alone!" I screamed, slamming it back down in the cradle.

It began to ring again.

. . .

The dead hooker was found in the early morning hours of May 24, propped up on a bench in Applegate Park. She was naked as the day she was born, her knees tied with twine to the armrests so her ravaged privates were exposed to anyone who was unlucky enough to pass by. Her raven-black hair was sheared off, probably with the knife that had killed her, and tossed about like birdseed on the grass. Her insides were unraveled and spread out along the dirt path along the lake, and in her head where her eyes used to be were two red roses.

And I felt as responsible for her death as the man who had done the deed.

I immediately regretted sending the hunting knife off to the police. Not that I should have held on to it, but I shouldn't have lied when I wrote I had come across it in the park. This was a terrible coincidence, and I feared that the mailed-in knife would wreak havoc with their investigation.

I blinked, and all of a sudden I was seeing the world through Pearce's dead eyes. He was up at the Crowley property. The wolf charged forward, becoming all he could see.

"No!" cried Pearce, but it was too late. The vision ended.

All this shit was really fucking me up. I needed to see Alice. She was the only thing left that made me feel at least the slightest bit normal.

I took a seat on the edge of the soft bed and lit a cigarette. There was a part of me that was tempted to take all my clothes off and ravage Alice the second she walked through that door, but there was another part of me that wasn't feeling it at all. I also knew that after having lost a friend, just like me, she probably wouldn't be in the mood to do the nasty. It was unfortunate that there wasn't a union for hookers. She would have been able to take the day off.

Alice stepped into the room and closed the door behind her. She was wearing a long white nightgown and a pair of slippers.

She would usually come in with a smile on her face no matter what the circumstances were, but not on this day. There was only so much she could pretend. I patted the bed next to me and gave her my cigarette.

"Tough day?"

"Yes," she said softly. "The police have been in and out, and Mama Snow's worried about what's going to happen."

"Are they gonna shut it down?"

"Never," said Alice. "You'd be surprised who comes here."

"I'm worried about you," I said.

"*She's* not. She's worried about business." She put her head on my shoulder. "I'm glad it's you tonight. I don't know if I'd be able to deal with anyone else."

"Were you and Josie close?"

"As close as you can be, living this way," she said.

I lit myself another cigarette. "We don't have to do anything tonight. I just wanted to be here with you is all."

"How come?"

"To make sure you're okay."

She laughed.

"You don't have to do that. Leon's here."

"I know," I said. "With all that's going on, I just wish you didn't have to do this. They're saying on the TV that no one's safe now, and this isn't exactly the safest . . . you know . . ."

"I know," she said, "but I can't just stop."

"What if I asked you to?"

"What?"

"Just till all this is over. Just so I know you're okay?"

"Marley . . ."

"I don't know. Maybe you can stay at my place for a while. I got an extra room and all. . . ."

"I couldn't."

"Maybe, like, if you wanted to, I could drive you around. Pick you up at home, drive you home in the morning. Just so you don't have to be alone."

I regretted asking. I knew just by her expression how much I had made her uncomfortable.

"Marley," she said, "that just wouldn't be appropriate."

I hung my head.

"I know."

"I know you know. There's a line . . ."

"I know," I said, cutting her off. "I just don't want anything to happen to you."

I could have told her how much she meant to me. I could have told her that if I lost her, I wouldn't care who the wolf went after, because I'd have no reason to go on anyway. But I didn't. I'd have been out on my ear faster than lightning.

"I can take care of myself," Alice said.

I'm sure Josie Jones had said the same thing a thousand times, but I didn't press the issue. Before long, we went to bed, and in the morning I left with a little bit of pain in my heart, just like I always did.

By the time I got to work, two things had happened. One, the trucker whose knife it was had contacted the police when the knife made an appearance on the news as a possible murder weapon. He claimed ownership of it, and stated on the television that he had been robbed of it almost three weeks earlier. He was not charged with anything.

Two, since the Rose Killer had struck too close to home for me, I decided to keep an eye on Alice. She had been unwilling or unable to accept my offer of protection. I couldn't let a little thing like acceptance stand in my way. I had lost too much. I couldn't lose her too. And maybe, just maybe, she would lead me to the bad guy.

FIFTEEN

Alice left her house at seven-thirty in the evening, got behind the wheel of her Honda, and drove to work. I was right behind her in the truck.

She parked on the corner, several doors away from Mama Snow's, and walked the rest of the way. At the front door, she was greeted by the monster known as Leon, who actually smiled. I drove past the house, made a U-turn, and parked on the far corner for my nightlong stakeout. I had a full view of everything, like a mountain bird.

Before long, the sky grew black.

It gnawed at my soul knowing she was in that house for all those hours with men that weren't me. There was a part of me that understood what she did for a living, the fact that I paid her just like everybody else. But there was another part of me that longed for something more than that. It was the part of me that cared and was much more likely to get me into trouble. What made those long, dark hours worse was that the radio didn't work in the truck. I couldn't very well keep the overhead light on, so I sat in the dark all night, stewing in my own crap thoughts, and watching German cars pull up to Mama Snow's one after another.

As midnight came and went, I got to thinking about the war.

At night in Vietnam we spent a lot of time staring into the longest, blackest night, waiting for something bad to happen, like hearing a twig snap, or hearing a bang and realizing someone just died. We couldn't smoke because the snipers would be able to put a bullet in your face. The glow at the end of a cigarette became a beacon for VC—it meant an American was taking a drag.

It felt the same as I watched Mama Snow's house from the cab of my truck. Sitting in the dark, waiting for something bad to happen.

I couldn't think about Vietnam without thinking of the ambush. It was in that ambush that I should have died. Instead, I became a monster. It was a triple-canopy jungle. The sunlight reaching the ground was scarce, and further obstructing our field of vision were patches of bamboo and elephant grass. Those conditions alone were terrifying. Every nook and cranny was a potential hiding place, every anthill a potential airhole for the tunnels that were probably running directly under us. Cambodia was just a handful of hours west on foot, we were that close. We were knee high in mud and foliage, a few miles away from where they wanted us camped that night.

It started off with Chandler's head getting blown off.

As his limp body tilted and fell to the wet earth, we all ran for cover because we didn't know where the shot had come from. We set our rifles to rock and roll and began spraying the green hell to our front.

Before long, we figured out there was more than one sniper. There were at least two. Shots started raining down on us from different directions. We didn't know where was safe, and everyone was screaming.

The second man to die was the radio man, Talbot. The enemy always went after the radio man. More so than a commander, the radio man was the prime target. Talbot caught one in the thigh, and he started screaming, dragging himself through the brush so someone could relieve him of the radio. Someone ran over to him to get the radio off him. As long as there was one man alive, that radio was more important than bullets. It was the only way to let anyone know where we were and that we were under attack. This was a fucking ambush.

Baxter—who made the run to get the radio—lost his jaw in a plume of gore. I had never seen anything like it, a man with a surprised expression in his eyes, and everything below his nose just a deep, red hole. Blood pouring out like puke from a mouthless cave. His eyes asked if he was okay, and then he just curled up in a ball and died. Didn't make a sound.

As that was going on, Conrad caught one in the shoulder, and Talbot caught another one in or close to his liver. We fired into the trees, and the sergeant kept screaming for someone to get on the horn so we could get some air support. By this time, Talbot was dead. In all, he got hit three or four times. Conrad was dead. Chandler was dead. Baxter. We lost four men in no more than five minutes.

The radio was sitting there in the dirt. We set off some smoke for cover, and this other guy, Morris, made a move for the radio. He went down hard, and when the smoke cleared, the radio was toast. Shattered and lost in a hail of bullets, like us.

Night fell. We couldn't hardly see the man in front of us. We were trapped like fish in a barrel. Every once in a while, someone would shuffle in his little cove, his few square feet of cover, and shots would ring out. Tracers from the treetops.

Vietnamese snipers lived up in those trees for God knows how long. It was their land, and it was in their blood, and they knew every inch of it. We were like parasites out there, getting picked off one by one for our trespasses. The sergeant ordered us not to talk because the snipers knew how the sound bounced in the jungle.

As the hours went on, we resorted to throwing stones out into the night. Shots would ring out, and tracers would mark a trail through the darkness. When we thought we saw where these shots came from, we'd let loose with our rifles, but it was almost more dangerous shooting our guns because of the small flashes of burning powder that would ejaculate from our weapons when they discharged.

We lost Poe, and we lost Wells after that.

Wells died slowly, from a gutshot, and he kept moaning and crying for his mother.

"Please, Hooper, I want my momma. Oh, God, man, it hurts!"

He was twenty years old. He kept screaming, and Sergeant Hooper started to crack up. He kept whispering to the kid, "You're going to give us away, you sonofabitch."

When the kid wouldn't shut up, the sergeant whispered, "Someone give him a fucking shot."

No one knew where the shots were, the morphine. They were probably on one of the bodies, so the sergeant made the decision to have someone shoot Wells, to put him down for the good of the men. I'd later learn that wolves in the wilderness have the same policy for sick members of the pack.

No one made a move to shoot Wells.

Wells kept screaming, "I don't wanna die, I wanna go home!"

The sergeant shot him, and then Wells just moaned. The sergeant shot him again and again until he didn't make any more noises.

A few minutes later, we heard a lone shot, and when someone called out for Hooper, he didn't answer.

That's when our worst fears became a reality. Our only hope was Charlie Company coming to look for us, but we knew it wouldn't happen until first light. We were on our own, and I doubt anyone thought we'd make it through the night. I can't communicate the feeling of what it's like being surrounded by boys—being just a boy yourself—and knowing that it's only a matter of time until you and everyone you know is going to die. Everyone started whispering prayers. In the distance, the dark, we could almost hear the snipers laughing at us.

I didn't pray. I thought of Doris.

Unbeknownst to me, my father had died a day earlier. He'd been hit by a bus backing into a space on the lot where he worked. He was rushed to the hospital, and spent the better part of his last day on earth in the intensive-care unit. Anyone else caught under the wheels of that bus would have died instantly. It takes an extraordinary amount of punishment to kill a Higgins man, and getting crushed under the bus was enough, but my father lived long enough to talk to his wife, and to pray that his only son was already dead. In a cruel twist of fate, I wasn't. And then my father died.

From the moment he died to the time that I myself was trapped and waiting to die, the spirit of the wolf crossed continents, perhaps as an invisible specter, or as a fast-moving storm cloud, and came to me in that jungle. I wonder if it watched me as I cowered there in that narrow ditch where water once flowed. I wonder if it laughed at the fear I had of my own mortality. Out in the jungle, the glare of the full moon barely came through the blanket of trees that shielded us from that exquisite, damning light. The only thing we could see were the tracers that got fired at us every few rounds.

I had my arms around Ritter, and he had his arms around me, and there we were—huddled down and waiting to die. We didn't want to die alone. No one does. You can have your friends and the people you didn't get along with, but when the pearly gates are in your sights, everyone's on the same team and you have to be brothers.

Men were crying. Someone whispered Ritter's name, and Ritter lifted his head up just a fraction of an inch. A subconscious reaction to his name being called through the silence.

Shots rang out. A tracer burned a brilliant hole through his cheek, and before his head exploded, it seemed to glow from the inside out like a jack-o'-lantern. His head literally exploded like a ripe melon. The smell of burning hair filled my nostrils, and Ritter's hot blood washed over me like a wave. A spilled drink. I could feel it in my eyes, and I could taste it in my mouth. I breathed in deep, and let out a bloodcurdling scream.

Ritter's body fell against me, and I pushed it away. I pushed it away as if the death that had infested it, had consumed it and claimed it, would wash off on me. Like it would contaminate me and I would be the next to die.

He could have *the fucking ditch,* I remember thinking deliriously.

I jumped up like I was on fire. I had to run. There was nowhere to run, but that was the moment that the combat broke me. I couldn't even think like a man anymore. The force guiding my legs to run belonged to an older, more primitive urge.

The men began to shout. "Higgins, get down!"

I couldn't respond. Language wasn't mine to use anymore. I felt hands pull at my pant legs, but these feelings just produced more fear. In my mind, they were the hands of the dead trying to pull me into hell.

More shots rang out—many—and I felt a bullet rip through the meat between my neck and my shoulder. My arm went hot and dead. More hot blood hit me in the face, only this time it was mine.

I instantly felt the loss of blood. My frantic steps stopped, and I fell to my knees. I felt like I had never felt anything else in my life before that, even the heavenly touch of my Doris. In a way, nothing had ever been more real than that gunshot, or more meaningful. In front of me, tracers zipped past my ears and burrowed holes into a tree. Strips of burning bark flew through the air like sparks. In that darkness it looked like a fireworks display. I was entranced, just . . . lost up there in my headspace. I threw my head back and cried.

Through a clearing, I caught the full moon in my eyes. The moon was pure white, save the spots of gray that dotted its pale and powdered face. I thought it was heaven, seeing that pearly moon fill the sky. I knew that somewhere, somehow, my Doris was looking at that same, plump moon, watching it with her beautiful blue eyes, wondering where I was, and hoping against all hope that I was safe.

In the blink of an eye, the moon turned from white to silver. My hysteria broke long enough for me to scream, because the pain of a thousand deaths had hit me. I saw my hand explode from the wrist down, and there was something else underneath it, but I didn't know what. A moment later, I was gone.

I came back to the States not long after, not knowing what had happened that night, not knowing what to tell the brass about how I had survived the firefight. I thought I was crazy. They did too, which was why they sent me back.

I shouldn't have come back. My father never should've had children. When he *did* have children, he should've killed the both of us. He should've lived one more day so I could've died in that moonlit jungle. I should've stayed down, or taken that round to the head for my friend Ritter. I never should've come home, because I never would've known guilt.

Alice walked out the front door and shuffled down the block toward her Honda. She got in, made a turn, and headed north toward home. I followed. It was just after four in the morning.

Once her front door closed behind her, I drove home, slept for a couple of hours, and got up a little after six to get ready for work myself. I was exhausted, but there was no rest for the wicked. That night I would do the same thing all over again.

Midnight again on Carpenter Street.

With every car that pulled up to see one of the girls in the house, there was the possibility he was a sick and sadistic killer. I kept my eyes open for a car with out-of-state plates, but they all looked local to me. As far as I knew, there wasn't even any proof that the Rose Killer had set foot in Mama Snow's. He very well could have come upon Josie Jones on the street somewhere, or at a coffee shop, or a red light.

Too many variables. It had never been my fucking forte to consider variables. I was a broad-strokes kind of guy, and yes, I can admit it now, it all made my head hurt.

It occurred to me that instead of the killer being from out of town, he very well could have been a local man who traveled around the world to do his dirty work. In that case, he would have been working too close to home now, which means he would have snapped recently, not caring anymore if he got caught. Or maybe he was just plain crazy. Was there anyone in town who fit the bill?

As if lightning had struck me dead in the brain, I no longer saw the darkened street ahead of me, but the outside of a dilapidated house somewhere not far away. I was experiencing another one of Pearce's memories. . . .

Pearce approached the house slowly. Not because he was afraid—the resident wasn't known to be especially violent—but because there was so much to take in. The resident's lawn was painted green. Not a single blade of grass grew. It was literally all green paint thrown across the bare dirt.

Pearce laughed, and before knocking on the door with his big, hairless knuckles, he peeked in through one of the broken windows. He could see a room painted blue in the space between the curtains. Up on the wall was one of those ridiculous posters seen in schools all across the country—a little kitty cat hanging by its paws from a clothesline or some such thing. The caption read "HANG IN THERE!"

Pearce sighed. This wasn't going to be easy.

Just then, the sun broke out from behind a squadron of clouds, and whereas the room once shone to him through the window, it was now obscured. All he could see was his face in the reflection. He looked at himself and smiled, curious to see how young he looked just then, even though he seemed tired around the eyes.

How strange it is, how a man spends his life looking in a mirror, only to think he will be the only person to ever see what he sees.

I see it too, if I just so happen to kill you.

Pearce stepped back to the door to the house and hammered it with his fist. Immediately following that, he stepped to the side and rested his hand on the gun latched on to the side of his duty belt. If the tenant was crazy enough to start blazing away, Pearce didn't want to get shot through the door. It's what he was trained to do.

Several long seconds passed. Pearce was about to knock again when the door creaked open.

"Hey, Officer," said Crazy Bob. "Everything okay?"

Crazy Bob was wearing a pair of dirty blue jeans and a wife

beater. He was covered from head to toe in green paint. He was, needless to say, the guilty party.

"Bob, right?"

"You got that right. What can I help you with?"

"Well," said Pearce, "your neighbors thought I should come by to see how you're feeling."

"I feel marvelous," said Crazy Bob. "Fantastic, even. Never better in my life."

Pearce cleared his throat and stepped closer.

"We'll see about that," said Pearce.

As suddenly as I had been forced into another man's memories, I found myself back behind the wheel on Carpenter Street. I lit another cigarette.

Before I knew what I was doing, I started the truck and was heading south. I knew where Crazy Bob lived. And they didn't call him Crazy Bob because he was the most predictable motherfucker in the world, either.

Picture, if you will, all the times you've driven through a really nice neighborhood in your life. The kind of neighborhood where in the winter months the Christmas decorations outside the houses will be elaborate and expensive. Where in the summers, boats are parked in the driveways. Where, through the windows, you could see the people who live there have honest-to-God chandeliers in the house, like at a fucking opera house or something. Now picture on this beautiful, upscale kind of block a single house that looked like it had been strafed and bombed by a fleet of F-16s.

That would be Crazy Bob's house. I passed it in the truck, saw there was a light on inside, kept driving, parked on the corner, and walked back.

Because of Pearce's memories, I felt as if I'd already been there, but I never was. It was very dark, but I could see that there were some patches of grass growing up on his lawn—a drastic shift from when Pearce had visited the place years earlier. I walked over the lawn to the window that Pearce had once looked in. It was just around the side, and, coincidentally, it looked into the one room that was lit from the inside. I was shocked by what I saw through the curtains.

The room was painted bloodred, and a bare lightbulb hung from a wire in the cracked ceiling, swinging back and forth like that scene in *Psycho*. The kitty poster wasn't on the wall anymore, and probably hadn't been for some time, but instead there was something in that room far more interesting.

Crazy Bob's back was to me. He was wearing a pair of jeans and a dirty T-shirt. His beer gut hung over his pants like a threat. In his right hand was a six-gun. A Magnum, by the looks of it. I swallowed.

Seated before him was a naked woman coated with sweat. Her legs were long and her breasts were just short of gargantuan. One of them had a red dot on it. That was blood, which ran in a fine trickle from her heavy lower lip. She was blond, and had enough makeup on to be mistaken for a member of Kiss. Regardless, it was apparent that the woman needed some saving from this madman. I would not let another woman die by this monster's hand. I presumed those were her clothes littered about the floor, only because they were surely too small for our friend Bob.

I had not anticipated anything actually going down when I swung by the lunatic's house. I merely wanted to do some recon. This, however, was not going to be recon. I wished I had brought a disguise, but then I figured it probably didn't matter. The chances were fair that no one was going to make it out of that house alive anyway.

I snuck to the back of the house. There was a door back there that led into the kitchen. I jiggled the doorknob, and the door opened silently. I breathed in deep and stepped in.

The stench hit me first—the smell of roaches. Then I heard Crazy Bob—thought to be harmless all these years—quoting scripture. Some business about the end times.

I slowly crept through the house. Mounds of plaster rested in the corners because the ceiling was caving in. I figured the house would collapse inside a year if it was left to its own devices. I could hear the woman breathing heavily.

I stopped at the open door to the red room.

Bob was calm, but I didn't know how alert he was, or how quick he was with the six-gun. I wondered what it felt like to truly kill a man. I hoped I wouldn't have to find out. *Fuck it,* I thought, and rushed him.

He didn't see me coming. My right hook from hell sent him into the far wall, and he dropped the gun on the floor. The woman screamed. With Bob off balance, I drove a closed fist down into his gut, and he doubled up. I followed that up with some quick punches to the back of his neck, and then he was down. He didn't even know what the fuck was going on. The heels of my cowboy boots did the job of knocking the motherfucker out cold. The woman screamed again.

I picked up the gun and trained it on the murderous sono-fabitch on the floor.

"Stop!" the woman cried.

I turned to her. I had almost forgotten she was there.

"Are you okay?"

In retrospect, I guess it was pretty obvious.

"No," she said, "I am *not* okay! Don't you dare shoot him! I love him."

"What?"

"How could you do this to him?"

"Are you fucking kidding me? Do you know who this guy is?"

"He's my husband," the woman said.

I lowered the gun.

"Husband?"

"You killed my husband."

"No, I didn't. I almost did, but . . . I didn't even know Crazy Bob was married."

"He is. To me."

This had not worked out the way I wanted it to.

"I thought . . . I thought he was the killer. I thought you were a captive."

"He's no killer. He's harmless."

It apparently didn't matter to her that I was holding a loaded Magnum.

"This is how we roll," she said. "And can you stop looking at my tits?"

"Sorry."

"You *should* be sorry."

"I am," I said. "I'll just . . . I'll let myself out."

I had obviously made a horrible mistake—I seemed to be getting good at that. I had been so sure that I had been witnessing the murder of another innocent person, but it turned out to be, well, the way Crazy Bob liked to roll with his old lady.

"By the way," I said, "where was the wedding?"

"There wasn't one," the woman cried. "We're married in the eyes of the Lord."

"Okay. How long?"

She thought for a second, then asked, "What day is it?"

I hesitated before saying anything—just for comedic effect, because what else could I do—then said, "Forget I asked."

I snuck back out the back door and took the gun with me.

Alice got home safe that night.

That was all very stupid of me, I admit that, but my heart was in the right place. I could only hope that Crazy Bob was crazy enough not to contact the law about my little bit of business with him. At least he was eliminated as a suspect in my eyes.

The next morning, there was an article in the paper that said a person of interest had been arrested the night before. I was giddy with joy; but by that evening my hopes had been squashed.

The police had picked up a bum in Applegate Park. They didn't know who he was—he was one of these fellows who must have come into town on one of the freight trains—and they had found a bloody knife in his possession.

After what must have been a heated interrogation, the man admitted that what was on the knife was blood, but it belonged to a dog. He had killed one to eat. In his mind, he was performing a public service and getting himself fed at the same time. He led the police to the animal's remains, and his story must have checked out because by nightfall he was no longer a person of interest, but he *had* been placed in Bonham's—the hospital for the mentally degraded that rested far to the northwest and looked about as cheery as a tombstone.

Several days came and went with no good luck for anyone. The killer was still out there, and the only consolation was that no other bodies had turned up. Alice came and went from work under my watchful guard every night, but in my mind the temperature was rising, and it wasn't just because the summer was upon us. There were ten days left until the next full moon filled the sky. Ten days left for the police to do their job. Ten days for me to find a needle in a haystack. Ten days left before someone died.

SIXTEEN

On the night of the thirty-first, Alice got to work at the same time as always, and, as usual, wasn't visible to me in my truck until the time she stepped out the front door just after four in the morning. The streets were dead. You couldn't even hear the crickets.

Alice said good night to Leon at the door, shuffled down the steps, and made a left at the curb. Her Honda was not parked on the block. In fact, it was parked two full blocks down. When she got to work that evening, there were several spaces she could have taken, but chose not to. I don't know why. I could only presume that Mama Snow didn't want so many cars on the block anymore. Maybe the police were giving her hell since Josie Jones died.

I was parked in my usual spot at the far end of the block, and I had a clear view of everything ahead of me. Alice was walking away from me on the opposite side of the street. Leon, instead of going back into the house right away, kind of watched her as she went down the block. I have to presume that he and I both saw the same thing at the same time.

At first it was nothing more than a shaking bush. Seconds later, a man in dark clothing emerged. Alice had passed the spot where he now stood just a few moments earlier, and was about twenty paces ahead of him. The man in black stood still on the sidewalk and watched her. Then he started to walk toward her.

I got out of the truck and closed the door just enough so no one would notice that it hadn't locked. I didn't make a sound. With Crazy Bob's Magnum at my side, I rushed down the block.

Leon was doing the same thing, except he was such a hellish creation that he didn't need a weapon—his pan-sized hands were practically designed by Reagan's Star Wars program. Leon saw me across the street and stopped in his tracks. He must have seen the gun in my hand. I held out my hand for him to stop and then waved him back into the house. I didn't want any witnesses. He wrinkled his brow, then nodded and went back to the house. He knew what I was doing.

I crossed the street silently. I tucked the gun into my pants. Up ahead, I could hear Alice's high heels clacking on the sidewalk. She was oblivious to the man on her trail, and he was oblivious to me as I came up behind him, grabbed him by the collar, and punched him as hard as I could in the stomach. A rush of drunk air belched forth from his mouth, and he fell onto the closely cropped front lawn of a beautiful house. I knelt in front of him and raised the gun to his head. His eyes were crossed as they focused on the long barrel, the night-light shining off of it. I raised a finger to my lips.

"Shhh."

I heard Alice's footsteps halt as I knew they would. She had heard the man get hit. She must have turned, but saw nothing—the man and I were hidden from view by tall bushes. Soon, she went back to walking.

I waved the gun.

"Get up," I whispered.

The man was my age, and disheveled. His dark clothes were filthy, and a slight beard hid a weak chin. He reeked of alcohol.

"Why did you hit me?"

"Shut up," I said. "Get up and walk."

The man got up slowly, his eyes not once leaving the gun, and then I pointed toward the backyard with my finger. He walked. I walked behind him, the gun in his back.

I couldn't tell you which one of us was sweating more, him or me. My heart was racing like a greyhound, I was so nervous. I had waited so long for so many nights, hoping and praying for the man of my dreams to appear from the ether, and here he was right in front of me. I couldn't believe my luck.

As we snuck around to the back of the house, I wondered what it would be like to truly kill a man, to wrap my finger around the trigger of the gun, to pull the trigger that sent the bullet through this man's organs. Would he scream when he died, or would it be so quick for him that he wouldn't even have time to think of all the women he'd killed? Would he willingly tell me what I needed to hear—what kind of hoodoo bullshit he had been involved in to make him untraceable not only to the fuzz, but to the wolf—or would I have to beat him to know what I needed to know?

The man's hands were shaking at his sides. I could see that even in the dim light. I'm sure he wasn't used to dealing with armed men, just defenseless women.

Behind the house was a basketball hoop hammered onto the outside wall. There must have been kids inside. I told the man to stop, and he did, but not soon enough. A bright light shone down into the yard—a motion detector. Someone would see us soon enough.

"Please don't kill me," the man said. "I didn't do nothing."

"Bullshit," I said softly. "You just answer my questions or it'll be over before it begins. I could shoot the wings off a fly if I wanted to, so you just be nice and still."

The man swallowed.

"What's your name?"

"Mickey," he said. "Mickey Hanson."

"Mickey. I've been waiting a long time to meet you."

"Man, I don't even know who you are. I don't have any money."

"Don't play stupid," I said. "I know who you are."

"How?"

"Motherfucker, don't you read the papers? You're the Rose Killer."

"Who? Me?"

"What did you do to cloak yourself?"

"What?"

"Just answer the question."

"I don't know what you're talking about."

I raised the gun to shoulder level and took it in both hands. I knew that I would land on my ass, firing such a piece as that Magnum. The man began to cry.

"Please don't kill me," he said.

"What made you invisible?"

"I don't know what you mean."

"What was with the church break-ins?"

"I don't know."

"Have you ever been to the state of Maine?"

"No, man, I swear . . ."

The smell of urine filled the air. That, coupled with the look in the man's eyes, told me he was probably telling the truth. *Damn it.*

"Why were you following her?" I asked.

"I wasn't following nobody."

"Now I *know* you're lying."

I pressed the gun into his forehead. He shook.

"I just . . . I just wanted to say hi."

"Bullshit. You *are* a sickie, ain't you? Just not *my* sickie."

"I'm not a sickie."

"Stop lying."

"I swear. Every once in a while there will be underwear out on a line, and I'll have a look, but that's it. It's not my fault . . ."

Up on the second floor of the house, a light went on.

"Shut up," I said. "Quick, take off your shoe."

"Which one?"

"Just do it."

He took off his left shoe and tried to hand it to me. There were no laces, and the heel was so worn down I almost felt sorry for him.

"Put that fucking thing down. I don't want your stinking shoe. Give me your sock. I want it."

"There's no money in there," the man said.

"I want the sock, I said. Give me your fucking sock."

With shaking hands he slid the scummy sock down his ankle and held it up to me like a peace offering. There were holes in it. I took the sweaty sock with my left hand and stuffed it into my back pocket. There was something else in the pocket, I didn't know what. Then I remembered—Anthony's photographs.

"I got your sock now, motherfucker," I said.

"Take it," the man said.

"Oh, I took it, man. It's mine now. But remember this, you fucking sickie: I own your life now, man. I won't forget you. And if I ever see you in this town again I'm gonna shoot the balls off you and stuff 'em down your throat."

The man swallowed again.

"Okay," he said.

"Now get the fuck out of here."

The man took off like a shot in the night. In a second's time, I couldn't even see him anymore.

This was another mark against me. I'd be striking myself out of the game soon enough if I couldn't help it. Up high, the window opened, and a middle-aged man in glasses looked down into his illuminated backyard. There I was with a loaded gun in my hand. I smiled and waved.

"What are you doing down there?" he said.

"Defending the public," I responded before disappearing myself.

When I got home that night, I dropped the keys on my makeshift coffee table, checked the four locks on the door, then checked all the windows. Everything looked fine, so I started the shower going.

As I was undressing, the phone rang. I pulled my pants back

up, went into the living room, and stared at the phone. The gun was next to it. I picked up the phone.

"Hello?"

"Getting home kind of late, aren't you?"

I hung up. Whoever was calling me was also watching me. This wasn't good. It was the kind of thing that made you want to drink.

SEVENTEEN

Midnight on Carpenter Street. Yet again. With the clock rolling over, it was now June 3. One week to go, and the police were doing no better than me when it came to getting the Rose Killer off the streets.

The front door to Mama Snow's opened. Leon stepped out with a cup of coffee in his giant hand. He crossed the street and came over to my truck. I lowered the window and took the cup.

"Nothing?" he asked in a deep, tremulous voice.

"Nope." I took a sip, then said, "You know, if you and I put our heads together, we'd be unstoppable. You should help me."

"I don't know you, and that's the way it's going to stay."

"Because you say so, or *they* do?"

"Because *I* say so."

"Okay," I said. "Still, for a vampire, you're all right. Thanks for the coffee."

Leon smiled and walked away. He was a man of few words, but he knew what I was doing out there.

I drank the coffee in one gulp. I was exhausted, had been running myself ragged since this whole affair started. By four, when Alice stepped out, the coffee had worn off, and I was tired. I guess that's why I didn't do such a good job of following her home as I usually did. At a red light I was stupid enough to pull up right behind her, no car in between.

When she got to her building, I was still driving right behind her, not thinking. She stopped short, and I almost drove into the back of her car. Before I knew it she had gotten out of the Honda and was standing outside my driver's-side door.

"What the fuck are you doing?" she said.

"Oh, hi, Alice," I said, doing a poor job of pretending like I had just run into her out of the crystal blue. "What's going on?"

"Are you completely stupid, or just when it comes to following someone?" She was genuinely upset. "I guess this is why I haven't seen you around at the house for a while. You were too busy being every other fucking place I was."

"I wasn't following you, Alice, I . . ."

"What?"

"I was just driving you home."

I couldn't think of anything else to say.

"Marley, do you think I haven't noticed your truck lately?"

". . . Have you?"

"Yes, Marley. I see your stinking truck in my dreams. I don't like being followed, especially since Josie died."

I sighed. "That's *why* I've been following you, Alice."

"Well, I don't need your help, okay? How did you know where I live anyway?"

"It's a small town. I'm sure you know where *I* live. . . ."

"I don't, and I don't want to know. This is a total invasion of my privacy."

"I'm sorry," I said. "I just don't know what else to do. I don't want anything to happen to you. . . ."

"Stop right there," she said. "Don't keep talking. I don't want to hear what you have to say."

"Alice, please . . ."

She stuck her finger in my face.

"If I see this truck again, I'm going to call the police," she said, her voice loaded with venom. "This is sick."

"It's not sick," I said.

"It's scary. This is just plain fucking creepy."

I thought I was beyond having my heart broken, but that's what it felt like. She began to walk back to her car, but I called her back.

"Alice, wait."

She came back to my window. I opened my dash and took out the Magnum. Her eyes grew wide, but then I took it by the barrel and held it out the window.

"Take it."

"I'm not taking that, Marley. What the hell are you doing with that thing?"

"I'm not doing anything with it. I want you to take it. Please."

"This town doesn't need a vigilante, Marley. Put the gun away."

"Take it," I said, hard. "I was doing this for you, no one else. If you don't want me around, fine. But it doesn't mean you shouldn't be safe."

She reluctantly took the gun.

"I . . . I don't like it when people cross lines," she said. "I don't know what kind of fantasy you have going in your head about you and me, but I don't want any part of it. There's a time and place. This is my real life. You're not in it."

"Fine," I said. "But be safe. Keep your eyes open. While you still have them."

I peeled away.

The way Alice spoke to me, it felt like a betrayal. It was impossible for me not to think of my mother.

When I came back from Vietnam, she wasn't there to meet me at the train. As you know, I was labeled a burnout, unfit for service. I was the sole survivor of my entire company. They had all been killed—ripped apart—and Charlie Company had found me wandering the jungle naked, incoherent. The only dressing I had was my tags. They tried to ask me what happened, but I didn't know. I didn't remember for a long time.

At the train station back Stateside, I was expecting people to fuck with me, because I'd heard stories from some of the guys back in California about men coming home and getting spit on, getting hit with eggs, getting red paint spilled on them, but no one messed with me. It was like I wasn't even there.

My friend Ben picked me up in his Thunderbird and drove me

home. I was happy to be back home where the air smelled familiar, the faces were friendly, and I didn't have to worry anymore. I had my life back.

The house I grew up in had flower bushes all around the front, a few trees. When Ben pulled up outside, I looked at the house and smiled. It looked like a postcard. I got out with my bag and went up the walkway.

For a second, I froze. I thought I saw someone behind one of the trees. My heart rate immediately sped up, and my mouth got dry. It was just my imagination, but it took me a moment to accept that I wasn't in hostile territory anymore.

I rang the bell and waited. I heard a dish break inside, and after a minute or so, the door opened. It was my mother. I said, "Hi, Mom," and I began to cry.

She began to cry too, and then she grabbed me and wouldn't let go. She had lost a husband, and though I was there in her arms, she had lost a son as well. I was not the boy who had gone off to war. I had come back a monster, but I didn't know it yet. I thought I had some kind of disease because of the two blackouts I'd had, including the one the night of the ambush. I put my stuff down in my room, and then we got in the car and went to see Dad.

His grave was new and clean. The letters spelling out his name and dates were recently etched, and the edges were sharp. We put flowers down, and then, once she washed away her tears, she left me there with him so I could have my time.

I had nothing to say. I wasn't one of those people who went to a grave and related my problems and worries, and I could never imagine how anyone could. I turned around to see where my mom was, what she was doing. I could see her where we parked, her back turned to me. I looked down at the grave.

"What kind of man were you to think it was good to send me out to that fucking madness?" I hissed. "They think I'm crazy. I'm having these blackouts, and I wake up God knows where, and *I'm* starting to think I'm crazy too. All I wanted was to have a life, and this war . . . It's for nothing, Dad. I watched guys die for a fucking jungle. Why did I have to go through that? How did it build my character? I'm sorry you left Mom alone, but we'll worry about this later. I have to see Doris. If she'll still have me."

I spit on the grave and walked back to the car.

"I need to see Doris," I said to Mom.

We pulled up outside Doris's house. My mother and I hadn't talked the whole way. I was seething, and she had something on her mind. I didn't know what. She said, "Do you want me to wait here for you?"

I said, "No, I don't know how long I'm going to be."

"How will you get home?"

"I'll walk."

"Walk? But . . ."

"I've done it a thousand times."

She was afraid. Of what?

"Okay," she said. "Should I make dinner?"

"I don't think so. I want to go out with Doris."

"All right," she said.

"What's the problem?"

"Maybe Doris isn't ready to see you."

"You know, that's some fucking thing to say to me."

"Don't talk to your mother that way."

"It's almost like *you're* not ready to see me."

"Marlowe . . ."

I got out of the car and slammed the door. She drove off slowly. I felt like punching a hole in the world.

I jumped up the steps outside Doris's house, just like I always did, just like I'd dreamt of doing since the day I left home. In that moment, I realized how lucky I was that I had made it home at all. Thousands didn't. Doris's mother, Gladys, opened the door.

"Oh, Marlowe!" she said, and she hugged me like I was her own son.

"Hey, Mrs. Moran. How are you?"

She rushed me into the living room to shake her husband's hand. He was happy to see me too. An American flag was up on the mantel, along with a picture of me, and a prayer tucked into the frame. I almost cried seeing that these people had prayed for me.

After a few seconds of pleasantries, Doris appeared at the top of the stairs and our eyes locked. She smiled, instantly shed tears. I ran to her, and she ran to me, and there, on the middle of that staircase, the loving embrace that I had been waiting for so long had become a reality. We kissed, and only then did I feel like I belonged. Only then did I feel like I had survived the war in Vietnam.

She had been working at the Coleman Building as a typist, just to put money aside for when I came back. I had a savings. We were going to go off and find a place to live, maybe even go to college.

Up in her room, Doris saw that something was upsetting me. She said, "Honey, what's getting you down?"

I said, "Nothing, just something my mother said. She said you might not be ready to see me."

"Oh, that's a terrible thing to say," said Doris, her voice going way up high. "I've never been happier than right now. But your mother . . . she's been through a lot, what with your dad and all. But they were acting strangely after you left."

"How do you mean?"

"Well, you know how I was always making pies for your mom and dad, and I promised not to stop doing that while you were away? Well, I was doing that. Every Sunday I went over there with a fresh pie, and I talked with your momma in the kitchen, but after a couple of weeks, she said I shouldn't come around anymore. That it wasn't necessary, and, well, I haven't really seen either of them since. When I'd spot them at the market, they'd pretend they didn't see me, but I know they did."

I knew it was truth.

"Let's not worry about that now," I said. "Let's go out tonight. Just you and me."

"Oh, Marley, I'd love it!"

"Great. I'll pick you up on the bike. If it still runs."

"God," she cried, "I'm so happy you're back."

We kissed. I buried my face in her hair and whispered, "I want to marry you, Doris."

"I know," she said. "That's why God brought you back."

I walked home. Once I got there, I went right up to my room without saying a word to my mother. Years later she would tell me that she had waited for me in the kitchen with my father's gun that day. She was going to put me down right when I came in, then take herself out, but she lost the nerve.

I changed into my old clothes and went down to the garage to check out my bike. I removed the tarp, poured some gas into it, checked it out. It still purred, so I took it out and rode around town till it was time to pick up Doris.

That night, she and I made love in the woods, and her body should've tasted sweeter than anything I'd ever known, but there was a part of me, a sincere part of my core being, that must've died or gotten itself blown out in combat, because everything I did felt a little more cold and dead than it ever had before. I did not yet know about the beast, but something bone-deep inside me felt wrong, alien, sinister. Staring down at Doris, her pale skin glowing white in the starlight, I almost felt like I had to protect her. Not from anything on the outside, some presence among the trees, but from myself. There was this little voice inside of me crying out in alarm. If I was at all intelligent, I would have listened.

Again, I thought of my father, and how I wished he was still around so I could blame him for that dead part inside of me, and hit him hard across the jaw for it.

I got home after two in the morning. My mother was still up, smoking in the living room. She said she needed to talk to me. "About everything," she added.

"Will that include how you two brushed off Doris while I was gone?"

"Maybe."

"Great, let's hear it."

She stamped out her cigarette and leaned forward on the couch.

I said, "We're going to get married, you know. That was always the plan."

"I know," she responded. "But there's a lot you don't know, and a lot you need to understand before you start trying to make a life for yourself, Marlowe. There are things that I need to say to you that I never in a million years thought I'd have to say. This was something your father, God rest his soul, was supposed to speak to you about, but . . ."

"But what?"

"But he's not here anymore, Marlowe. You are. And this was never . . . I don't know how to do this, but you . . . you're not the same man that you were when you left."

"I know," I said.

"I don't think you do. Otherwise, you wouldn't be here now. What exactly happened that got you sent home, Marlowe?"

I sat down across from her on the other couch. "We were surrounded by snipers. They were picking us off like flies. I thought I got shot, and I blacked out. All the men were dead when I woke up, and I was the only one that made it out of there. I can't remember what happened, but the brass didn't want me out in the shit anymore, so they sent me home. Case closed."

"Without a scratch," she said. "Don't you think that's a little odd?"

"I don't know." That was the exact same kind of question the military had asked me. "I've tried not to think about it," I said, grinding my teeth.

"Maybe you should. That wasn't the only time you've blacked out, was it?"

I wanted to ask her how she knew that, but I was too fucked

up, too angry. I walked away. If she had told me the truth that night, I think I would have killed myself. I was younger then, more rash. I wouldn't have thought twice about it. Instead, it was still a secret, and bad things were to come. It was that rashness that led me to move out just as quickly as I had moved back in. The way the family had treated Doris in my absence was inexcusable. I didn't want any part of that household anymore.

The next morning I got a suitcase together and moved into a cheap motel with the money I had. It was one of those kinds of places where you pay by the end of the week, or they took your stuff and beat the living hell out of you. There weren't any families in there or anything like that. Mostly drunks and men who'd gotten kicked out of the house for whatever reasons men do things they shouldn't do.

I made a promise to myself not to get a haircut for at least a month. The promise ended up stretching on for years. Doris and I made plans to go away for a while, somewhere nice, just her and me, but that was still a few weeks away.

I was not a pleasant man at work on June 3. I had not slept at all that night, even though I got home by five. I was so upset about what had gone down with Alice that I couldn't sleep a wink. Then all of a sudden the sun was up, and I had to be at work. There was nothing new in the papers, just the same old public outcry to the authorities, who, according to some of the op-ed pieces, were resting on their laurels. I was highly agitated, tired, and I needed a drink. It was scaring me how much I felt like I needed a drink. Abe did what he could to make me feel better, but there was nothing short of a magic potion that could have worked. I guess I was teetering on the edge of an abyss.

I was in the kitchen, using a wet towel to clean off the grill. Steam blasted up, and I could feel my forearm getting burned, but I didn't care. I usually didn't because there would never in a million years be a lasting mark, but this was different. This was penance.

The phone rang. I never answered it because of my tendency to casually curse during conversation, or sometimes even when no one was around. Abraham answered the phone. I heard him ask who it was, and then he came back to the kitchen through the double doors.

"Phone's for you," he said.

"Who is it?"

"Some dude."

"Did you get a fucking name?"

He shrugged. I swallowed. Took the phone.

"Yes?"

"Hey, killer," said the voice.

I hung up.

Abraham saw me grinding my teeth. I told him to get the fuck out of the kitchen. A second later the phone began to ring again. I picked it up.

"Be seeing you," said the voice.

I hung up.

I grabbed my pack of cigarettes and walked out of the kitchen. I had to get out of there. "Hey," shouted Abe, "where the hell are you going?"

"I gotta go," I said.

"But Carlos ain't here yet."

"I gotta go," I repeated. I got in the truck and took off.

Like old Bill Parker I was circling Old Sherman Road. I couldn't stop myself from doing it because it felt right. I knew it felt right for him too, and that's why he did it.

When I got home it was after six. The second I walked in, the phone rang. It was with this phone call that I stopped teetering on that edge and finally fell. I picked up the receiver, and the voice said, "I'm sure Frank won't be happy that you left early."

"I'll see you in hell," I said.

"I'm counting on it, because I'm going to make you pay for what you did."

"Who the fuck is this? Why are you doing this to me?"

"I'm the tooth fairy, Higgins."

"Why don't you come on over, then. I got something under my pillow for you."

"Well," said the voice, "I've already left something there for you."

I hung up and rushed into the bedroom. My heart was beating in my ears. Everything looked the way I had left it in the morning. I walked over to my bed and lifted up the pillow. There was a note, folded in two.

"Oh my God," I said out loud.

I lifted the piece of paper and unfolded it with my shaking hands.

It read, "IT'S OVER."

I ran into the bathroom, where there was a small window that I had never wanted to nail shut because when I take a dump it is truly deadly. The window was halfway opened, the tiny little lock on the top of the frame was hanging on by one screw. Probably jimmied from the outside by a fucking flathead screwdriver. I clutched the doorframe for balance and screamed. A second later, the phone rang.

I pulled my truck into the parking lot of the first bar I came across. I couldn't take it anymore. There was a time for being a stoic motherfucker, and a time for getting trashed and beating someone's head in. This was a time for the latter.

I came in through the door and was greeted with honky-tonk music playing a bit too loud—just the way I used to like it—and the warm glow of a dozen neon beer signs. Sawdust littered the floor in mounds. It helped with the ambience by taking your attention away from the drunks passed out in the corners. I sauntered up to the bar, and the bartender came on over.

"Howdy," he said. "You look pretty down. What's going on, partner?"

"Oh, you know, lost my best friend, lost my whole way of living . . . all very Old Testament kind of bad things going on."

"Sorry to hear that." He chuckled, as if I was kidding.

"Gimme a shot of whiskey and a pint. Whatever's cheapest," I said.

"I'm sorry, partner, I can't do that."

"Do what?"

"I can't serve you any alcohol."

I was flabbergasted. "Why the hell not? This is a bar, ain't it? Ain't that what gets done in these fucking places? Gimme a drink, goddamn it. I got cash money, just like every other sonofabitch in here."

My attempt at getting wasted was not working out as planned.

"I'm sorry, I just can't do it."

"Well . . . *why*, man?"

"Last time you was in here, you fucked this place good and proper, and we can't go on and let that happen again, can we?"

"Oh, you prick. What is this, a joke? Where the hell did I set foot in?"

"This is Cowboy's Cabin."

"No shit."

"No shit. No, sir."

"Well," I shouted, "I guess I'm just gonna have to get one of these slim motherfuckers at the bar to buy a drink for me. What do you say, boys?"

Four younger guys in designer outfits sat down the bar from me, a few other guys filled up some tables behind me, and I was in the mood to rumble. More than anything else, I wanted one of these boys to do their best to kill me in hand-to-hand combat. The four guys looked at me, shook their heads no about buying me a drink, and looked down, then went back to drinking.

"Well, fuck each of you and all of you, then," I shouted.

"Sir," said the barkeep, "I think I'm gonna have to ask you to leave."

"You know, it's been a while since I've heard that. Let's hear it again."

"Will you please leave?"

"Don't ask, pissant. Do it. Or try, if you think you can."

I put my dukes up.

All of a sudden, I saw bits of wood flying past my head from behind me. A second later, I felt pain, and I realized someone had just busted a pool stick off my head.

I turned around, and the guy there looked awfully familiar. Someone, some time, had broken that nose of his good and proper. I tasted blood in my mouth, coming from somewhere up high on my head.

"Excuse me," I said. "Did I ever fuck your sister?"

His two friends grabbed me from all sides and dragged me outside.

"Was it something I said?"

They went to work on me out in the parking lot, all of them. Bounced me off so many cars, I knew what flies felt like on country roads. They even incorporated a belt and a tire iron into the beating.

"You like that?" one of them shouted as he jammed his boot into my stomach.

"I like it like your mother likes it," I grunted. "Do your fucking worst, faggot."

The next thing I knew, I was handcuffed to a metal rod running along a gray cement wall. I was lying on a wood bench. A bright light burned overhead, and two of the guys that had vandalized my ass were cuffed to another rod on the wall to my right. They were immaculate. All I could see of myself were my hands, which looked like they had been run over by a pair of dirt bikes.

It had been a long time since I was behind bars. It didn't bother me, being behind bars, but it bothered me that it had to happen in Evelyn, and not some other hick place that I could pass a fake name off in.

I looked at the two men and said, "Hey, I know where I know you guys from. You're Moe and Curly. Where's Larry?"

"He runs like a jackrabbit," said Curly.

"How you boys feeling?"

"Fuck you," said Moe. The other spat at me.

"That's not very civil."

"You broke my nose a few years ago," said Moe. "The dang thing never healed right, man. I've been waiting years to get my hands on you, and by the grace of God that time finally came."

I laughed, though it made my head hurt some.

A uniformed cop came to the bars and banged his nightstick against them. Behind him stood Van Buren in a suit with his detective's shield pinned to a black holder fastened to his belt. The suit was no work of Italian finery, but cost a hell of a lot more than the brown layer of shit I'd worn to his partner's funeral.

His shoes were shined and creaseless. New. He was wearing a wedding ring, and a gold watch was apparent at his wrist. He had close-cropped hair and was a little younger than me. Instead of a cop, he looked like a tax collector. He didn't have the kind of face that made you feel either scared or comfortable. In fact, it made you feel like taking a wild swing at it just to get it out of sight.

The uniform opened the cell door, and the suit stepped in behind him with his hands in his pockets as if he were the coolest, most dangerous guy in the world.

"Get up," said the uniform to the two other men.

They stood, and were forced to lean forward since they were cuffed to the wall.

Their cuffs were removed. The uniform then removed the cuffs from the rail and put them in his back pocket.

"Get out of here," said the uniform. "Get your shit at the desk."

They began to walk past the detective.

"Hey," I said, "those pricks assaulted me. You're letting them go?"

"You gonna press charges?" asked the uniform.

"You bet."

"Too bad," he replied.

I looked at Van Buren. His eyes smiled.

The two little fighters left the cell and disappeared down the hallway. The uniform turned to Van Buren and asked, "You need me here?"

"Of course not," he replied in a calm voice. "We're just going to talk. Isn't that right, Mr. Higgins?"

"Sure," I said.

The uniform left, and then it was just the detective and me. He came over and sat next to me on the bench, but not before methodically adjusting his pants around his thighs. "That's quite a shiner," he said, pointing at my face.

"I wouldn't know," I said.

"Are you in any pain?"

"Am I in any pain? Yes I am. I think I have a boo-boo or two." I laughed. He did not.

"Do you know why you're here?"

"Can't say that I do," I said, "unless it's become a crime in this country to get the shit kicked out of you."

"No, it's not a crime to be beaten, Mr. Higgins."

"What's with this 'Mr. Higgins' shit? You know my name. Use it."

"You are Mr. Higgins," he replied. "That's what I'll call you. In return, you will call me Mr. Van Buren."

The man never liked me since the first day we met at the supermarket.

There was this beautiful woman in the produce section, feeling up the pineapples, and I couldn't take my eyes off her. She smiled at me. Then her husband got pissed off. That was Van Buren. I was never forgiven for that.

"Mr. Higgins, it is not a crime to be beaten, but this matter is not as simple as that. As you see, the two men who attacked you have been released. Everyone who was at the scene of your latest incident has stated that you were the one who instigated this fight, and it would seem like the only difference between this incident and those in your past is that you didn't get your little fists up in time."

"Are you trying to be cute with me?"

"No."

"Can I have a cigarette?"

"No."

"Instigating something is different from busting a stick off someone's head, cop."

"Maybe, but this is my investigation . . ."

"What investigation?"

"Quiet. It is *my* investigation, and such matters that you discuss are merely semantics in this case."

"Semantics? What happened to my face is semantics?"

"It would seem."

"I don't think I like you."

"And Evelyn doesn't seem to like you, Mr. Higgins. You see, some people around here seem to have some memory lapses, but I know you, and I know what you're capable of, and I know how violent you can be when you drink."

"I didn't drink."

"Says you."

"I didn't do anything."

"Didn't you?" I didn't say anything. "That's what I thought. But I'll be merciful tonight, Mr. Higgins. I'm going to let you go."

"Well, in that case, you can go fuck yourself."

He laughed. "No, I won't be doing that tonight."

"Why, your wife ain't gonna touch you."

His eyes grew red with fire. He put his finger in my face and said, "You watch your mouth with me, you dirtbag."

I lunged and bit his finger, to which he yelped and quickly drew away.

With the other hand, he slammed a fist into my jaw. I winced, and he grabbed a fistful of my hair. "You bastard," he said. "You're going to go down for what you did, you hear me? I know exactly what . . ."

Just then, the uniform appeared in the doorway, and said, "Everything okay in here?"

Van Buren sat up and backed away from me, said, "Yes. We were just having a chat. Weren't we, Mr. Higgins?"

"Yup," I mumbled.

"I don't think Mr. Higgins is ready to go just yet. Why don't we keep him till five or so. Then, make sure he gets home okay," said Van Buren.

"You got it," said the cop.

"Give him the whole nine yards."

"You got it," said the uniform.

Van Buren stalked out, but not before turning to me and saying, "We have an honest-to-God killer running around this town, Mr. Higgins. Big news. But don't forget. I've got my eye on you."

Then he was gone.

At five o'clock in the morning, the uniformed cop came to the cell door and unlocked it. He told me to stand, and then he undid the cuffs. He perp-walked me over to the desk, gave me back my stuff, and took me out to the parking lot.

"Where are you taking me?" I asked the cop.

"Home," he said.

"I can walk."

"Not in your condition. Get in the car."

A black-and-white had pulled up to us. Inside were two young cops. He opened the back door.

"Watch your head," he said.

Not a word was said the whole ride home. When they got to my block, they flashed the lights and sirens and came to a stop outside my home. Everyone was sleeping, but because of the ruckus, lights went on and people came to their windows to see what was going on.

This was a blatant tactic by the police to embarrass me and discredit me in the eyes of my neighbors. I didn't appreciate it, but the two punks driving the car weren't paid to be the sensitive ones to my situation.

I got out and walked to my front door quickly, dizzied by the fight and the blue and red lights bouncing off the front of my house.

The door locked automatically behind me once it closed. At that point, the lights and sirens stopped, and the police car disappeared in the dark.

Van Buren had it in for me. I couldn't imagine it was because he still held a grudge about his wife digging the way I look in a pair of jeans. It had to be something else, but I didn't necessarily want to stick around to figure out what it was.

The cruelty of all this was that I hadn't even had the chance to have a drink before I got in a bar fight. I could have taken that as a sign that I shouldn't be hitting the sauce again, but I'm nothing if not tenacious.

EIGHTEEN

I got out of the shower and combed my hair back in front of the mirror. All in all I didn't look that bad. One of my eyes was a little puffy, like it was a little more tired than the other, and there was a cut at my hairline.

Instead of putting myself through the trouble of having to sit down and get back up, I decided to instead make my morning pot of coffee and get ready for work.

Despite the head start on the day, I still got to work a few minutes late. I had to walk to the bar to pick my truck up, after all. At the restaurant, there were three cars already in the lot. The first was Abraham's Buick, complete with his Bob Marley bumper sticker. The second was Frank's. And the third car in the lot belonged to Carlos, the cook with the evening shift.

I walked into Long John's, and the little bell jangled above my head. Abraham was behind the counter, and Brian the life insurance guy was sipping a cup of coffee, standing by the windows. Through the long window I saw Carlos, surrounded by steam. Seated at one of the tables was Frank.

"What's going on?" I asked him. "Am I finally getting a shift change?"

Frank raised himself from the seat with what looked like great effort. I hated him effortlessly, he was such a bum. He said, "Why don't we talk outside."

"Let's not," I said. I had a bad feeling. "What's going on? Why is Carlos in my kitchen?"

I looked at Abe, and he looked away.

"Frank," I said.

"Marley," he replied. "It isn't your kitchen anymore. I need to let you go."

"What? You've got to be fucking kidding me, man. How the hell can you do this to me in front of Brian?"

"I told you to come outside, you idiot. . . ."

"Hardball, eh?"

"No hardball, Marlowe. . . ."

"Why the hell are you firing me, man?"

"Our agreement when you took this job, Marlowe, was that you would be out on your ear if you ever got in trouble with the law, and that's what happened. Honestly, I'm surprised it took so long."

Jesus, I thought. Van Buren must have been holding a *serious* fucking grudge for him to contact Frank about my arrest.

"In case you didn't notice, I got worked over like a two-dollar whore. I didn't do anything. I was the victim of an assault."

I pointed to my swollen eye.

"Sure," said Frank. "Just like you're a victim of goddamn sexual harassment. I don't need to hear it."

"Like a two-dollar whore," I repeated.

"I can't have any sympathy for that," he yelled, "and you look as ragged as you always do."

"But it's my fucking *job*, man," I said.

"Not anymore."

Brian stood up and said, "I personally think the world of Marlowe. He's a splendid man. I think you should give him a second chance."

"Yeah," I said. "Have some fucking compassion, man."

"Compassion! Who gave you the job in the first place? What's the first thing you do when the only man that saw a lick of good in you went on and died? You got drunk. It's bad enough you harass the patrons when you're sober. No one needs to hear a booze-hound like you rant and rave in the middle of my goddamn diner. Now get outta here before I call the police."

"Well, you're not even willin' to entertain the thought of being a humanitarian today, are you?"

"No," he said, and he lit one of his awful cigars.

"I'm sorry," Carlos said through the long window.

"I know," I said. "It's not your fault."

I turned to Abe and said, "Any words of encouragement?"

"You're not black," he said. "You'll get another job."

I smiled, but I sucker-punched Frank in the stomach anyway. He collapsed back into his chair and gasped for air. His face turned as red as a brick. Abe rushed out from behind the counter and ushered me out of the restaurant as quickly as he could. The bell jangled, and then we were outside. Abe pushed me down the few steps outside the restaurant. It wasn't a fight he wanted. He was just being a peacekeeper in the only way he knew how.

"What the fuck do you think you're doing?" he asked.

"Nothing."

"It don't look like nothing, you crazy asshole. Why'd you have to do that?"

"He thinks he's better than *me*? Fuck him."

"No."

"You think he's better than me?"

"No, Marley, no one's better than you. Now go home, and I'll do my best to keep this guy from calling the cops. How does that sound?"

"Fine, but I got friends on the force," I said.

"No, you don't," he said.

He was right. "Damn, Abe, you didn't have to say it like that."

He came down the stairs and slapped me on the arm. "Marley, I feel for you, man, but you gotta pull your shit together. You can't go on and let yourself fall apart because of these external factors, man, you know what I'm saying? I know you're hurting, but you've got to be a big man here."

"I know. I just can't help it."

I felt like crying right there. I couldn't believe I'd been fired.

"I lost my fucking job, man. . . ."

"You need someone to talk to, you know I'm here for you," he said.

"I know, bro. You never liked Ozzy, but you're an okay guy."

"Yeah, and you never liked Al Green."

"I don't even know who the fuck Al Green is," I said.

"If you did, we wouldn't be here right now. Now, get outta here. And, Marley?"

"Yeah?"

"Be good. There's a lot of people in this town who remember how you used to be, and they don't fuckin' like you. Don't justify that shit with some stupid-ass behavior like the shit you just pulled in here, okay?"

"Arright."

"What would do you good is a little bit of church."

I was driving on Old Sherman Road, my mind spinning in a hundred different directions. If my radio had worked, I would have been informed that there were still no developments with the Rose Killer case, and there was no comment from the police. Luckily, my radio was on the fritz. I didn't have to hear it.

I hit a pothole, and my head hit the roof of the cab. It hurt, and I squeezed my eyes shut for just a second. When I opened them again, I saw there was a man in the road just ahead of me. I hit the brakes hard, and the truck skidded to a stop just feet in front of the man.

He was old, and wearing a tattered suit and a baseball cap. Over one shoulder he had a plastic bag full of cans he'd picked up from the gutters. In his hand was a long stick with a nail driven through the end. It was the fucking Indian.

His eyes glimmered with wisdom and dirty secrets, like they were laughing at me for not knowing what he knew. I should've hit him.

"Do you want to die, old man? Are cans that important that you'll stand in the middle of the fucking road?"

He looked at me like I owed him an apology.

"What the fuck are you lookin' at, you old bastard?" I shouted out the open window. He said nothing. I knew he wouldn't. "What are you doing?"

He came over to the truck, to the side, to my window. He was holding that stick up like a weapon.

"Waiting for you," he said in a low, cracked voice.

"The fuck does that mean?" I sneered.

"You drive these roads . . . like a mad wolf, white man. I know which way you come. Your darkie friend gave you some excellent wisdom, and . . . you'd be wise to follow it."

"Yeah? What would that be?"

"External factors have destroyed the balance."

"Fuck did you just say?"

"Outside forces are at work, Higgins. Be aware . . ."

"How the fuck do you know my name?" He smiled, ignored the question. "How do you know about me?"

The toothy smile on his face turned into a perfect moonlike crescent.

"You sinister little bastard," I said, opening the car door, my fist clenched at my side.

Just then, I heard a noise like the wail of a clarinet, and caught a movement in the corner of my eye. On the other side of Old Sherman, right where the woods meet the road, was a wolf, watching me. It was gray, with blue eyes so piercing my heart skipped a beat. It looked at me, yawned, then padded into the maze of trees, out of sight. When I turned back to the old man, he was gone.

What did that damn Indian mean about external factors? Wasn't it a strange coincidence that Abraham had just said the same thing earlier that morning? Abe also said I should go to church. At that point, a lightbulb went off in my head, and church didn't sound like a bad idea at all.

The church I went to wasn't just any old church, but the one that had been broken into the night that Josie Jones disappeared.

I knew which one it was because I had read the article several times.

It was all the way on the west side of town on a very quiet block. Just a few homes here and there, and the church took up one whole corner. Off to the side was a playground. Past that was a church-type school, where the kids wore uniforms. The street was empty, and I couldn't imagine it being any different in the dead of night. The cross on top looked nice and even, and all the stained-glass windows were clean. No one had seen or heard a thing when the place got busted into, but I needed to satisfy a curiosity. Maybe something had gone down they didn't mention in the papers. If there was semen all over, or a swastika or some such thing, I can't imagine the churchgoers being anxious to know about it. But I had to know. It couldn't just be a coincidence that a church break-in occurred on the same nights as the disappearances. I could have been grasping at straws, but something told me I wasn't. After all, there was a mighty strange incident that had happened years before I moved to Evelyn, and it involved a church.

It was 1988. The bodies of three children had been found in a drainage ditch just a few miles outside of Chicago. Two of them had been there for several weeks. The third was fresh. The papers said there were no signs of sexual misconduct, but that didn't mean anything to me. When the full moon came around, the wolf knew what to do.

It visited the dumping ground, picked up a scent, and tracked it on the wind to a fellow named Jack Kaplan, who at that moment was joyriding on a Japanese motorcycle. He was a high school dropout with an arrest record loaded with drug charges and a couple of indecent exposures. Nothing serious, but that's just because he'd never been caught. Just like me.

The wolf stalked him till he turned off an exit and wound up in the suburbs, far away from prying eyes. On a quiet street, it sprang from the bushes, causing the man to fall from the bike.

He took off his helmet, saw what was coming at him, and took off like a bat out of hell.

Directly across the street was a church. He charged it, as if he would be granted asylum there. He kicked the door in and shut it behind him. The wolf entered the church just seconds later, but was unable to locate the man, who was just several feet away, hiding under one of the pews. This had never happened before. It was as if the wolf's powers had been nullified once it set foot on holy ground. Anywhere else in the world, it would have been able to find the man with its eyes closed, just on scent alone, but in that church, the creature was rendered almost human.

The wolf looked left and right, and roared in confusion. The hellish sound of the beast scared the man out of his hiding place, and he ran. The wolf followed.

To make a long story short, the wolf eventually chased the man onto the roof, where he jumped and died. This incident is unique and noteworthy for two reasons. One, something to do with the church legitimately fucked up the wolf's senses. Two, something to do with the church had prevented the wolf from ripping the man to shreds. Instead, it led him to his own doom. It was as if the wolf had obeyed some unwritten rule I knew nothing about, or if not, it seemed that Jesus put the kibosh on the beast's dastardly ways while it was on His turf. Maybe Jesus came down and said, "Hey, man, don't make a mess in here." I didn't know what to make of it at the time.

On another occasion many years earlier, I had taken shelter in a church on the night of the full moon. As night came down, the priest was alerted of my presence because I was screaming. I was changing, but it was happening more slowly than it would have in any other place. It hurt twice as much. I couldn't move. The priest helped me outside to wait for an ambulance. The changing process then sped up, and that's when I killed him.

I climbed the stone steps to the church and opened the heavy wooden door. The church had a high ceiling that was designed to look like the inside of a boat, like Noah's Ark. There were pews on each side, and all the way down at the other end, the altar. A big, hungry Jesus hung on the wall behind the altar, and there were candles all over the place. Right in front of me was a big vat of holy water, like a birdbath. I dipped my fingers in the stuff and smelled it. Smelled like water to me.

There were two women seated in one of the pews, both dressed in black, like widows. I didn't want to look at them. What I needed was a priest or something, not atmosphere. I didn't know if there was some office located somewhere, or any kind of fancy legwork I had to do to get the man's attention, so instead, I cleared my throat. Loudly. It didn't work. So I did it again. The two widows looked at me.

I cleared my throat a third time. A man in black poked his head out from behind one of the columns. I waved, and he strolled over with a plastic smile on his face. He was my age, with his short brown hair combed to one side, and a pair of wire-rimmed glasses perched on the edge of his nose. He was trying to look older than he was. The hell of it was that I recognized the guy, and then I remembered: He had done the services for Pearce.

"Good afternoon, sir," he said. "What brings you to our house?"

I blushed. I just then realized I didn't know how to address him.

"Hey, Padre," I said, to which he frowned, "you don't know me, but I was wondering if I could just ask you a few questions about some stuff. It won't take but a minute."

"Certainly, sir," he said. "Time is not an issue here, because the time is always right to find yourself in God's house."

I said, "Sure, man. Whatever you say."

"What is your denomination?"

"My what?"

"What church have you attended in the past?"

"Oh. Well, honestly, Your Honor, I'm not here about, uh, to inquire about attending your services and whatnot."

"Oh," he said sadly.

"You see, I'm inquiring about the break-in you guys had here a while back. This was two weeks ago, this happened."

"Yes, I remember. Do you . . . do you have any information regarding . . ."

"Actually, I was hoping to get some information from *you*."

"Are you with the authorities?"

I evaded the question. "The article in the local papers pointed out that nothing was stolen from the premises. Is that accurate?"

"Oh, yes. Nothing was taken."

"How sure are you? All the crosses are accounted for, all the candles? Little things like that?"

"Yes, but . . . I have to wonder why you're asking."

"I don't know if you're familiar with the killings that have been going on . . ."

"Yes, as much as anyone else in Evelyn . . ."

"The break-in here happened the same night that Josie Jones went missing. The prostitute. On the night that Gloria Shaw, the first victim in Evelyn, disappeared, there was also a church break-in, with nothing taken. Allegedly. This was also the case over in Edenburgh. Don't you think that's odd?"

"I didn't realize . . ."

"It's a strong coincidence."

"My," he said. "It certainly is."

"So, what I'm asking is, are you people sure that nothing was taken?"

"Oh, yes. Quite sure. Everything was accounted for. The surprising thing is that our poor boxes weren't even tampered with, much less broken into. When people feel compelled to force themselves into a church, it is usually to, um, gain the contents of those boxes."

"But that didn't happen?"

"No."

"Was anything done? Anything moved, or replaced? Anything at all out of the ordinary? A note, a stain, a footprint?"

"Definitely not," said the priest.

"Okay," I said. "Thanks for your help, Reverend."

I turned to walk out of the place before he tried to convert me.

"The name is Peter," he said.

"Rock on, Peter," I called back.

My chat with Peter proved to be another strike against me, one of about a million I had accrued in the last few weeks. Just as I got home, the phone was ringing. I didn't want to pick it up, but I just couldn't help myself.

"Yeah."

"Welfare can help with your bills," said the voice.

"I'm going to welfare your fucking face."

The man laughed, then hung up.

Made me realize that I still had a drink coming to me.

NINETEEN

The man with the broken nose turned when I tapped him on the shoulder. My right hook from hell sent him flying through the air like a kite. He landed on the edge of the pool table, then dropped down to the floor like a bag of wet clothes. His friend from the jail cell got a kick in the balls that brought him to his knees, and the other guy that did the job on me in the parking lot the night before got a left hook to the jaw. He dropped his weight down and brought his shoulder into my guts. The momentum carried me into the edge of the pool table, which screeched back along the floor. I dropped a double-ax-handle onto the back of the man's neck, and he fell to his knees. A boot to the face left him sleeping on the floor. When I looked up, Curly was running toward the door.

I caught him in the parking lot. He was digging through the trunk of his rust-colored Mercury, and when he set eyes on me, he stepped back from the trunk with the tire iron in his hand. He swung with it once. I ducked under the arc, and then delivered an uppercut that sent him back on his heels. He dropped the tire iron. I grabbed him by the shirt and threw him headfirst into the open trunk, then retrieved the tire iron.

"You got me," he said, his hands up.

"Give me the fucking keys," I said.

He fished the car keys out of his pocket and handed them to me. Then I slammed the trunk lid shut. He pounded against it with all his might, but his efforts were futile. I got behind the wheel of the car, guided the car out of the parking lot and into the street, and then turned on the radio. "Take It Easy" by the

Eagles was playing. I was always a big Eagles fan, so I turned the volume up as loud as it would go. The sound blocked the noise of the man trying to hammer his way out of the trunk.

The street sloped gently down to the south. With the car in neutral, I pushed it and got it going. After a few steps, the momentum carried it toward the center of town at a slow speed.

I strolled back into the Cowboy's Cabin and took a seat at the bar on one of the stools. There was this real pretty college girl behind the counter, not the scumbag bartender from the night before. Her mouth hung open in a perfect O. I bet she'd never seen such work done before in her life. Her hair was short and dyed purple. She had on a really tight-fitting Rolling Stones shirt, which I was able to forgive her for because she had big tits. I loved the Eagles, but hated the Stones.

"Hey, darling, what's your name?"

"Autumn," she said softly.

"Autumn, I'd like a drink."

"I don't know if that's a good idea," she said.

I laughed. "Please?"

A hand came down hard on my shoulder from behind, and a voice said, "Don't worry, sugar, I'll keep this guy out of trouble."

I turned my head, ready to throw down, but it was Anthony Mannuzza, the asshole with the camera.

He was all duded up in black slacks and a crayon-green button-down shirt. The shirt was made of a shiny material, like silk, and hanging from his neck and one wrist were thin gold chains. He wore a gold watch with a sweeping second hand, and his dark hair was slicked back with sweet-smelling oil. His prettyboy Euro-trash face was perfectly shaved and preened, like a broad's legs. He even pulled some of his eyebrows out to give them that regal look, and he would've been a ladykiller if he wasn't such a goddamn fag.

"Well, if it isn't Jimmy Olsen. Take any nice funerary pictures lately?"

He smiled, said, "Oh, you saw that? I was trying to keep myself on the down low."

"That was a man's burial, prettyboy."

"Well, hey, what's the big deal? There were a hundred fucking guys taking pictures out there. Pearce must've been a popular guy."

"You have no idea."

"Believe me, I wasn't taking pictures for me, man. I swear."

"I know. For the book, right?"

"Right," he said, smiling. "There you go."

"Arright, well, I'm gonna have to hit you anyway."

Autumn cut in with, "Aw, c'mon, don't start now."

I said, "Arright, darling. I'll hold off. For you."

She smiled. Anthony started breathing again.

"Marley, I think you need to relax," Anthony said. "I know just the thing."

I looked at him. He had fire in his eyes.

"What the hell is that supposed to mean?" I said. "You tryin' to get cute on me?"

We walked out of the Cowboy's Cabin, and he led me to his Mach 1. I got in the shotgun seat, he got behind the wheel, and we took off.

"I saw what you did to that guy in the parking lot," he said.

"And?"

"And you're fucking psychotic. I like it."

I smiled and lit a cigarette. "That was nothing. You should have seen me when I was *your* age."

After about five blocks, we saw the twirling lights of a police cruiser up ahead. As we got closer we saw that the Mercury had plowed through a white picket fence and had come to rest against a parked minivan. The officer was apparently so distracted by the music coming from the stereo—it was "California Dreamin'" by the Mamas and the Papas now—that he didn't realize a man was locked in the trunk. As we drove by, Anthony lost all composure and laughed so hard that he cried.

He brought me to this little place on the edge of town I'd never even heard of. We pulled up outside the place and there were maybe only three or four cars parked in front. Nice cars, not the usual Toyotas or Fords that dominated the roads of Evelyn. These cars were the few fancy cars in town, the BMWs, the Jaguars, the lone vintage Ferrari painted cherry red no doubt purchased by some pitiful millionaire going through a midlife crisis.

The building was a small log cabin tucked in behind the trees all the way at the end of Liston Street. An electric lantern hung from each side of the wooden door, and that was the only illumination. There was a wood plaque by the door where the mailbox would be. It said "Rose."

"What the fuck is this," I said, "a gay bar?"

"No, it's not a gay bar. I'm not gay, man. I don't know why you keep saying that."

"Because you're a fucking fruit, that's why."

"Whatever. I'm not going to argue with you, mister-fucking-violent."

"Well, what's the story with this place?"

"You'll see. But before we go in, tuck that shirt in. They're kind of picky about appearance."

I was wearing a pair of dirty blue jeans, a white T-shirt with a pale denim shirt thrown over it. Work boots. "What, are they gonna try to make me put on a fucking jacket with a crest of arms on it?"

"No. Don't worry about it. You're with me."

"Whatever. Lead the way. All I know is, I need a drink."

Before we reached the door, it was opened from the inside by a large, well-dressed bouncer in a black suit and shirt. He was shaved bald, but had a peach-fuzz mohawk atop his head. This guy at the fancy bar was just one big muscle in a three-piece suit. He shined a flashlight in our faces. When he got to mine, he grunted.

"Don't worry, Hyde," said Anthony, "he's cool. He's a legend."

Anthony palmed this guy a twenty, and he let us pass. The inside was a large room lit only by candles placed on every surface. The walls were wood. There was a full bar, and maybe eight or ten small tables with just as many chairs. In the back were two doors. One seemed to lead to a kitchen, or a storeroom, the other, I didn't know. Probably a bedroom.

There were four well-dressed men seated individually at tables, drinking. Classical music was playing softly on a stereo. What caught my eye more than anything were the girls. There were five of them, all young, all pretty. One was wearing a black body stocking, one wore nothing more than a red bra and thong. Another was wearing a schoolgirl's skirt and white shirt, and the other two were wearing negligees—one blue, the other black. "Jesus," I said.

"Am I still a fag?" asked Anthony, smiling.

"I don't fucking care," I said.

"You never knew about this place?"

"If I did, I'd live here."

Anthony led us to an unoccupied table, and we sat down. The girl in the schoolgirl outfit came over.

Anthony said, "Hi, Samantha. You look nice."

"Thanks," she said robotically. "Who's your friend?"

"This is Marlowe Higgins."

She and I shook hands. My hand had its own, separate orgasm—a tingling upon touching her, like when you carry heavy groceries for too long.

"You look a little rough," she said to me.

I couldn't take my eyes off her body. I couldn't respond.

"Wait, I think I know who you are," she said. "You work at Long John's, right?"

"Uh, yeah," I said.

"Great food," she said.

"Thank you. I don't recall ever seeing you."

"I don't dress like this every day," she said, as if I were an idiot for not realizing that. "What would you guys like?"

"You," I said.

"Actually," said Anthony, "this is my friend's first time here, so I think we should start off with a couple of wet kisses."

"Sounds good," she said. "Who would you like?"

Anthony whispered in my ear, "She's the hostess. Let me do the talking, okay?"

"Sure," I whispered back.

"Can you get me Sharon, and, uh, for my friend here, uh, let me see . . . Marley, who looks good to you?"

"Jesus," I murmured.

"Samantha, if you could get Patty over here for my buddy, that would be great."

"Sure," she said, and padded off.

"Anthony, what did we just order, and how the hell am I going to pay for it?"

"Don't worry. I got you covered."

"You trying to butter me up for your fucking book or something?"

"No, man. You just don't get to meet a lot of cool people when you're constantly traveling."

"Sure," I said. I didn't care, one way or the other.

At the least, I was getting free drinks, and at the most . . . I couldn't even imagine. Before long, the girl in the body stocking and the girl in the red thong came over to our table. The Red Thong carried a bottle of whiskey and two shot glasses. Body Stocking took a seat on Anthony's lap. The red thong came up to me and straddled me in my seat.

"Hello," she said.

She nestled into me while Anthony and Sharon talked, and she poured out a shot of whiskey into the shot glass. Then she passed the bottle to her friend, and she did the same. Anthony was running his hands up and down that girl's body, and no one was doing anything, no one came over to throw him out of the joint for getting fresh, so I put my hands on Patty's hips and rubbed her legs.

She knocked the shot back, then came forward and put her mouth to mine. She spit the shot into my mouth. I drank it out of her, then sucked at her sweet lips for what was left. At my right, Anthony was doing the same.

It had been years since I had a drink, and after that long, that one shot hurt me like fire. It burned my throat, my chest, and burned a fire behind my eyes, like a preview of what hell would be like. I could immediately feel the stuff swishing around my brain, making me a little stupider than I usually am, but I didn't care, because my friend was dead and my life had gone completely down the toilet. I'd lost my job, the girl I loved didn't want anything to do with me, and unless the Rose Killer popped up somewhere and said, "Here I am," the wolf that lived in the place where my soul used to be was going to kill some innocent person in five days. I think I was entitled to a drink.

In the back of my mind I saw one of Pearce's memories. In it, I was a little bit younger, a little more angry, and he was pointing at me, saying, "God gave you a choice, man. You don't have to drink." He truly believed it.

We had seconds on the wet kisses, and then the girls left the table, leaving the bottle of whiskey behind. I started laughing, caught up in a rush of hormones like a teenage boy.

"You like?"

"I love," I responded.

"It's crazy, isn't it?"

"What's that?" I asked.

"Women," he said. "For hundreds of years these creatures have struggled with the 'male establishment' to have their equal rights and their equal wages, and to not be seen as women in a man's world. They've tried to do whatever they could do to erase the supposed myth of chicks being sex symbols. Burning bras and all that. But one look at any magazine blows all that women's-lib shit right out the window, and then you walk into someplace like this and you see that absolutely nothing has ever changed and it never will. Women are always going to be looked at in biblical terms, as seducers, as temptresses, as creatures who can't be trusted, and it's all their own fault. It's amazing. They're all crazy. Every single one of them."

"That's a pretty dank view, man. Especially after having a drink fed to you by a girl that looks like that."

"It's true. I mean, I've worked in big cities, man. New York, L.A., all over the place. And lately, I've been going all over the goddamn country for this photo book, and truly, there are some unique places in this world, but it really is the same everywhere. It really is. It's sad."

"I know," I said. "It *is* the same everywhere. There ain't a good place left anywhere in this goddamn country."

"I'll drink to that," said Anthony. "Lord have mercy."

"Never has, never will."

We knocked back our shots.

"What's it cost to screw in this place?"

"More than you and I have," said Anthony. "But that's the point. Keeps the low-bloods away, and the few yuppies in this town coming back. The yuppies know that they're the only ones that dip their wicks in these broads. I guess it makes them feel like these broads are some more things that they own. That pair of wet kisses was twenty bucks, times two, plus tip."

"Damn. And you don't want anything in return? You're a better man than me."

"Probably not," he said.

"How did you find this place? You're not even from around here."

"I keep my ear to the rails. I listen. And I look. I like being nosy, I like exploring. That's the whole point of the book, is the finding of places that no one's ever seen or heard of. Kind of like an unknown America kind of thing. The obscure. The little things that people don't see, I see. And I take pictures."

"Like that tree."

"Yeah, like the tree. My cover shot."

"Have you taken pictures in here?"

"Why? You want copies?"

We laughed.

"I asked, but they don't allow cameras in here, but," he said leaning in close, "that doesn't mean shit to me. I got all kinds of equipment in my car. I got a camera the size of a typewriter, and I got a spy camera the size of a pen. If I want a picture, I get it. I've been doing this a long time. I don't fuck around. Before this, I always did fashion photography for magazines, and I tell you the God's truth, the kind of women in that business are all whores, every single one of them. You look at any model in a magazine, and you can pretty much take it to the bank that she fucked her way into that picture, onto that cover. It's amazing. So you take your pictures, and you get your perfect shot. You take some pictures for fun while she's naked, you know, because it's basically a given that you did your thing with her, and you know the pictures are going to look great, and then when she sees them, she doesn't want you to have them. Meanwhile, she's fucked half the building, but a couple of pictures drive her up the wall because she's worried about her reputation. What the hell is that?"

"Who knows?"

"Women," he said. "You see the girls in here? You give any girl the chance, *any* girl, even a fucking nun, and she'll end up like this. Selling it. They're all the same, and it's like this everywhere."

"Whatever." His rant was starting to get to me. "Maybe you're just bitter."

"Bitter? What could I be bitter about?"

"Who gives a shit? You could be bitter about coming off like a queen, or not getting laid, or who knows? You sound like a fucking pig."

"Oh yeah? As I recall, you more than welcomed that wet kiss from the chick in the thong, Marlowe. You're right here with me, so don't play high-and-mighty with me. We're in this shit together. We're kindred spirits. It's just that I'm the one that's keeping this real. I'm not bitter. I'm a realist. You seem to have some romantic fucking view of sex relations, but you don't practice what you preach, so don't give me that shit about bitter. If anything, I prefer the word 'sardonic.' It's much more sophisticated."

"Whatever."

"*You're* bitter," he fired childishly.

I laughed. Of course I was bitter.

"There you go. Actually," he said, "you know what? There's only been one town in this whole country that I've been to that didn't have one loose woman in it, one brothel, or one strip joint, or even a girl painted up like a fucking whore. Marshall Falls."

"Huh?"

"Marshall Falls, New Mexico. If there's one place where women haven't degraded themselves, it's there, and believe me, I looked."

"I've never even heard of it."

"Of course. That's why I went there. The population is maybe a thousand, or less, even. Right in the middle of nowhere. You want to know how the town got that name?"

"No."

He laughed. "I'll tell you anyway. It's a good story."

"Don't."

"A hundred fucking years ago, this Robin Hood–type bandit named Marshall—they don't even know his full name—bit the bullet there. He had a band of thieves together that robbed the trains that rolled across the vast lands, and with the goods, well, he basically took care of this little, starving community of religious types. Not Mormons, but something crazy like that. It wasn't even a town, it was a fucking wasteland. He got shot, and he died, and some other bandits buried him there and put a marker over him. Decades later, a legitimate town started up near the grave, and when they found that grave, the weather had eaten half of it away, and the only words left on the marker that anyone could fucking read were 'Marshall Falls.' And that's what they named the town. Some historian pieced that shit together. Ain't that great?"

"Yeah, kid, it's the greatest thing I've ever heard."

"Every town has a story. Even a shitty little flyspeck like Marshall Falls. This place seems to have a few. That's why I've stuck around so long."

"Well, ain't we the lucky ones."

"Damn right," he said.

When the girls started blowing out the candles, we left. Anthony and I were both extremely drunk, but my supernatural metabolism had me in a little better shape than him. I took the keys to his Mach 1 and drove us back to where my truck was parked. When we got there I was ready to get myself home, but he stopped me.

"Let me show you something," he said, and he led me around to the trunk of his car. There were about a half a dozen cameras back there in the trunk, rolls and rolls of film, and a bunch of wires, batteries, and boxes, all kinds of crap. All kinds of crap were stacked up in the backseat of his car too, but I couldn't see what any of it was because of the poor lighting. I figured it had to be his clothes.

He started moving shit around, and then opened this one box. It was full of eight-by-ten photographs of places around Evelyn. He started flipping through them, and then pulled a few out. They were the pictures of Pearce and me, the ones he had taken at the restaurant.

"Here," he said, "you can have them if you like."

I took them and flipped through them slowly. The shots were taken in rapid succession, and going through them was like going through a small flip-book. Pearce and I slowly giving the finger to the prettyboy cameraman. One of the last times either of us had smiled. "Thank you," I said, meaning it.

"Don't worry. I have doubles."

I switched the pictures to my left hand, took a deep breath, and decked Anthony with my right hook. The shot sent him back into the side of the car, and he fell on his ass. A tear of blood leaked from his lower lip.

He shook his head, then looked up at me with an expression of pure rage. He looked like a different person, but the look was soon pacified, because he knew in that moment that anything he could possibly do would be futile.

I shook out my knuckles, then said, "Thanks for the drinks, but you had that one coming for those pictures no matter what."

"Fuck you," he grunted.

I lit a cigarette and walked back to my truck. I put the pictures on the passenger seat.

"We all have a job to do," he shouted. "It's nothing personal."

I took off.

"We all have a job to do, nothing personal," I said to myself.

It sounded true, I thought, plowing into someone's mailbox.

TWENTY

A loud banging woke me from my deep, drunken
sleep. That was another reason I used to love to drink so much—
it made the bad dreams go away. I was so out of it, my head went
back down to the warm pillow, and I was out again.

Seconds or years later, I wasn't sure which, the banging came
back, and it was anger more than anything that gave me the motivation to get out of bed. Some motherfucker was at the door,
and they were going to suffer for it. The skull-and-crossbones
sticker wasn't on my mailbox for nothing.

On the other hand, I thought I recalled leaving a puddle of
vomit at the mailbox too, and that didn't so much have any signif-
icance that I could think of, except letting people know I'm an idiot as they walk by.

I slipped on my pair of jeans, grabbed my baseball bat from
the hallway closet, and went to the front door. I was barely able to
walk straight. The pounding continued. My head felt like it was
full of lead pellets. Buckshot.

"Stop it!" I shouted.

A male voice I couldn't place said, "Open the door. Now."

"Oh, I'll open it, scumbag."

I undid the chain and four locks, and as I ripped that door
open, I raised the bat to shoulder level, aiming to score a homer
with this bastard's head.

It was a guy in a gray suit and polished shoes. Sunglasses. Short
hair. A wedding band on his finger that he twirled without realizing it.

"Detective Van Buren," he said. "Remember me?"

"I've tried not to," I said. "Leave me alone."

"You want to put that bat down?"

"No," I said.

"I can make you."

"Have it your own way."

He didn't make a move. He was smart.

"What the fuck do you want, cop? You woke me up."

"It's two-thirty in the afternoon, Higgins. What happened to your precious job serving gruel at that hellhole on Main Street?"

"Fuck you," I said.

"I won't be doing that today," he said, smirking.

"Is this what you came here for? To wake me up? To joust with me? I don't have time for this shit."

"I think you do," he said. "I think you have plenty of time to talk to me."

"Sorry, I don't think I do."

"We can do it here, or we can do it at the station."

"Listen, son, I've been hearing that line longer than you've been alive, arright? Don't give me that shit."

"Listen, Higgins . . ."

"No, you listen, cop, I don't know what you want, but you're seriously fucking up the Zen-like flow of my day here, and you can't really talk to a man when he's holding a baseball bat, so get the hell off my porch."

I went to slam the door in his face, but he put his foot in the doorway. The door bounced off of it and swung back open.

"You don't have a porch," Van Buren said.

"Oh, you're cute," I said, surprised at his audacity. "You must be handicapped, like, mentally, to pull that shit on me."

"You scuffed my shoe, Mr. Higgins. I'm not happy with that."

"Drop dead, lawman."

"You're going to hear me out whether you like it or not," he said.

"I already don't like it."

"How about you let me in. We can talk like gentlemen."

"I don't think so. Move your foot and write me a letter. The building number's on the door."

I made a move like I was going to slam the door again, but his foot didn't budge, and I wasn't about to wail on a cop unless he swung first. So it seemed we were at an impasse, as Proust would say. I couldn't crack his head open without feeling provoked, and he couldn't come in or pull out to talk to me unless he saw a table behind me covered in cocaine and plutonium. But why did he want to talk to me? Was it for something I'd done at some point? Something they suspected me of? Whatever it was, there wasn't enough proof around for this cop to get too fresh with me.

"Arright," I said, "I have a serious fucking headache, man. What's it going to take for you to go away?"

"A few minutes of your time."

"Is this about the other night?"

"Not quite. . . ."

"The Indian?"

"What?"

"Nothing."

"Let me in."

"Fine, you fucking . . ."

"Now lose the bat."

I turned and threw the bat back into the house. It landed on the couch, bounced, then rolled across the floor. I turned back to the cop.

"Happy, asshole?"

"Yes," he said.

He looked like he was about a hundred and sixty pounds. A lightweight. Grandmothers would describe him as "slight." If I'd ever seen him on the street, I'd have dismissed him as a twerp.

In the blink of an eye, this little bastard bum-rushed me, right in my own home, and I let him do it by ditching that damn bat. One of his hands came up quick and locked around my face. The other hand pressed into my sternum, and he ran into me and pushed me all the way back into the house. We fell into the recliner, and the recliner tipped back and over. When the dust cleared, the cop was still on top of me, and he'd somehow slipped a pair of meat hooks on me.

"You fucker," I hissed. "Get these fucking things off of me. Now."

"I told you I'd make you lose the bat," he said, smiling. "Idiots like you always think the same. They expect violence because that's all they know. How to be a goddamn brute. It's that limitation that makes you all so fucking stupid."

"Fuck you."

"That's why criminals get caught."

"Get these cuffs off me."

"And that's why scumbags like you always make a mistake."

"I'm going to have your fucking shield for this, man. What the fuck is this about? What are you talking about?"

He got up, put his foot on my chest as if I were a big game trophy and someone was about to take a picture. "Pearce was my partner, Higgins."

"Good for you!" I yelled. "What do you want? A medal?"

"We worked together for a long time."

"This is police brutality, man."

"That's what this is about," he said. "About Pearce."

I forced myself to calm down a little, then said, "Fine."

"Good," he said.

"Good. Can I get off the fucking floor now?"

"No."

"Can I have a cigarette?"

"No."

"Well, fuck you, cop. You come in here, you wake me up, you attack me, you break into my home and take me fucking hostage. And now I can't even smoke in my own home. That's it, man. It's on."

He came down fast and wrapped a hand around my throat. "Shut up, you fucking worm," he grumbled. "This isn't your home no more, you hear me? Now shut up. You say one more word, I'll bury that bat in your butt."

I couldn't answer him because he was strangling me. It was probably for the best.

"Pearce was my partner, but more than that, he was my friend. He was my little kid's godfather. Why? Because he was a good man. The best man in this goddamn town. I know that. Everyone that ever met him knew that. In another day and age, he would've been the one to nail Capone or some shit like that. He was a good man and a good cop. And now he's dead. So I have to ask myself, if he was such a great guy, what was he doing spending time with a piece of trash like you?"

He eased up on my throat long enough for me to hack out, "Baking cookies."

A slap across the left side of my face stunned me.

"Marlowe Higgins. I pulled your record, you know. You're not an upstanding citizen, but there have been worse. But scumbags like you are sneaky, like worms." He got up off me and set up the recliner. Took a seat in it. "It alarms me that there are so many gaps in your activity. So many years without paying your taxes and whatnot, without having a residence, a paper trail. What were you doing?"

"I was going door to door for the Mormons."

"I always wondered what Pearce was doing, wasting his time with a piece of trash like you. When he told me, uh, quite a while back that you and he were acquaintances, I honestly thought he was full of shit, because, hey, everyone on the force had heard of you. You're the guy with the mean right hook, right?"

"You'll find out soon enough," I said.

"I followed him one night. Again, no time recently, but quite a while ago. I couldn't even tell you when. And when I followed him, he drove right to that shitty little diner you got fired from . . ."

"It ain't a fucking diner, man. . . ."

"Shut up! Just shut the fuck up already, Higgins. You'll have your time to talk, and with any luck, it'll be from behind bars or over a fucking hole dug for you. He drove to that shitty diner, and, hell, he actually ordered a cup of that muck you people call coffee, and he talked to you. I could not believe what I was seeing. I have to admit, it got me worried, my partner socializing with a connie like you. Goddamn, I was worried he was taking drugs out of evidence for you, but guess what's missing from your rap sheet?"

"Rhymes?"

"Drug charges."

"That too."

"Seeing that made me happy, and I thought nothing of it, this weird association of his, that is, until this Rose Killer came to town."

Hearing that made my skin crawl. "Now listen up, cop, if you think . . ."

He moved like a cat, and before I knew it his foot was pressed into the side of my face. "What part of 'shut up' are you having a hard time with?"

I groaned from the pain. After a few seconds he got off me and sat back down.

"From a crime scene like the one up at the Crowley property, you'd think a guy might call his wife, or his special lady, just to tell her he may not be home for a while. That's what any man would do, especially when you have federal agents crawling in and out of your asshole, and that's what Pearce had done a million times at crime scenes. But what did he do when they found that poor woman up there? He called you. Why is that?"

"Oh, you mean I can talk now?"

"Briefly, yes."

"Well, it seems that our good buddy Pearce liked bouncing his cases off me. I think he felt better talking to me than you because I had a better relationship with your wife than you did."

Detective Van Buren turned red, which made me happy on the inside.

"Maybe you should have tried following *her*," I said.

"You sonofabitch!"

He jumped up again, toward me, and this time he reached

inside his jacket. Out came the police-issued handgun. He grabbed a fistful of my long, flowing hair with one hand and pressed the barrel of the gun into the side of my nose.

"Do it," I said. "Do it."

"It's not over, you piece of trash. They may have put my friend in the ground. We may be in the middle of nowhere, with all kinds of creatures doing God knows what out in those woods, but you mark my words. I will not rest until you're the one in a cage. I don't trust you. And I don't know what Pearce was involved with you for, but I will not allow his memory to be tarnished by whatever the fuck you two had going on. I don't know why he called you from the crime scene, but if you had anything to do with that murder, I'm going to find out about it. Why? Because you're a fuckup. You're all fuckups, and I'm better than you. And when that time comes, when I find what I'm looking for, enough to put you away, you'll have nowhere to run to, and nowhere on this fucking earth to hide. Do you understand that, *man*?"

"Do it now."

"Don't be so greedy, Higgins. Your time will come. And then it will be over."

He got up and put the piece back in the holster under his jacket.

"You're the one that's been calling me, aren't you?"

He smiled.

"I knew it," I said. "You're a twisted sonofabitch, you know that?"

"Let's keep this little chat between you and me private, okay? If you go to my people, you'll only be hurting yourself more, because I can guarantee they won't listen to a word you have to say about this. And I'll find out."

"Figures."

"Don't make it hard for yourself. And remember, whatever you've done, you could always turn yourself in, save me the trouble of having to come down on you, because it's only a matter of time."

"Great."

"You may be wondering what my motivation was, coming in here and showing you what a little connie you are, huh?"

"Not really. I kinda presumed you had the wrong house to begin with. . . ."

"You're a funny guy, you know that? Remember some of these lines when you're in prison getting drilled up that hairy old ass of yours. But anyway, I'm here just to let you know that I'm going to get you. It may not be today, and it may not be tomorrow, but it's coming and there's not a goddamn thing you can do about it. You bastards always fuck up, and I'll be there when it happens. I just wanted you to know that. You've started saucing it up all over town, Higgins, getting into punching matches with all the lowlifes in this town, just like old times."

"Hardly," I said.

"Shut up. That tells me you're weak, you're already running from something up in that feeble old head of yours, and that tells me I won't have to wait long to put those hooks on you again. I'm going to be watching you. Wherever you go, I'll be over your shoulder. I'm going to be so close to you, I'll be like cancer, practically inside you. And I'm going to break you."

He turned and headed for the door.

"Hey!" I shouted.

He turned his head.

"Pearce *was* a good man," I said. "The best man I ever met. It doesn't mean anything to you, but I had nothing to do with anything. More important, neither did he."

He said nothing, just turned his head back and went for the door.

"Hey!" I shouted again.

He stopped.

"What about these fucking handcuffs? Get these fucking things off me."

He fished around in his pants pocket until he came up with the key. He held it up to the light, let it glisten.

"This goddamn Rose Killer has to be stopped," he said. "I don't know where he came from or where he's going. I don't know if what's been going on down here are copycat killings. The feds think it's the real deal, though. The one thing I'm sure of is that the killer is still here."

"How do you know that?"

"We found another body," he said.

My mouth fell open on its hinges.

"I almost wish it was you, but I know where you were last night. In a way, it's a shame," he said, then threw the key at me. It landed by my feet. "But I'll find out what your involvement is in all this. In regards to the handcuffs, get used to 'em."

"What exactly do you think I've done?"

He walked out as if I'd said nothing.

The TV confirmed what Van Buren had said. There was another body. Her name was Betsy Ratner. She was a teacher for second-grade kids at one of the local schools. She was twenty-eight years old. She was a single lady, though from the photos they showed she seemed to be a rather pretty girl with long dark hair and wide, innocent eyes. She had gone out with some of her girlfriends last night, and drove home somewhere in the neighborhood of two o'clock in the morning. She was inebriated, but comfortable enough to drive home alone.

Shortly after two o'clock in the morning, her car rolled down her driveway, went across the street at a speed of five miles an hour or so, and went into a car parked across the street, which set off the alarm. The police were called, and when they arrived they saw that the driver's-side door to Betsy Ratner's car was hanging open. There was a spot of blood on the driver's seat, and several more drops on her driveway, but no Betsy Ratner.

Her body was found at the crack of dawn in Wild Oaks Cemetery, naked and posed on Detective Daniel Casey Pearce's grave. Two wild, red roses were stuffed into her hollow sockets.

This murder was different from the Rose Killer's previous kills for several reasons. Right off the bat, the evidence pointed to a blitz attack, hence the blood on the driveway and the unsubstantiated report that a bloody log was found in the bushes outside the house. He must have knocked her out in a hurry. All previous evidence pointed to mutilation occurring postmortem. Differing from other instances, the body was found in a matter of hours instead of days. This in itself was an oddity. It was as if the killer hadn't been as methodical as he usually was, didn't take as much time as usual. I reckoned this incident was much more impulsive than those in the past. There was a more urgent need for him to do what he did than was typical. Because of this rushed feeling to the crime, it felt much more sloppy than it ever had.

That was a good thing. For all I knew, the police might have a print or a witness that they weren't revealing to the media. I was hoping that was the case because there were only four days left until the next full moon, and I had failed once at taking the Rose Killer down and more people died because of that. I didn't want it to happen again.

It meant something that the killer had left his victim's body on Pearce's grave. Pearce was in charge of the cases here in Evelyn, and the killer would have known that. He also knew the body would have been found quickly, which meant it was all for show, a big and personal "fuck you" to the world. Pearce's fresh grave was turned into a crime scene. Off-limits to even his wife, who visited it every day, just so his soul could bless their unborn child and keep it safe.

I drove like a bat out of hell to my newsstands to get the papers. These had a little more information than the TV reports, and more pictures. In one of the pictures of the crime-scene tape around Pearce's grave, I saw Anthony Mannuzza taking his own picture off to the side. At that moment, I regretted ever taking a drink in the first place, but especially with him. The man was a prettyboy, but he was like a wraith, sneaking to and fro to take his goddamn pictures. I vowed I'd never touch the sauce again. I'd made a horrible mistake.

I also learned another interesting tidbit: That same night, St. Mark's Church had a window smashed in. Nothing seemed to be missing.

Even the church break-in, if it was, in fact, related to the murders, seemed to be rushed. Usually a lock was busted, not a window.

The *Harbinger* interviewed one of the feds, who said the same thing they always do: It's only a matter of time now. This will be the last victim. Turn yourself in because it will be better for you. I wondered if anyone ever fell for it. I wouldn't.

In the distance I heard sirens screaming.

The murder dominated the town. The police didn't know what to do, and the people knew it. I could see it on the streets as I drove back home. The cops were rounding up the drunks, the hooligans, and the vagrants, shaking the trees out of desperation, hoping a miracle happened. It wouldn't.

When I got home, I knew I had some cleaning to do. Van Buren had been the sonofabitch that broke into my house. I would have preferred it to be an ordinary, run-of-the-mill psycho, because anything that cop could find would be called evidence for whatever he thought I was involved in. He knew I had a gun. He knew I read. He also knew I had articles about all the murders up on the wall. I had to get rid of all of it. The articles got burned in the fireplace, along with any miscellany I had floating around— bills, receipts, old fake IDs I'd been holding on to. I knew the police had some way to make traces of blood glow in the dark with certain lights and chemicals, but there was no possible way for me to do a job on the house that would throw off such an inspection. If the cops did come under Van Buren's insistence that I was behind every unsolved crime since the end of the war, they would certainly find blood in my house, and that wasn't a good thing.

On the other hand, everything Van Buren had done thus far

had been illegal. Not admissible. But would that matter if I was actually arrested for something? I'd still be behind bars for at least a little while.

If only the wolf had revealed to me its memories from the night my friend died. For all I knew, the wolf knew exactly what had happened that night, but it was not being forthcoming. I was in the dark, and I had no idea what to do. All I knew was that it wasn't over, no matter what Van Buren's crazy note said. There were still some variables floating around to help me get to the bottom of all this.

TWENTY-ONE

In the morning I drove out to the Pearce house
with a fresh bouquet of flowers. I'd never been inside the house
before, but I knew where it was. I'd driven by it a thousand times,
and always slowed down when I did, just to make sure no one was
snooping around outside when Pearce was at work.

The house was white, with dark blue shutters fastened to the
frames of all the windows. A hedge encapsulated the house, and
a weeping willow about twice as tall as the house overshadowed it
from the left. I cleared my throat, then knocked on the door.

No one came, so I tried the bell.

I heard it echo inside the house, and then I heard footsteps
come closer. Soon, the door opened, and there stood Martha,
blue-purple bags under her puffy eyes, her hair matted, like she'd
done nothing but sleep since the funeral. The sad fact that a dead
body had been planted on her husband's grave only made things
worse.

Down the block, two plainclothes policemen sat in an unmarked car watching the Pearce household. Some probably
thought the planted body of Betsy Ratner was a warning to
Pearce's widow. I could only imagine the sizes of the bricks they
shit when I went up to her front door.

Martha wore a white, nappy robe, and slippers. Her belly
came out so far, I could've reached out and touched it. "Mrs.
Pearce," I said.

"Hello," she said, a tinge of anger to her voice.

"I, uh, just wanted to pay my respects. I got you these."

I handed her the flowers. She took them, smelled them quick, and then lowered them to her side. She hesitated, then said, "Thank you."

"Don't mention it," I said. "I was wondering if I could come in for a minute, talk with you for a minute."

"Now's not a good time. I have people over, and . . ."

"I hate to be a pain, Mrs. Pearce. I know you're not my biggest fan, but I know you're alone right now. Yours is the only car parked out there, and the house is silent. Now, I can understand it if you don't want me in your home, but . . . hell, I'm trying to be really sincere here, ma'am, and, uh, I just need a minute of your time. Truly."

She cleared her throat, looked behind her, then out onto the street to make sure the cops were still there. "A minute," she said. "No more."

"That's fine."

She stepped aside and let me pass. I went into the living room and took a seat on the couch. The house was spacious and decorated with the intent of making the place look cozy. Big pillows all over the place, a huge kitchen. A big television. Everything made of oak. A true home. Up on the fireplace mantel was a picture of them at their wedding, a picture of her, and a picture of him, younger, in his dress uniform. I knew the other pictures were of their parents, because I remembered a memory of Pearce's when they were decorating the place. I even knew what they kept in every drawer in the house. Mrs. Pearce came in and slowly lowered herself into a chair. She didn't offer me anything to drink, nor did I expect her to. Danny and she usually kept at least a dozen different kinds of tea in the kitchen.

"What do you need?" she asked.

"I don't need anything. I just wanted to talk a minute. I wanted to say that I'm sorry that you and I never got along well. Pearce was a great guy. I mean, that's all they say on the TV, but for those of us who knew him, it really was true. He was too good a man to be a cop. And, uh, his partner, Van Buren, he's kind of got a personal vendetta against me. I won't get into it, but I'm wondering if he's said anything to you about me . . . that kind of sounds like he suspects me of anything."

"How can you come into my home and ask me a question like this?"

"I'm sorry, ma'am, I don't want to upset you."

"I think you should leave."

"Please don't say that."

"Get out."

"No, ma'am, this is important. More important than you know."

"I want you out."

She was crying now, and getting loud.

"Mrs. Pearce, please."

"Out!"

"No. I will not get out. For the baby's sake, don't get yourself worked up. I'll be out of your hair in no time." I didn't ever expect to yell at a pregnant woman. "Now, listen, you and I never got on, but your husband and I did, and he was a damn good judge of character, and I think you ought to respect that right now and hear what I have to say, if for no other reason than he would have. Okay?"

She got quiet.

"Okay."

"This Van Buren guy is after me," I said. "Has he talked to you about this?"

"Yes."

"What has he said?"

"He thinks you got Danny into something bad, and maybe that it got him killed . . ." She broke down. "I told him Danny wasn't like that. Danny would never involve himself in anything illegal. The job was his life, but his partner wouldn't listen to me. He thinks I'm hysterical."

"Why is he so concerned about Pearce's reputation?"

Mrs. Pearce said, "The blue line at work," and left it at that.

"On the night that the first girl died, do you know what Van Buren was doing, or where he was?"

"No, but he did call that night. They always talked at night.

They laughed for a few minutes, talked about work, and that was it. Same as always. Why?"

"Don't worry about the why of it. Uh, on the night that Danny died, do you know what he was doing up there at the Crowley property?"

She didn't answer for a long time.

"He said if he was able to make this case, it would make his career, and . . . not only would he avenge all those poor girls, he'd do what the feds couldn't do, maybe write a book about it. He said if he was able to catch this guy, we'd never have to worry about money for our little girl. He said we'd be set. And so he spent all these hours up at the scene, just . . . trying to put it all together in his head. He wanted this guy, Marlowe."

"And what about Van Buren?"

"Van Buren," she said hesitantly, "is not a good detective. But . . ."

"But what?"

"But I know what you're thinking, and you shouldn't be. He has problems."

"What kind?"

"No one knows it, but he takes crazy pills. He's a paranoid. I'm not supposed to know that, but I do."

She jerked forward for a second, then put her hands on her belly. That one crease appeared on her forehead.

"Are you okay?"

"Yes," she said. "She just kicked."

I held my breath for a second, and watched her watch herself. I didn't belong.

"Do you want to feel?" she asked.

For a brief moment, I wasn't me anymore. I was Danny, seeing her through his eyes. His hands became my hands, and in this memory she was just a little bit lighter around the waist. He reached out to feel his baby.

"Uh, is it safe?" I asked. Danny had said the same thing once.

"Yes."

I got up and crossed the floor. I bent down and put one hand on her stomach, softly. She grabbed my wrist and pressed my hand more firmly against her. After a few seconds, I felt the baby shift inside her. It was as if the baby was able to recognize me by my aura, and I made it so unhappy with my presence that it tried to swim away. Maybe it knew that I killed its daddy. Or maybe it felt its daddy inside me.

I looked at Martha, and Martha looked at me, and I began to cry. I backed away.

"Thank you for your time, Mrs. Pearce. Thanks for having me."

I went for the door. I didn't belong that close. She struggled to get up quickly.

"Wait," she said.

I stopped. My insides were compelling me to get as far away from the unborn child as I could. I didn't belong near children.

"There's something you should have. Hold on one minute, let me find it."

"Sure," I said, and I waited there at the door.

After disappearing somewhere in the house for a handful of minutes, she came back with a manila envelope that was sealed with duct tape. It had my initials on it, in marker. She handed it over.

"Van Buren doesn't know about this," she said. "Danny told me a long time ago that if anything ever happened to him, I should make sure that you got this. It's been changed to different envelopes, because he was always messing around with what was in there, and, uh, he even went so far as to put a piece of his hair there, on the edge of the tape, to make sure no one ever opened it. Do you know what it is?"

"No," I said.

I'd never had a memory of Pearce's regarding the envelope, but I could feel it hanging there like a thread on the edge of my brain. My heart went crazy in my chest. She looked at me, and that moment seemed to last ten thousand years.

She never liked me. I always had to presume that it was

because to most people, I was nothing but a common ruffian, a drunk, and she resented the fact that her man put a great deal of trust in a bum like me. Now he was dead, she was a widow, and she still didn't know what the hell was going on.

Her baby had no father. She was all alone in that house, and the world that had granted them so much had gone crazy, turned cold, and taken back all that it could. It wasn't right, and it seemed that there was no one out there who could help her.

Justice was dead. The law had proved to be useless in protecting her man, or the people of Evelyn. The power over life and death had been taken from the hands of the good and put into the hands of a very evil entity. No man had been able to stop him. No one had come close, and it was never going to stop. That only left one option open to put an end to this thing.

Even if Van Buren wasn't following me, he'd find out sooner or later that I'd paid a visit to Pearce's wife, but she wouldn't say anything about the envelope. I knew that much. I swallowed a lump in my throat.

"Mrs. Pearce, it's time for me to go. Thanks for having me. I know it seems this whole town has gone to hell, and I know that it seems like everything is hopeless, but I just want you to know that it's not over."

I went home with the envelope. Once I was in my recliner with a cigarette burning, I opened it up with a pair of scissors. I pulled out over a dozen black-and-white photographs, each of which had a medical report stapled to the back.

Each photo was of a crime scene, the oldest of which was three years old. The most recent photo showed a skull at the base of a tree. The report on the back said it was the remains of one Bill Parker.

In flipping through the pictures, I found that all the bodies depicted belonged to all the people I'd killed in Evelyn over the years. All of them, except the ones they'd never found, but it was close enough. Detective Danny Pearce had me pegged.

I closed my eyes, and there was Danny . . .

He was looking in the bathroom mirror at the Pearce house. He was wearing a pair of blue jeans and a black sweatshirt with a hood. A pair of eyeglasses, though they weren't prescription. An idiot's disguise, like mine. He walked out of the bathroom and went to the kitchen, poured himself a Thermos full of coffee. Looked out the window to see a full moon. The clock on the microwave said it was nine o'clock.

Martha padded in, not yet pregnant, and asked him where he was going dressed like that.

"That's top-secret," Danny said jokingly, and then he gave her a kiss and went out to the car.

He drove to my place and watched the house. A couple of hours later, he saw the wolf walk out the front door, hunching its shoulders as it did so, so it could fit, and then it sniffed the air and took off like a shot in the night.

Pearce had had his suspicions because of my brilliant insights into the suspicious deaths of several people. He, unlike all the other rubes on the force, happened to realize that most of the town's disappearances occurred on the night of the full moon. Maybe it was only natural to watch me, to see if the guy he'd taken under his wing was, in fact, a serial killer himself.

What he saw shocked him so badly he pissed in his jeans. He hadn't been so scared since he saw a bear attack someone when he was a boy. Not even the hostage situation at the jewelry store had scared him that bad. But now he knew. Now he knew why some people got mauled, why some people just simply vanished, why there were some nights I just didn't feel like talking on the phone. Why I didn't want anyone in the house. Why I'd never had a tattoo, even though I seemed like the type that would be covered with them—the tattoos would never grow back after the change. He never tried to put me down, and he never tried to stop me. Why? I closed my eyes and rummaged around in my brain to figure that out.

Pearce, upon discovering my true nature, knew that no one

would believe him. He knew that what I did, and how, were things that could not be explained by science or legitimately discussed in a court of law. Arresting me for being a supernatural killing machine would have been ridiculous. No one would have believed it, and if so, how would I be prosecuted? Further, the only evidence that I had been the one who had killed all these people would have been the microscopic flecks of blood in and around my house. Everything else would have been circumstantial. Any case against me wouldn't have held up under close examination.

After having thought about my dilemma in purely legal terms, Pearce began to contemplate this unique issue in another light. He was a man who had never approved of vigilantism because he was a man of law and order through and through, both because of his military service and his career as a cop. However, even he wasn't immune to a certain duality of character. Knowing I could never be stopped, he didn't so much see my continued freedom as a way for the town's trash to be eradicated as it was a way to ensure the fact that the criminals his police force couldn't catch wouldn't be able to commit their particular crimes over and over again. That was how he rationalized allowing me to live.

In his darker moments he admitted to himself that he was in a way living vicariously through me. After all, I was wholly capable of crossing those lines that he, as a police officer, had to steer clear of. He sometimes envied me for this, which, when his head would clear, disgusted him.

I wondered if Pearce and I had ever really been friends, but I knew we were. However, the purpose of this friendship was twofold. One, he liked my company, and two, he felt obligated to keep tabs on me. Feeding me information about cases he knew he wouldn't be able to solve was his way of manipulating me, and I didn't even know it.

Why, I asked myself, *was he up at the Crowley property if he knew the wolf would be out that night? Did he see it as two heads working toward the same end?*

Pretty much. He thought he'd at least be safe.

And why did he leave me the envelope? To rub my face in it? To prove he wasn't as bumbling as I might have thought? No. It was so if anything ever happened to him, I could avenge his death.

"Well, knock me the fuck down."

I looked down at my hand and saw it explode, but it was all in my head. It was time. The wolf was going to give me the memories of that night that I'd been hoping for.

They say birds can see colors in the spectrum that people can't, and that dogs can smell things that people can't too. The wolf experienced the world more fully than any man could ever imagine, and on those occasions in which its memories would bleed out and seep into mine, it was as if I was given the power and the privilege to see this world through the eyes of God, or at least a notable competitor to his title and throne.

In living day-to-day, I see the world as I always have, but because I know of how it *could* look, it has lost its shine, its flare, and its magic. It is dull, lackluster, and rusted, and I always know that there are things that dwell just below the surface that I, in my human form, could never put my finger on. The taste of metal filled my mouth. I tasted . . . I tasted blood . . . I *changed*.

The beast rose on its own two legs from the murky red puddle that still steamed on the floor. It howled low, grunted, and quickly swept the house for signs of life with its ears, its nose. It smelled my detergent, it picked up the mouse living under my kitchen sink by the rustling of dust bunnies, the minuscule pitter-patter of tiny feet.

The beast made the decision to leave it be. It knew it had a target in the Rose Killer, and even if it didn't have a target, it would not have settled for the death of an animal. It smelled the collected smoke from my years of cigarettes, permanently clogging the air in the house, and living in the walls and fabrics. The beast wrinkled its wet nose and let out an animal sneeze.

It lurched through the house slowly and left through the front door, stooping its shoulders to fit under the frame of the door. Once it was outside, its ears perked up; it breathed deep and bellowed. The night glowed and screamed with life. Like I'd trained it to, it closed the door behind it before taking off into the night.

It ran at speeds beyond my comprehension, faster, perhaps, than the great cats that prowl the prairies of faraway lands. Through backyards, dark roads, then the woods that surround the town of Evelyn, and finally, the open road, it ran. Wind kissed it, streaking trails through its thick, dark hair. The moonlight came down, washing over it like a mother's love.

The sounds and smells of an entire world enticed it, beckoned it, pulled it in a million different directions, but the beast was focused. The beast knew what it had to do. It was hungry for it. It had the intent. Thank God for that.

The wolf reached Edenburgh and quickly found the spot where that poor girl had been found over there, the backyard to the house with the swimming pool. As it had done countless times before, it got down low on all fours and smelled the ground, leaving drips of snot and spit on the crushed blades of grass. With its tongue, it picked up the soil, rolled it around in its mouth, all with the purpose of picking up the scent, the taste, the smell of the perpetrator. Once it had that, the bells would toll and it would be only a handful of minutes or hours before the target would meet his destroyer.

After several seconds, the wolf wrinkled its brow, clenched its giant fists, and growled somewhere deep inside it. It spit out the soil and howled. It was mad. It was a feeling, a sensation, an instance that had never occurred before, and the beast didn't know what to make of it. The beast was frustrated. It hadn't picked anything up.

How is that possible?

The beast angrily went on to what it felt was the next possible spot to help it along, using the same kind of reasoning skills one would expect only real people to be capable of. In the blink of an eye, it stood upon Judith Myers's grave, breathing heavily. With fingers stretched and claws bared, it went to the business of digging out the coffin, hoping in its own, animal way to get a scent off the dead girl's body.

When it got to the shell of the coffin, six feet down, it pulled the lid off the casket. The beast looked down, and there rested the young, dead lady. Like a burnt piece of paper, she had begun to turn a darker shade around her edges—her eyelids, her fingertips, her lips. She was discolored, as if she were covered in a fine layer of soot. Her dress was stained by dirt now, and as the beast took her by the back of her neck more carefully than I ever imagined it could handle something, the stitches in the dress where they had sewn it around her stiffened form began to pop open.

The beast lifted her up. As she bent at the waist, the beast heard cracks. To its otherworldly ears, they sounded like firecrackers. It smelled the putrid fumes of chemicals and death rise from her like angry phantoms. Her dress fell away to one side, exposing a dead breast. The wolf groaned low, and hunched up, almost as if it were ashamed of itself, or sad for what had happened.

Its left hand sliced the dress away from the body, exposing rows of thick stitches along the chest and lower regions, forming a Y, as if it was a question branded into her so she could remember to ask God that, just in case she happened to run into him.

More dank smells, almost too powerful for the wolf. It wanted out of that grave, but it would not go. It smelled her down there, privately, up along the blackened stitch holes, and up further still to the eyes, or, more accurately, the sockets where eyes used to live and swim and dart. Where beautiful eyes used to see, to know, to wonder, to radiate joy and love, and watch the rain come down.

The eyes saw the killer. Could that be why he took them?

The holes had been stuffed with cotton and glued shut, heavily caked with makeup, giving the impression that nothing had been done to the face. With the grace and precision of a surgeon, the beast, with one gleaming nail, plucked through the gunk sealing the eyeholes and opened them up. It brought its nose up close, close enough to leave wet marks, and smelled there in the dried and putrid pits.

Nothing.

The beast crawled out of the hole and screamed. Before taking off into the night, the beast laid the lid back down and filled in the hole by kicking the dirt in, like a cat in a litterbox. The beast was now in a rage. It had struck out twice, unable to get a lead on its target, and it was now getting close to seething. It felt . . . *denied*. The anger was rising, and it was running out of options.

With nowhere else to go, the wolf came back to Evelyn, racing through the darkness of the woods along the northern edges of the town. A million animal eyes watched it dart past them, unafraid. They knew. There was a communication there. There was only one prey for that night. No substitutes.

When the beast reached the perimeter of the Crowley property, it slowed down to a careful, silent stalk, kept low to the ground, all senses focused out on the horizons. It smelled the ground, the occupants of the great house many, many yards away. It heard the occupants, sleeping, breathing deeply and slowly. To the south, it heard the low rumble of a car engine, tasted the grainy tang of gasoline fumes on the air. It heard a cough. Picked up the scent of meat loaf.

It was crawling now, down on its hands and knees. With its nose twitching, it came up to the spot where she died. It could at least smell *her* there, the scent left behind of Gloria Shaw, but nothing else. No *one* else. The beast was . . . *lost*.

And that was it. It knew it. The scent of its prey was gone. It had vanished to such a degree that not even the wolf's otherworldly senses could pick it up. The target was gone, and without a target, the beast was without anchor, without guidance. It cried. It roared.

The beast heard a twig crack behind it, and it turned. Pearce was there, standing right there, his gun drawn and pointed. He did not fire. His eyes were wide and filled to the brims with fright. With its uncanny hearing, the beast heard a rumble in the man's belly as loud as a passing train. The man spoke.

"Don't," Pearce said, stepping back slowly. "Get back. I'm not the one you want."

The wolf rose up, towering over Pearce by a foot, if not more. Its veins, its teeth, its very being called out for blood.

"We're in this together," said Pearce. "Don't come closer."

The lust could not be denied. That's what it *was*.

"Don't make me," cried Pearce. "Don't fucking move."

The beast howled in his face. There was no more mission. No more target. Just the core-deep cry of its purpose. To kill. That's all there was inside it. Everything else, in that moment, was gone. The beast felt nothing but the need for blood, nothing but hunger, and the flesh in front of it that could satiate that calling. Pearce was just in the wrong place at the wrong time. It could have been anyone.

The beast got into a striking stance and lunged. Pearce yelled my name, "Marley," and his finger tightened around the trigger. "No!"

The sound of metal moving inside the gun was like a spring being compressed in a mattress. He was not fast enough to fire a single shot. He died quickly.

The beast bit into him and drank as the life force evaporated from Pearce's body. In its bones, the beast could hear—feel—his dying pulse. The smell of shit filled the air. The beast gnashed, lost in it, and when it drew back its head to catch the moonlight in its scarlet eyes, it moaned with what I could only call sadness. It did what its nature made it do, but it knew somewhere in its hide that it had done wrong. Still, it could not stop. Like a glutton, it lapped at the hot blood around the corners of its mouth and went back to work on the body.

The spell broke. I was shocked back to reality as if I'd been hit by lightning. I was shaking, and I couldn't stop. I needed a drink, but there would be no more of that. I lit a smoke to calm my nerves.

Why couldn't the beast get the scent? It certainly had tried. It had something to do with those church break-ins, I was sure of it. I needed those police files, or at least a man on the inside, like Pearce was. Someone who could feed me the information I needed. Someone to check back and go through all those Rose murders to see if a church break-in coincided with all of them and if anything was ever boosted from any of these places. Maybe nothing was stolen, but maybe something was left behind at one of these churches, some clue as to who this man was. Maybe someone had been caught at some point busting into a church. Maybe it was the Rose Killer.

The church angle was a lead, as was this Polaroid box that was found up at the Crowley property. I couldn't count on the beast with this next full moon, that much was clear, and it wasn't even the monster's fault. This target was a wraith. A fog. A ghost. He had some kind of trick up his sleeve that protected him from the wolf. I wasn't used to being proactive—Lord knows I wasn't good at it—but for me, for the girls, and for Pearce, I was going to get the Rose Killer. The only question was how.

I put my cigarette out, lit another, and came up with a plan. Just like Nancy Drew.

I tore the envelope, the pictures, and reports to shreds and put them in the fireplace. I lit a match and watched it all burn.

TWENTY-TWO

Detective Van Buren arrived at the Evelyn Police
Station just after nine. It was a two-story building erected in the
forties, and up on the second floor was where the Rose Killer
Task Force was situated. That's where he was off to, I supposed. I
was watching him from across the street, blended into the crowd
of television and radio reporters who had set up tents outside the
front of the building. When they were on the air, it was from the
"frontlines."

I watched Van Buren get out of his car and go in. I had no idea
where he lived—he wasn't in the phone book, and after riffling
through Pearce's memories I couldn't come up with it—but I
needed him, so I at least had to know which car was his.

It was a maroon-colored Ford hatchback with a bumper sticker
that read "Life's a Beach." Just for that and that alone I wanted to
punch the guy in the stomach until I broke all the bones in my
hand. But again, I needed him, and in order to get him to help
me, I was going to have to lie through my teeth.

When it got dark out, I snuck into the precinct parking lot and
jimmied open the door of his car by sticking a hooked wire between the window and the frame. I thought it was great, me
breaking into a car after so many years, and where was it? A cop
parking lot. Better still, it was a cop's car, and he hadn't even set
the alarm. I couldn't help but laugh. I had a sharp knife on me
from my kitchen drawer. All I had to do was wait.

He came out through the back door at midnight. He looked
exhausted. His black suit was wrinkled, and even in the dim light

of the parking lot the bags under his eyes were evident enough that I almost felt sorry for him. Almost. I felt pretty bad too, having spent one whole evening hiding in the back of a car, but I'd gotten good at hiding out the last few weeks anyway, so it could have been worse.

He got to the car, got his keys out of his inside jacket pocket, unlocked the door, and got in the driver's seat. He started it up, then tapped on the radio. Dylan's "Lay Lady Lay" came on.

The idiot sighed.

Before he switched into drive, I got up off the backseat and sprang forward. He saw movement in the rearview mirror and went for his piece, but I was already upon him, the tip of the knife poking a tiny little hole into the underside of his neck.

He stopped breathing.

"Higgins," he sneered, "you motherfucker. You're going to get yourself killed."

"Don't get your panties in a bunch, chief, just keep your hands on the wheel."

"I told you you'd fuck up, and guess what? You just did. I'll kill you for this."

"Not if I kill you first."

I put more pressure on the knife.

"Okay, okay," he grunted. "What the hell do you want?"

"Well, I want you to drive, man. Get us outta here. There's too many cops here."

"Oh, really? At a police station? You've got to be fucking kidding me. . . ."

"Can the sarcasm. It doesn't go with the suit. Drive. And don't do any bullshit signaling to anybody. No flashing headlights, no secret wave, none of that, cuz I'll cut your fucking head off. You copy that?"

"Yeah, I copy."

He put the car in drive and eased out of the space. We got to the street, and without direction from me, he made a left, avoiding the circus show outside the precinct. When we got a little

farther away, I reached into his jacket with my free hand and re-
lieved him of his piece. With that, I put the knife in my back
pocket and sat back with the gun trained on the side of his head.

"You're not such a big man now, are you? Not without your
fucking gun."

"Fuck you, Higgins."

"No," I said, "you won't be doing that today. Keep going till we
get to Old Sherman. From there, I'll direct you further."

"My wife knows I'm on the way home. She knows my schedule."

"Tight leash, eh?"

"Higgins . . ."

"Just drop it, okay? You'll be getting home soon enough, given
you don't fuck with me. Now, just focus on the road. Safe driving
saves lives, you know."

We got to Old Sherman Road. We took that about a mile north
to where there was this little dirt road that went about a hundred
yards into the woods and ended in the middle of nowhere. Why it
was there in the first place was anyone's guess. We took that little
road to the end of the line, and then I ordered him out of the car.
The point of the gun never strayed from his body. I came around
and stood about ten paces in front of him.

It was pretty funny, if you got to thinking about it. In the last
few weeks I'd held guns on more people than I ever had in my
entire life.

We were in the middle of darkness, perfectly concealed. The
only light came from the car, and I think this made Van Buren a
little more nervous than he was when we were driving. For all he
knew, there were wild dogs in those woods. Dogs that . . . well . . .

"Black Is Black" started playing on the car radio.

"I love that song," I said.

"Okay already," said Van Buren. "Get to it."

"Arright. Well, first I want to apologize for the inconvenience.
Your wife didn't want you seeing me in the house. But basically,
I'm going to need you to do a couple of favors for me."

"Me? Do favors for you? You've got to be kidding me."

"I'm for real, man. The way I see it, you pissed me off good and proper. Came into my home, cuffed me, treated me like a fucking scoundrel. Threatened me, even. You were the one making all those crazy phone calls, and you busted into my house and left that fucking note. I didn't like that. I didn't like that one bit. You and I gotta even up."

"I don't owe you shit, Higgins."

I fired a shot into the trees. He jumped. It was time to spin my web of lies and hope he fell for it. "You do owe me, cop. You have no idea. You see, I know you take crazy pills, and something up in your brain is way offtrack. You've been dedicating all this time to my ass when you could have been tracking down the killer. Instead you've been satisfying your dementia, and innocent people have died. All the while you've just been making things more complicated than they ever had to be."

"Who told you about my medication?"

"I got sources, you prick. I'll run it down for you. The arrangement Pearce and I had? You wanna know what it was? You wanna know how we were in cahoots? I was his garbage man," I said.

"What the hell is that supposed to mean?"

"All those cases you boneheads never solved? *I* solved 'em. Motherfuckers never got brought in, but they got taken down all the same, and they're all buried in these woods. Every single one of them."

"My God."

The gullible prick.

"Yeah, that's right. You think you're dealing with some run-of-the-mill punk? No, I've killed more men than you've ever talked to."

"You sick . . . *bitch.*"

"I'm not sick. I'm a public servant, just like you. Vietnam made me a machine. I'm just doing my job for America. Making the community safe. This shit with the Rose Killer has gone on long enough. Pearce knew it. He knew the feds couldn't get the job done. That's why he enlisted my aid, man. I'm gonna end it, and you're gonna help me. Pearce was helping me, now it's your turn."

"Fuck you."

"You wanted to know the deal, now you know. What are you gonna do? Play high-and-mighty with me? I think not. You're not Mr. Untouchable yourself. Your prints are in my house, as are your handcuffs, also with your prints on 'em. How'd they get there? You're gonna fuck with me, I'll fuck you right back. You can't turn me in, because the second you do I'll bring this town to its fucking knees. How do you think the public will react when they find out their tax dollars have been going to an executioner? You can't do that to Pearce's memory, man. You can't do that to his wife. His unborn child."

A minute passed.

He said, "What do you want?"

"I want your wallet."

"Why?"

"Just do it. Gimme the fucking wallet."

He fished out his wallet, then threw it to me. I took out his license, pretty much just for show. I looked around in the sleeves a little more, then chucked it into the open car door.

"Now I know where you live," I said, "and I know what your kid looks like."

"Okay," he said, "that's enough."

"What's the boy's name?"

"That's enough!"

"Not quite. You're going to get me the information I need, just like Danny did. If you don't, or if you fuck with me in any way, I have a number of bombs—I won't tell you how many—planted throughout this town. A signal needs to be sent to these bombs every twelve hours. When a signal isn't sent, say, if I'm arrested and unable to, or injured, or something like that, then the bombs kind of take it upon themselves to blow up. You copy?"

"Yeah," he grumbled. "You're the goddamn devil, Higgins."

"Only if one of those bombs happened to be planted in the school where your little boy learns his letters, Van Buren."

"Monster."

"You have no idea," I said, "but at least my first name ain't Clancy. You must have gotten beat up a lot as a kid."

"Shut up."

"You may not want to help me. You may want this to be personal. But if you feel like you can still be a hero in this, just think of the hundreds of innocent people in this town that will die by fire if my bombs go off. Now, I need to know everything there is to know about that Polaroid box they found up at the Crowley property. Everything. And I need to know if a church break-in occurred on the same night as all the murders."

"A church break-in?"

"Yeah. It happened this time, with Betsy Ratner, and with Josie Jones and Gloria Shaw. The same thing also happened over in Edenburgh. You fuckers have the resources to go through the archives of all these cities to see if this correlation goes all the way back."

"Shit . . . you're right. It *did* happen last time, didn't it? Let's say I get this information for you. Then what?"

"That's it. I take care of business, and whatever happens after that happens. This evil prick might kill me, or I might kill him. If it's the latter, I'll get out of Evelyn before his body goes cold, you have my word on that, but this thing I'm doing, I'm doing it for Danny. When this is over, no matter how it plays out, I sure as hell won't be a problem for you. I guarantee you that much. We can pretend this little meeting of the minds never happened."

"You take care of business? What about the case?"

"Fuck the case. You see, that's why Pearce was a good man. He put his job aside for this business on the side. What I do . . . what *we* did . . . it wasn't for any case, it wasn't for his job, it was for the greater good. One less disease in the world. You understand that?" It was close enough to the truth that I didn't need a poker face.

"When do you need this by?" he asked.

"What? Pal, we're going back to the precinct right now."

"No, we're not."

"Don't fuck with me," I said, leveling the gun at his privates, "and don't give me that shit about your wife missing you. . . ."

"No, Higgins. I can't go back now. I punched out and I've been fucking shot at. I can't go snooping through the fucking computers without one of the feds seeing me, asking me what the fuck I'm doing back so soon. I'll do what you're asking, but I'm not going to lie to the feds for you."

I thought for a second. There were less than forty-eight hours until that full moon started to shine. Shit was coming to a head.

"Fine. Tomorrow. I'll call for you, we'll meet somewhere. No funny business."

"Fine," he said.

I popped the clip out of his gun and ejected the cartridge in the chamber, threw it all into the dirt.

"Be good," I said, and I walked back down the road.

TWENTY-THREE

I watched from the shadows as Van Buren got in his car and took off. I didn't trust him, but he felt like my only hope. With any luck, he'd take my insane blackmailing scam seriously, and do what he was told to do.

After he was gone, I walked across Old Sherman and went a few blocks east to where I had my own truck stashed. On the passenger seat, under a blanket, was my rifle. The extra shells were in the glove, as was Van Buren's pair of handcuffs.

For the rest of that night, I drove all through Evelyn, hoping just like the cops that I'd catch the bastard in the act. The business with the church break-ins and the Polaroid box was good information—the only lifelines for a drowning man—but the chances of any of it panning out and leading me to the Rose Killer were slim at best. All I could do was hope and pray that all the girls in the world were behind locked doors that night.

I didn't want to think about what would happen if my plan didn't work. In my mind, I was attacking on two fronts. First, this fucking guy was still my target. The wolf very well could get him, but because of this invisibility he seemed to possess, the only way to get him would be for me to know exactly who it was. I needed a name, a face. My only hope of that was if Van Buren came up with something. An arrest for one of the church break-ins, maybe. It was my job as a doomed man to take this Rose Killer down with me, because if the beast truly had gone haywire, I was going to have to kill myself, and God knows I didn't want to do that.

I called the precinct at two in the afternoon and asked for Van Buren. He clicked on a minute later. "Van Buren," he said.

"You get my presents for me?"

"Yeah, but I'm in the middle of something right now. I can't get away."

"You're going to have to. Maybe you don't realize there's a man out there on the verge of killing someone's daughter, huh? And me to boot, gunning for you. Meet me where I took you last night. Half hour. No excuses. Or fireballs will fill the sky. I do not give a shit, cop. Just do it."

I hung up, hoping he wouldn't call my bluff. I lit a cigarette, got my gear, and went out to the truck.

I drove my truck all the way down that little dirt path and parked it off to the side. In the daylight, being lost in the trees was enchanting, pretty, even comforting. At night, I noted, you couldn't help but want to run as fast as you could toward the nearest metropolis. Being in the woods at night always made me think of Vietnam.

I left my weaponry and whatnot on the seat, but I wanted it near just in case I needed to put the fear of God into Van Buren, or if he brought the cavalry, we could shoot it out. Maybe they'd put me down once and for all. . . .

He came down the path in his hatchback about ten minutes later. Even in daylight, it was impossible to see us from Old Sherman. I was thankful for that. I was leaning against a tree, a cigarette in one hand and the other slung over my belt. He got out and closed the door behind him. One of his hands immediately went under his jacket, as if to go for the piece he kept there.

"Chill out, cop," I said.

"Just stay back," he said sternly.

"Give me what I asked you for. What did you come up with?"

"I didn't have the time to check all the way back, but a church break-in occurred on the same night or the night before every murder outside the state of California."

"Knock me down," I said.

"Good work, asshole."

"Thanks," I said. "Was anything ever stolen?"

"No. Petty vandalism at the most."

"Like what?"

"Spit. Broken candles and so on."

"You should have the spit examined, see if it matches the fluids taken off the girls."

"Spit isn't saved from petty property crimes, Higgins. Try again."

"Anyone ever brought in?"

"No."

"Suspected?"

"No. Try again."

"Any witnesses to any of these break-ins?"

"Nope."

"No surveillance footage or anything like that?"

"Nope."

There was nothing there to help me just then, but at least I was right. That would get me far in life. "The Betsy Ratner murder seemed much sloppier than the others. Was any evidence left behind? Fingerprints, a puddle of pee, anything like that?"

"No. The guy is good."

"But he . . . he's fucking these girls, yeah? You guys have his seed. . . ."

"Yes, Higgins, we have his 'seed,' as you so lovingly call it."

"What are the chances of me getting my hands on that?"

I had to ask. The scent the wolf would get from that little Baggie of play-pudding would get the job done.

"No chance," Van Buren responded. "It's all been sent out to different labs, you sick, sick man."

"Do you have addresses for these labs?"

"What do I look like to you, a goddamn directory?"

"What about the Polaroid thing? No prints?"

"No prints," he said.

"No hair? None of that?"

"No."

"Do those Polaroid boxes have serial numbers? Would you be able to figure out where it came from?"

"Yeah, the feds did that the day we found it."

"Where was it from? Around here?"

"No."

"Where?"

"It doesn't matter."

"Why?"

"Don't worry about it, Higgins, it didn't pan out."

"Don't fuck with me, man, just tell me."

"A fucking bumwater town, Higgins. No murders happened there, so whatever. People weren't on the lookout, so no one down there knows a damn thing."

"Just . . . *where?*"

"This fucking shantytown in New Mexico. Marshall something or other."

I swallowed hard. A heavy meal I couldn't recall eating plunged its way into the lowest areas of my belly.

"Marshall Falls," I said.

"Yeah, that's it. You know it?"

"Vaguely," I replied.

"I'd never heard of it."

That sonofabitch prettyboy was mine. "Well, knock me the fuck down," I said.

With that, Van Buren rushed me. This time with a football tackle that sent me back into the dirt. He jumped on top of me and gave me three right jabs to the face. Four. Before I knew it, he was going crazy on my face with short punches. I got a thumb in his mouth, hoping to pull his head down, but he bit it.

I grabbed his ear after that, and twisted it back. I could feel blood on my fingertips. He screamed. With that, I brought a leg up over his head and kicked him off of me. He went flying onto his back. We both got up, he more slowly than me.

"You sonofabitch," I hissed.

"Your ass is mine, Higgins," he said calmly. "You think you can get away with this shit? Blackmail me, threaten my family? You're not making it out of these woods."

"Let's not get dramatic," I said. "You're a jerk, but you ain't no killer."

"We'll see."

I rushed him this time. He threw a handful of dirt at me that he'd palmed, hoping to get it in my eyes, but he failed. I faked, then came up with a left hook that spun him on his heels. Before he fell, I grabbed him by the shoulders and delivered two swift knees to his guts. A karate chop to the back of his neck. He went down on his knees. I punched him in the forehead.

He drove an elbow up into my crotch. I lost my breath.

He pulled on me by my belt and came up with an uppercut. My teeth met like chimes. My face vibrated. He followed the uppercut up with a series of gut shots. Lefts, rights—all of them left me wishing I'd had breakfast just so I could have thrown up on him. I backed up into a tree, wheezing. I saw his hook coming from a mile away—he put so much of his weight behind it—that I had time to duck. His fist rammed into the tree, and he let out a scream. I grabbed him by the lapels of his jacket, and then I head-butted him. Once. Then again. I let him fall in a heap, his nose a bloody mess.

I limped away, toward his car. I was going to take the keys out and chuck them in the woods, just to be an asshole, but I was interrupted. He came up behind me and cracked the butt of his handgun off the back of my head. I got dizzy and stooped forward. He used my momentum against me and hurled me onto the hood of his car. My head cracked his windshield. A little bit of blood got in my eye.

I rolled onto my back, saw him lunging. I raised my leg and let him run into my boot. It made contact with his jaw, and did enough damage that he had to take the time to shake out the cobwebs. I rolled off the hood, got a kick to my knee, but it grazed without breaking bone, and with him off balance, I took advantage. My right hook came out of nowhere and met his jaw like an atomic bomb.

He went down and didn't get up again.

I went through his pockets, found his cuffs in a belt holster, and cuffed him out of spite. Then I took his badge. He started to come to.

I grabbed him by the collar and said, "Keep your boys in blue away from me. There's a lot more people at stake here than your goddamn family, and that's a fact."

"I can't let you go," he mumbled.

I brought a foot down into his face.

"You're gonna have to. You have too much to lose, cop. Let me do my job."

Back in the truck, I looked at myself in the rearview mirror. I wasn't as inconspicuous as I'd been five minutes earlier. With the blanket on the seat, I wiped the blood off my face. My hands were shaking, but I felt great.

"Anthony," I said. "Anthony, Anthony, Anthony. Time to pay the piper."

TWENTY-FOUR

The sun came down in brilliant rays, and the air
was warm. There was a slight breeze. On any other day, it all
would have been enough to make you happy to be alive, but to
the citizens of Evelyn, the daytime had become nothing more
than a handful of hours in which they felt just a little bit less
afraid. Me? I was in good spirits. I was bleeding out of my face,
but I knew who the Rose Killer was.

I still didn't know what the deal was with how he had been
able to conceal himself from the wolf, but it didn't matter too
much anymore. I knew his face. I knew his name. I knew his car.
Hell, a little bit of his blood had run onto my hand when I
knocked his lights out in the parking lot. He was as good as dead.
But still, I wanted him. He had caused too much pain and chaos
in my life for the wolf to have all the fun. I wanted a little piece of
him just for me. All I had to do was find him.

The whole situation with the bloody face was kind of pressing,
though. I couldn't very well go around town looking like I'd gotten intimate with an ugly stick, so once I drove back to Old Sherman Road and the civilization on the other side of it, I headed to
the closest deli. There was one just a few blocks away.

I walked in, and the old man behind the counter took one look
at me and opened his mouth. "Son," he said, "you're not looking
like you're doing too good."

"I can't complain," I said, and went back to one of the coolers
to grab myself a bottle of water.

I took one of the few remaining dollars out of my wallet,

slammed it on the counter, and headed back out. It was there on the sidewalk that I saw someone I didn't expect to see again.

She was wearing a pair of sweatpants, sneakers, and a tight white T-shirt with a picture of Jimi Hendrix on it. Sunglasses hid her beautiful eyes from me. I stopped dead in my tracks.

"Hey, darling," I said out of habit. I kind of instantly regretted it.

She removed her glasses. "Hey, Marley," said Alice.

"You look good."

She laughed. "I wish I could say the same about you. What happened?"

"Oh, you mean this? Just been a tough day is all. . . ."

"Maybe we shouldn't be talking now," she said plainly, like she'd flipped a switch inside her and turned off her emotions.

"Wait, please, let me explain."

"Marley, you don't need to explain anything to me. It's not like . . ."

"Please don't say it, Alice."

She stopped.

"I need to apologize about the other day. About following you."

"That's fine, Marley. You don't owe me an explanation."

"I feel like I do. I know you have a line. It's something I've heard you say a thousand times, and I know you don't want to hear it, but I care about you."

She put her glasses back on to hide her eyes.

"You can think what you want about me," I said, "but there's more to me than you could ever imagine. There's a lot I would have liked for you to know about the real me, the me that's been kind of hidden away for so long, and I feel like now, *especially* now, with all that's going on, that's never going to happen. And I'm sorry about that."

"You sound like you're not going to be around anymore."

That was true, one way or the other. "That's right," I said.

"Why?"

"Things have kind of come to a head."

"What things?"

"Things."

"There are bands of men looking for the killer in vans and pickup trucks. They have chains, pipes, whatever they can get their hands on, I guess. I hope you're not one of them. This town doesn't need that kind of justice."

"I'm not a vigilante," I said.

"Marley," she said sadly, "what are you caught up in?"

"I wish I could tell you."

She turned and ran her fingers through her hair. "Everything's gone to hell so fast. These killings are ruining everything. He got Josie, and now I feel like I'm losing . . ."

"Losing what?"

I thought she was going to say she was losing me too.

"Nothing," she said. "When do you think it's all going to end?"

"Soon," I said. "I promise."

I headed back to the truck and said, "Be careful."

"You too," she said.

I got in the truck and took off. I poured some of the water on a towel and washed my face. It would have to do.

Anthony the serial killer had once told me that he had a room rented over on Lincoln Street, on the east side of town. After consulting the phone book at a telephone stand, I saw that there were three motels on Lincoln: the Golden Eagle, the Phoenix Inn, and the Night Owl Lodge. *All bird names,* I thought. What were the odds?

I pulled up to the first on the list—the Golden Eagle—ran in, and asked the lady at the desk if she had an Anthony Mannuzza staying there. Because of my busted face, she wasn't exactly willing to answer me like she would for a more handsome bloke, or maybe she—an oatmeal and Bible type—never took to "long-hairs."

"That's privileged," she said, the two words sounding like two parts to a single fart. If she were a man . . .

"Ma'am," I said, "the guy's a friend of mine. I know he's staying on Lincoln, but I'm not sure if this is the place."

"Well, maybe you better talk to your friend."

I took out Van Buren's detective shield and said, "Listen, lady, I don't have time to mess around. Answer the question."

She nervously went through the registry, then said, "No."

I began to walk out, but then realized the chances were good that he would've given a fake name, or maybe Anthony wasn't his real name to begin with. I went back and gave her a general description of the scumbag, and I probably used the term "pretty-boy" more than once. It still didn't pan out with her.

"So let me get this straight," I said. "Even though this guy isn't staying here, nor anyone that matches his general description, you were still unwilling to answer me when I came in here. How come?"

"You look like a rock musician," she said.

"I appreciate your honesty. More of a Hank Williams gal, are you?"

She smiled. I walked out.

At the other two places, I started with the description, and then said a possible alias was Anthony Mannuzza. These places didn't pan out either. There was the possibility that he was staying somewhere else entirely, but I didn't have the time to visit every single motel in Evelyn. I didn't want to expose myself that much, especially because I was using stolen police property to get my answers, and for all I knew, I was now officially wanted for assault. So I was shit out of luck, but not out of options.

I drove out to the edge of town to this little bit of land with a log cabin on it. The plaque by the door said "Rose."

This was the fancypants liquor-and-skin joint Anthony had taken me to. The lot in front had one car parked in it. It was a European car, and I didn't know whose it was. I parked the truck, then knocked on the heavy wood door. After several minutes, it opened, and that terrifyingly large bouncer in the black suit stood before me, his squinty eyes drilling holes into my brain. My head began to feel like that scene from *Scanners*. I wondered how often he had to resort to using his hands on people. I wasn't sure if I really needed to know, though.

"Hey, uh, Hyde, right?"

He didn't say anything.

"I need to speak to someone here about one of your customers."

"No," he said.

"Yes," I said, showing the badge. "It won't take a minute. Mind letting me in?"

He looked behind him, said, "Cop," and a female voice said something to him that I couldn't hear. He stepped aside, and I went in.

Seated at one of the tables was that Samantha girl, the one that was in the schoolgirl outfit the night I was there, but now she was wearing sweatpants and a large Buccaneers T-shirt. She was counting stacks of money and didn't seem to think anything of it that a cop had come to her establishment. She barely had the energy to look up, but when she did, she got angry, and fast. A look came onto her face that could melt paint off a wall. But she was still adorable.

"What the fuck is this?" she said. "You're no fucking cop. Hyde!"

The man grabbed me by the back of the neck and squeezed.

"Jesus!" I cried, sinking to my knees because I couldn't feel my legs anymore.

"What the fuck are you doing here?" she asked me.

"I need to talk to you for a minute," I grunted. I felt like I was going blind from the pain.

"Posing as a cop could get you in a lot of trouble," she said.

"My middle name's trouble," I said.

"Mine's Venus. Don't tell anybody." She flashed a smile, but just as quickly as it appeared, it was gone again. "What do you want?" she demanded.

"You know that prettyboy kid I was in here with the other night?"

"Who, Anthony?"

"Yeah," I said, "Anthony . . . *goddamn* . . . I'm looking to find him."

"Why?" she said.

"That's private."

"Not private enough that you didn't have to lie your way into my place of business, though."

"Well, that's true. You think you could tell this guy to let go of my neck?"

"No."

"Oh."

"What do you want with him?"

"Who? Anthony?"

"Yes, you twit."

"Well, he screwed me out of a lot of fucking money, and I want what's mine. That's all."

"Oh yeah? It looked like he was carrying *your* sorry ass the other night."

"It's poker money," I said.

"Whatever. You don't have to tell me. But he's a creepy little bastard, so I'll tell you what I know anyway. One of the girls asked him one night where he was staying. I pulled her aside, because I had a vibe about this guy. I told her not to go with him. She said she wouldn't, but later on that night I heard him tell her he was staying at a place on Barlow Drive."

"Shit," I said. The bastard had lied to me. "Do you know what place?"

"Do I look like I'd want to?"

"Which girl was it?"

"Helen."

"Which one was that?"

"The one in the blue thing."

"Oh," I said. "Any chance I can get her number?"

"You're a funny guy. No."

"Do you feel like calling her?"

"For you?"

"I'd certainly appreciate it."

"No."

"Well, please go on, then."

"At the time, I figured, well, fuck her if she doesn't want any advice. So she goes with him. And the next day she showed up with bruises all over her goddamn back. The dumb bitch."

"Wow, that's harsh," I said.

"Don't tell me what's harsh, you fuck. Until you have a vagina, you don't know what harsh is, okay?"

"Okay," I said. "Whatever you say."

"Anything else you need to know before you're banned from my place?"

"Well . . ." I thought for a second. Then: "You married?"

She gave Hyde a look, and he lifted me up by my neck, carried me to the door, and threw me out on the grass. The door shut peacefully. Soon after, I heard Tom Jones playing in there. I think it was "Green, Green Grass of Home."

After a few minutes, the feeling in my legs came back, and I went back to the truck. The sun had dipped below the horizon, and the sky was a deep royal blue. Time was running short for me. I needed a cup of coffee.

I didn't see Frank's car outside so I pulled into one of the spaces, walked up the stairs, and went in. The bell jangled.

Abraham was behind the counter, and when he saw me come in I could tell he wanted to smile. "What the hell are you doing here?" he asked.

"I'm thirsty," I said. "I hear you make the best coffee in town."

I took a seat at the counter. This was the first time I had set foot in the place since I lost my job. I missed the place, the normality it represented for me.

"What happened to you?" he asked, pointing at my face. "Personality clash?"

"Something like that," I said.

Behind me, I heard, "Howdy, Marley."

Without turning, I said, "Howdy, Brian."

Abe poured me a cup of coffee, slid over an ashtray, and leaned in close to me.

"A cop came around asking about you. What have you gotten yourself into?"

"Nothing, except one bitchin' headache."

"It doesn't look like nothing."

I looked away. My head felt like it had been in love with a bag of rocks.

"Looks ain't everything, Abraham. If they were, you'd be the loneliest bastard in the world."

He laughed, said, "Fine, forget I asked. Am I gonna see you on the news one of these days?"

"I sincerely hope not. I'm not a bad guy, Abe. Things have just gotten complicated."

"I don't like complicated."

"Me neither. I got a question for you."

"It ain't complicated, is it?"

"Remember that fruitcake that came in here a while back? The prettyboy?"

"The prettyboy. How can I forget?"

"When was the last time you saw that guy?"

"Why? You two gonna run off together?"

"Something like that."

"Well, I don't know what to tell you, Marley. This hasn't been your most glorious month, man. I'm worried about you, and I don't want to get involved in . . ."

"There ain't nothing to get involved in. Just help me out. Have you seen the kid?"

"He was in this morning."

I smiled, said, "Did he say anything about leaving town?"

"No, not that I recall. In fact, he was looking for you."

"Was he? Good. Did he say anything strange? Did he talk about aliens, or communists, or Charles Manson, or anything like that?"

"I think I'd remember if he mentioned communism."

I got up off the stool and briskly headed for the door.

"You owe me for the coffee!" he shouted.

"I'm good for it," I said, and I left. Pearce had been the master at walking out without paying for coffee. It looked like I had stolen that little trait of his.

I had to go back to hunting. I had twenty-four hours to find the Rose Killer. A police force could scour the whole of Evelyn in a few hours, come up with whatever they wanted. One man looking for a single car would take a hell of a lot longer, but that's what I did.

I drove up and down the streets at random well into the night, keeping one eye open for that dusty, black Mach 1 that I had seen so many times before.

I saw Anthony everywhere and nowhere. My eyes were starting to play tricks on me. Up high, the big moon shone down like a warning. I decided that if the wolf took another innocent person, I'd go to the feds with what I knew about Anthony. It wouldn't matter if they believed me. Someone somewhere would do some kind of checking or other, and maybe find some proof of what had been going on. After that, I'd take myself out. I would almost have to.

I was driving east on Main, through the woods. When I got to the water, I took Campbell's Bridge across, got out of the truck, and checked the waterfront on that side of the river on foot. There were a lot of romantic places to park a car over there, to get it on without being seen, but I didn't see the Mach 1.

I headed back across the bridge to Evelyn.

When I got to the other side, my frustration got the better of me. I punched the dashboard as hard as I could, and with that, this eerie green light sprang up behind all the dials, and music filled the car.

The radio was working. Creedence's "Lookin' Out My Back Door" was playing on KBTO. I laughed out loud. The damn thing had been broken for so long, and all I'd had to do was drop a fist to get it going again. Things were looking up.

These bright headlights appeared from my left. A car was speeding toward me through the darkness. I figured it would swerve, that it was maybe some drunk kid tooling around the waterfront, but it just kept coming.

"Holy shit," I said.

The car made contact. A noise I'd only heard in movies filled the air, and the truck tipped over on its side, then came to rest upside down. Metal and glass shards perforated the air, tickling me with pain. I wasn't wearing my seat belt, so I got banged around pretty bad.

When I got my bearings, I realized I was lying on the inside of the roof, covered in glass. I looked out, and there were a pair of feet standing outside the truck. The feet wore clean, brown leather shoes. The car behind the feet was a blue or black four-door of some kind. I'd never seen it before. The front of it was sizzling with smoke and noise.

The legs attached to the feet bent, and Van Buren poked his head into the truck. His face looked a little worse than mine did, but after getting bounced off the walls of the truck I didn't know *how* bad I looked anymore.

"Higgins," he said, "need a hand?"

"You sonofabitch," I said, coughing. "I'd just gotten the radio working. . . ."

"Save it," he said. "It's time to end this. You lied about Pearce."

"You're forgetting the bombs, you fool. . . ."

"Bullshit," he said, and he pulled his gun with one gloved hand and fired two bullets into me.

The midnight hour came and went, leaving me behind.

I pulled myself from the wreckage, clawing at the dirt like it was sucking me under. The truck was smoking, burning. Every breath felt like fire inside me, and every muscle I moved made me want to cry in agony. I wasn't strong enough to take everything with me. I took the rifle and the handcuffs. I left behind the extra shells.

I was wet with blood.

Up high, the moon glared, calling me out. I had thunder in my veins. I went into the woods on my hands and knees. I had to hide. I had to rest. Just for a little while.

TWENTY-FIVE

When I came to, daylight was pouring down like rain. A rabbit was looking at me from about five feet away like it knew me. I grunted, and it took off.

When I sat up, my insides cried. I was caked in dirt, and dried blood held my shirt to me like a second skin. Leaves were stuck all over me, and I must have looked half buried. My chest was on fire. That's where the bullets were. I wasn't bleeding anymore—it would take a lot more than that to prove fatal for me—but I wasn't in the best shape of my life. I got up slowly, using the rifle as a brace; then, like a zombie cursed to walk the face of the earth, I stumbled west.

I figured I had to keep to the shadows, seeing as how the police were probably looking for me, or my body, more appropriately, and on the other hand, a guy covered in blood and holding a rifle wouldn't look like the most appealing thing to the townsfolk. I made it to Old Sherman, but kept to the edge of the woods. Behind me, smoke filled the sky. I had to presume that that was my truck, or if not that, then that paranoid sonofabitch Van Buren had torched the car he tried to kill me with.

As I made my way along the side of the road, I realized the whole situation was doomed. Van Buren—an officer of the law—had single-handedly ruined my chance at redemption. His paranoia had muddied the last month of my life, and with this little stunt of his, he had basically guaranteed an innocent person's death. In the shape I was in, and with no ride to boot, my chance was gone. The moon was going to come and go, and for all I knew, the chances were fifty-fifty that the Rose Killer would once again escape the wrath of the beast. The beast, in turn, would commit the same kind of atrocity that its lost target would. I was thankful I had the rifle. I might get the chance to use it after all.

A couple of hours passed. I'd made it perhaps no more than three or four miles. If I'd had any determination left, I probably would have gotten twice as far, but there was nothing left in me.

Even though my chest was on fire, I desperately needed a cigarette. I felt at my chest pocket, but it was empty. My front pockets were empty too. "Shit," I said.

I reached around to my back pocket. I didn't have any cigarettes on me, but I found something else. Anthony's folded photographs.

I took them out and flipped through them one by one. They were all pictures of the same thing—that stupid tree he'd found in the woods and allegedly wanted to use as his cover shot.

In one of them, a wide shot, something in the far corner caught my eye. It was a shack, a shanty, hardly any bigger than an outhouse. I'd never seen it before, but it clicked in my head. For him to do what he did with those girls, he needed somewhere to go. He couldn't have done the murders in his car—I had been in it, and it's not that the car was clean, because it wasn't. It was lived-in, but there was no blood. He would need someplace private where he had all the time in the world. I was willing to bet that it was that shack.

Just then, a feeling like lightning came over me, and I winced. I squeezed shut my eyes, and when I opened them again, it was nighttime.

The wolf was giving me something. A memory.

It knew where the shack was. The wolf had passed it before on one of its travels. It was not far from where I lived, about a mile into the woods past Old Sherman Road.

I emerged from the woods and crossed the road. The first car I saw was an old Chevy. It had been a long time since I'd had to hotwire a Chevy, but I hadn't lost my touch.

. . .

Berger Street dead-ended at Old Sherman, just like most streets did, and as I pulled up in my stolen Chevy, I saw the Mach 1 parked at the end of the street. I pulled over.

"Jesus," I mumbled, "knock me the fuck down."

I came up to the black car slowly, gun raised. I was hoping he'd be in there playing with himself, or doing something that would occupy his hands just as much.

No luck. It was empty. I didn't see him anywhere. He had to be at the shack. I could feel it in my bones.

If I could, I was going to try to subdue the sonofabitch. If that didn't work, I'd shoot him in the foot, force him to handcuff himself. Hopefully, he'd cooperate. He wouldn't be dealing with a girl. He'd be dealing with a very angry man with a rifle. With that, the beast could have its way with him. And if I had to kill him myself, then so be it. I'd never killed a man before, but I was as ready as I'd ever be.

I ducked behind the Mach 1. That way, if he was in the woods, he wouldn't see me. My heart was beating like a drum, and I was sweating like a pig. The holes in my skin where the bullets went in felt like they were being rubbed with salt. Every breath was an exercise in pain. The flames of hell were licking at me, getting ready for the big burn. I looked through the car's windows, all frosted and covered over with road dirt, hoping to see something highly incriminating, but all there was was a bunch of designer clothes and a few cameras. A Polaroid camera.

I came around the side of the car slowly, crouching. I had the rifle pointed into the trees, paying great attention as to whether anyone was watching me. Windows. Treetops. Bushes. The barrel of a gun could be pointing at me from anywhere. It made me think of my time in the war.

I had been ambushed once in the green. That was what was on my mind as I crossed the threshold and stepped into the woods on the far side of the road. I was young, then, and I didn't see it coming. I couldn't let it happen again.

I measured my paces, and moved carefully into the woods. I didn't want to step on any branches and give myself away. In 'Nam, a sound like that would have spelled doom. No one was going to get the drop on me now.

I went in deeper, till the road behind me was a dirty gray line in the distance. The sounds of birds and chipmunks filled the air. Up ahead I saw a squirrel jump from one tree to the next. Light came down in brilliant little bursts. The rest of the ground was hidden in shadow.

I became conscious of the sound of my own labored breathing, the smell of my own sweat. Somewhere, I could smell animal shit. The noises of the town were absent and behind me, and maybe never to be known again.

The tension was palpable. I was working on a level of awareness that made me think of Sergeant Hooper. As I continued forward, ever vigilant, a spiderweb tapped me in the face, and became stuck because of the sweat. I couldn't blow it off, and in that one moment my senses were so heightened that the feeling of that thing made me crazy.

I rested the rifle in the crook of my right arm and pulled away the webs with my hands. I heard a noise behind me. I knew it wasn't a deer—it was a man.

I turned quickly and fired blindly.

There was no one there. Taking the rifle in both hands, I stared down the sight and did a scan. I ran in the direction of the noise.

No one in town would have heard the shot, and if they did, they would have paid it no mind. It was just me and Anthony out there. In the distance, through the maze of trees, I could make out the shack. I had one shot left. I had to make it count.

I heard another noise to my side, and I began to turn to fire, but I wasn't quick enough. I saw a pair of hands holding a log, and the log was speeding toward my face. After that, all I knew was darkness.

. . .

Before I found the strength to open my eyes, I was roused from a deep slumber by the screaming of my limbs. I felt as if I were being stretched on a rack. Hell, I was almost *afraid* to open my eyes. I wasn't sure if what I would see would upset me too much, and for a second, I even had the thought cross my mind that the Vietnamese had gotten ahold of me.

"Wake up," said the American voice. "Wake the fuck up, you filthy redneck. Or I'll *really* get to work on you."

My eyelids broke the seal of sweat. My vision was busted in two, but soon joined up again. There was a bright light coming from the front that hurt, but as my eyes adjusted, I saw it was a lantern.

Anthony stood before me, leaning against the wall, and he had a long butcher's knife in his hand. He was playing with it, twirling it in his fingers, flicking the blade, picking under his manicured nails with it. He was wearing all black, like a burglar. Black running pants, a black sweatshirt. Black sneakers. For all I knew, he was wearing black underwear too.

I tried to move, but I couldn't. For a second I was worried that I was paralyzed, that he'd done something nasty with my spine. But I could feel, and I became aware that I could move my fingers. I then realized I was tied to a chair. My ankles were taped to the legs of the chair, my chest and waist to the back, and my arms were handcuffed behind me. I could feel the metal digging into my wrists, like old friends who always had to borrow money at the worst possible time. An extension cord was tied around my neck. The cord ran behind me, and the other end was tied to my feet. If I tried to bend forward, I'd choke. The bastard was ingenious. Anthony was smiling.

"Welcome back, Marlowe Higgins," he said in a low voice that was throbbing with anger.

"Prettyboy," I said, like that was his name.

"I guess you're the lucky chap who found the one guy in this shit-box town that everyone is looking for. You look like you had one hell of a day," he said, pointing at my various wounds.

"You could say that, you fucking devil."

"Take it back, it hurts." He laughed. "You know what they say. Sticks and stones. Sticks . . ." He sliced me across my left cheek with the knife. ". . . And stones!"

I cried out. He laughed, then licked the blade clean.

"You look like you lost a lot of blood already, so what's a little more? Besides, that one was for taking a shot at me."

Deep inside, I could feel the pull of the moon tugging at my bones, trying in vain to lure me to its light. I was in no position to oblige.

"Enjoy your final moments, Marlowe. Make your peace with God and all that shit. While I have a smoke, why don't you come up with a last request like in all the old movies, huh?" He pulled out his cigarettes from a hip pocket and lit one up. "I could never be accused of being a bad sport."

I started looking around. We were in the shack. That much was obvious. The slats in all the walls had spaces between them, and nothing was coming through except a cool breeze and the smell of the evening. Darkness. It was night.

The wood floor was covered in dust and dried blood. Blood was splattered everywhere, and there was too much for it to be just mine. Rose stems were scattered in a corner, their flowers gone and used in horrible ways.

Color photographs were pinned to the walls. I recognized Josie Jones in some of them, and the teacher in a few others. In some, they were alive, in some, they couldn't have been. In some, they were clothed, and in some, they were naked. The rest of the pictures must have been his other victims. In the corner behind him, a camera rested atop a tripod like a bird of prey. More than any weapon, that camera seemed to be his accomplice in this whole sordid affair.

I brought my head back and saw there was a window behind me with a strip from an old rug nailed over it. If one thin beam of moonlight could hit me, I'd change, but with things the way they were, I was fucked. Anthony could very well kill me.

I had to ask myself if things deserved to be any other way. Anthony had destroyed dozens of lives, and, if he were to survive another night, would probably go on to kill another one, two, or even a handful of innocent people before he was apprehended. But in that darkened one-room shack were two monsters. I had ended lives in the hundreds, and if events tilted into my favor, I would be responsible for perhaps thousands more before I perished of old age. We were each of us as bad as bad can be, neither one any better than the other.

We were two sides of the same coin. It didn't matter that I had tried, had, to a large degree, learned to control the wolf and had built a life for myself on the most salted and rockiest land. I had done the best I could given my circumstances, but I was still inhuman. So was the Rose Killer. No matter how hard each one of us tried to blend into the world around us, we deserved no part of it, and it would be much better off without the both of us, and when we were both dead, I knew we'd have the chance to maybe laugh about the old times in a very hot climate.

The fact was that the Rose Killer targeted and murdered people because he thought they were evil. I did the same thing. We both hunted. Neither of us could help doing the things we did, but the difference between us was that he liked it. Pearce's death wasn't my fault. It was Anthony's. That's why, I decided, he had to die.

"Hey, Anthony," I said. "What was with the church break-ins?"

He turned pale. "How do you know about that?"

"They don't call me Nancy Drew for nothing."

He thought for a minute, then put his cigarette out underfoot. "That's not something Anthony wants to talk about right now."

"What *does* Anthony want to talk about?"

"I don't know," he said, his eyes darting like frightened fish.

"Where's my rifle?" I asked.

"In the corner. I may kill you with that. Or I may cut you in half. See if you're as gutsy as you act."

"You'd be surprised."

"You have a wicked sense of humor, Marlowe."

Being almost immortal does that. He'd have to get truly severe on me to put me down for good. I thought he was the type of guy that wouldn't have a problem with that.

"How did you find me?" he asked. "I mean, how did you know it was me?"

"Marshall Falls, Anthony. You have a big mouth. That Polaroid box you left behind was traced back to a mom-and-pop shop down in New Mexico. It was that simple. That, and you hate women. I put two and two together."

"How did you find out about the box? I thought your friend on the force had died."

"I bet that didn't break your heart, seeing as how you used his grave as a fucking . . ."

"A frame," he said. "I never met a cop I liked. By the way, I put the bitch on his grave for *you*. You made me very angry that night by hitting me in the face. The bitch was the one who had to suffer for it. Now it's your turn. And what were you planning on doing? Blowing a hole through me like Charles Bronson?"

"Actually, I was going to tie you up first, but you stole my routine. This right here is the exact opposite of what I would've liked to have happened."

"Does anyone know you're here?"

"Does it matter? One of us is going to die here tonight. You know that, right?"

"I know. I'm the one with the gun."

The camera on the tripod made a noise. It was a video camera. He was filming this, the sick bastard that he was.

"You took pictures of all the girls?"

"Damn right. They're mine forever. All mine. No one else's."

"Why don't you tell me what happened, Anthony. Tell me what happened to the eyes. Help me understand."

"You never would, you fucking redneck."

"Try me."

He lit another smoke. "Women, Marlowe. More than any bullet

or bomb, they are the most destructive force on this fucking planet. I hate them so much . . ."

"Why the roses?"

"Roses for girls. I think it's funny. No one else seems to think so. Women's eyes can lie to a man's soul. They're all demons, those eyes. And roses are truly beautiful creatures, aren't they? Seems fitting enough, taking away the evil, putting in the . . . *true.*"

"And you filmed all this?"

"I'm documenting my journey. It's all about . . . this is what happens to a man when he's pushed too far. Watch the fuck out, because this will happen to you. That's the point. This is me doing what I want."

"Do you even believe your own shit? You sound like a fucking lunatic."

His face shriveled up—I didn't even recognize him—and he came at me with the knife again, screaming animal sounds I couldn't understand. The wolf might have.

He sliced me above my eye real deep, then planted the knife into a space between my ribs. It hurt so bad, I couldn't even make a sound. He drew the blade back out, and it shone red with my blood. Within seconds, I could feel my organs filling up with blood. With that, I got light-headed. I was dying. I was actually dying.

"And why the break-ins?" I asked, wheezing.

He went quiet again, then asked, "Are you trying to stall me?"

"I'm tied up and bleedin' on the inside, prettyboy. Do the math."

"The break-ins were to make everything right."

"How?"

"Holy water," he said.

"Holy water," I repeated. "Holy water . . ."

It must've thrown the beast off, that stuff. God knows how, and God knows why, but that had to be it. That crap must've "cleansed" the places or something. Washed away the sin.

"I needed the holy water to help the girls. I'm not a bad guy. I killed them because they needed killing, but I'm not fucked up.

I don't think anyone deserves to burn in hell forever, so with the holy water . . . I figured I was saving them, you know? Taking them out, but only physically. See?"

"Yeah, I see. You're out of your fucking mind."

Anthony swatted at my face with the knife again. I felt it run through the skin on my forehead. Precious blood ran down my face, and mixed in with the red pool that had formed in my seat.

The wolf was a curse, but the one single thing that it ever did for me that could be considered good, or kind, or merciful, is that after all these years it has never allowed me to remember what happened the night that Doris died. But I remembered everything else. I remembered the oath I swore to my friend's memory, and what had, in the end, brought me to that shack.

Anthony let the knife fall from his fingers. It stabbed the floorboard and stood erect. The boards were riddled by bugs and warped by years of rain. The shack had been left abandoned and standing in the middle of nowhere for God knows how long so this parasite could bleed the town for all its worth from a quiet little perch that was lost in the green. He picked up the rifle, raised it up, and pressed it into my forehead.

"Anthony, before you do me in, I have a request."

"Fuck you," he said.

"I won't be doing that today," I said, "but you said I could get a last wish, like in the movies. I have an easy one."

"What is it?"

"I'd like to see the moon one last time before I buy the farm."

He lowered the gun toward my chest. "Why?" he asked.

"I'm a hopeless romantic. It makes me feel like everything's going to be okay."

"Don't say I never did anything for you," Anthony said.

He went over, gun over his shoulder, and pulled the rug from the window frame, sending dust into the air. White moonlight hit the ancient glass and came through silver. The dust particles lit up and shone like a million little stars in that silver light. Like fireflies. Like angels. Like answered prayers.

It washed over me, shocked me like a current.

The blood that poured from my face began to bubble and turn to smoke. Anthony dropped the gun from his shaking hands and backed far away from me into the darkened corner of the shack. As he did so, he knocked the lantern off the hook in the wall with his shoulder. The light that came from it extinguished itself, died, and Anthony mumbled something low. A question lost to time.

"Anthony," I said with a voice that was no longer wholly my own, "there's more than one creature that stalks the night."

Anthony began to scream. He turned and struggled in the darkness with the latch on the door, but the thing was rusted, and his shaking, sweaty hands had no force to guide them right in the darkness.

Skin ripped. Muscles expanded. I screamed. My monster hands burst from the shackles he'd bound me in. The handcuffs bent, then gave way like rotten nutshells. With that, I tore the cord from my throat with the nails that had quickly protruded from the bleeding fingers of my right hand. The tape ripped away as my body grew, and I rose.

Anthony fumbled for the gun and fired the last bullet. It missed me completely and went clean through the ancient glass. He tried to fire again, but it didn't work. He sank to his knees, crying. Vengeance was mine.

TWENTY-SIX

His name was John Raynor.

He was raised in Las Vegas by a domineering woman who, while being deeply religious, imbibed drugs and drink like her life depended on it. Like most people who grow up to be deranged, he seemed to find a secret joy in starting fires and shooting cats and dogs with a pellet gun. If he was able to catch them, he would do experiments.

His earliest special memory was of his cousin, a girl named June. She was two years younger than him and was easily coaxed into games of doctor that went too far. He was acting out all the things he had seen his mother doing with strange men through the crack in her bedroom door.

When his mother found out about what he was doing with June, she filled a tub with scalding water to scorch away the sin from his privates. The burns on his legs never went away, and from that day on, he only wore long pants.

Eight months before the *federales* believed the Rose Killer spree started, he killed his first victim. It was a woman he picked up at a bar in Los Angeles. He'd bought her a few drinks so he could get her home. When they got to his apartment and the clothes came off, she laughed at his legs because the skin up to his thighs was red, as if constantly embarrassed.

He choked her. He didn't mean to. He had drunk just as much as she had, but the anger that always rested in the pit of his stomach like a molten ball suddenly flared to life, and he couldn't control himself. Immediately after, he broke down and wept. He couldn't believe what he had done. There was regret, but not for her. It was for him, should he ever get caught. Psychopaths *do* feel remorse, just not for others.

He checked her pulse, and was able to detect a faint heartbeat. He knew that if he brought her to a hospital, she would have him arrested. Then what would happen? He felt his only option was to make sure she never told, so he loaded her up in his car and drove west, to the water. When he found himself on a quiet block, the only witness the moon in the sky, he dragged her out of the car and stabbed her in the heart.

He became so consumed with worry about being caught that he started fucking up at work—he worked at a photo development lab in a menial position—and he got fired. It was then, with no more income, fear of losing his home, the life he had built for himself, that he killed another, and another, and another. Soon, there was no turning back.

The name he lived under on the road—Anthony Mannuzza—was the name of the cop who'd arrested him for disorderly conduct just days after he'd killed his first victim.

It was a woman who had burned him, a woman who had gotten him burned in the first place. It was women that always found his legs repulsive, no matter what kind of hairstyle he had, or how nice his clothes were. With all the blood on his hands, he had nothing left to lose, except his life, and that's where I came in.

When I woke up, sunlight was coming down. The air moved in a gentle breeze, carrying the scents of flowers and honey. The birds were singing, as if the world were perfect. It wasn't, but it was just a little bit better than it had been the night before.

My limbs were covered in dried blood, and as I stretched out naked in the tall grass, it chipped off like a layer of skin. I breathed in deep, coughed, and then smiled. I got up off the ground, using the tree as support. Once I was on my feet, I realized which tree it was. There, carved into it at shoulder level, were the names Johnny and June, surrounded by a carved-out heart. In the upper right corner of the heart was a hole. That was where my shot from the rifle had ended up. Ten yards past the tree was the shack, its one window blasted out, and its door slightly ajar. I walked over.

The wood door cried on its hinges, revealing a ten-by-ten room completely painted in blood. It was on the floor, the walls, the ceiling. It was so thick in some places that it had seemed to dry in layers—dry at the bottom and wet at the top. The photos along the walls were ruined, but there was a bag in the corner that I hadn't noticed the night before. It was probably loaded with photographs that had made it safely through the crimson rain. I went over and opened it, and sure enough, it was. Bundles of photographs. I didn't want to look at them, and I didn't have to. Everything the Rose Killer had ever done was in my head now, and would be until the day I died.

I stacked the pictures on a fairly dry spot on the floor, being sure not to leave big, bloody fingerprints on the edges, and took the bag. I would need it. Next, I righted the chair I had been tied to the night before and set the bag on it.

Shredded meat littered the floor like confetti, maybe a third of what it would take to make a man. Resting in the far corner, one stacked on top of the other, were a pair of human legs, un-touched, as if the wolf had wanted no part of them.

A fly landed on my hand. I blew it away. "Come back later," I said.

I rummaged through the ankle-high mess and came up with the keys to my house, but that wasn't all I was looking for. There were some things in that room that I needed to take with me—the definite signs that I had ever been there in the first place.

I picked up the bloodied clothes that had burst off of me the night before and found my skull-and-crossbones belt buckle un-der my torn-up pair of jeans. It was caked in blood, but still in one piece. I'd had the belt buckle for years, and truly dug it. It was coming with me. Everything else was reduced to rags. Every-thing went in the bag, like the busted handcuffs and my wallet and the pictures I'd carried around so long in my back pocket, but not the rifle, which went over my shoulder. I took the tape out of the video camera. It had been a long time since I'd seen a good show.

Last, I found John Raynor's torn pair of pants and went through the pockets. God was smiling down on me, because his cigarettes were dry. I lit one up, and then fished out his car keys.

I ran across Old Sherman Road in all my naked glory and got in the Mach 1, then drove it as deep into the woods as I could. I emptied out the trunk and everything from the backseat, and dropped it all just outside the shack. When I was done, I used my old pair of underwear to wipe down the doorframe and anything else I might have touched. My blood was technically all over the place, but there was nothing I could do about that.

Having everything in one spot was my good deed for the *federales*. I was only sorry I couldn't wrap a bow around the whole fucking building. I lit another cigarette, got in the car, and took off.

I got home just short of six o'clock in the morning. I was half expecting to see a cruiser parked outside the place, but the coast was clear.

I made a pot of coffee and jumped in the shower to wash away the blood. As I combed my hair in front of the mirror, I touched my chest. The night before there had been two bullet holes in it. Not anymore. I wondered where the bullets went.

Over a bowl of cereal, I watched the tape that John Raynor had filmed the night before. When the strip of old rug came off the window, I saw myself change. I'd never seen it before. Now I was not only seeing it on film but I was reliving the Rose Killer's perception of it as well. I wasn't just getting a show; I was getting a double feature.

Anthony got off the floor as the wolf took its first lumbering steps toward him, and he tried once again in vain with the latch on the door. The wolf threw a clubbing blow into his back, and he doubled up. The camera tipped over. The wolf then swatted him against the wall, and he sank to his knees. As he screamed, the wolf pinned his arms against his chest and proceeded to gnaw slowly at Anthony's face.

Before long, the killer passed out, and it was at that point, in which he no longer had a face to enchant with, in which his eyes hung like shining ornaments from their ruined sockets, in which he was no longer responsive to pain but lost somewhere up in his primordial brain someplace just short of death, that the wolf went on and took him apart.

Once he was dead and scattered about like the rags of my clothes, the wolf sauntered up to the camera, crouched down, and looked into the lens. With a deep breath it fogged up the lens, then roared, as if to say, "There you go."

It then raised its hand beyond the scope of the camera's eye, and turned the machine off. Watching that, I smiled. It was good to be a team again. But I destroyed the tape all the same.

After I finished my cereal and coffee, I put the bowl and mug in the sink. I would not have the chance to wash them. I went through the house gathering up my most treasured possessions— Doris's night-light, the one picture of her I had left, the eagle feather my mother had given me and which was my burden to carry for the rest of my days, my old leather jacket, the naked-lady ashtray, clothes, the Proust I hadn't finished reading—and loaded the trunk with them, then put the trunk in the backseat of the car. There was nothing else in the world I possessed.

I dressed in a clean set of clothes—jeans, cowboy boots, and an old flannel shirt—and locked the door behind me. I no longer had a home. And I no longer had a name. It was time for me to disappear. It's what I was good at.

I remember leaving home like it happened yesterday. I remember pounding on my mother's front door, begging her to let me in. She finally did. I hadn't seen her in weeks, not since I left in a huff and moved into that fleabag motel on the other side of town. Doris had come over to my room the night before with a travel bag. In a couple of days we were going to get on the bike and head out west toward the ocean. We were going to get married along the way.

My mother answered the door in her bathrobe, her graying hair up in a bun, bags under her eyes the color of bruises, like she hadn't slept since I came back from the war. I was hysterical, shaking, crying, and she carried me over to the couch and sat me down.

In a calm voice, she asked me what happened. I told her.

"Doris is dead," I said, weeping.

My mother lit a cigarette and blew smoke at the ceiling.

"You blacked out, didn't you?"

"How do you know?"

"By any chance," she said, "did you see the full moon last night?"

I saw an image of hell flash across her eyes.

"What does that mean?" I asked.

"Son," she said, a tear sliding down her face, "you should have died over in that godforsaken war."

"What was Dad supposed to tell me?"

She started it off with, "Well, Marlowe, you're not like other boys," and it went downhill from there.

She told me about my bloodline, how my great-grandfather had been a bounty hunter, how he had gone after an Indian who was called "the Mad Wolf." The Indian was said to be deranged and possessed of supernatural powers. He had left whole villages in ruins. My great-grandfather killed the Indian, but his life was cursed from that day forward. When he died, his son inherited the curse. Down the line it went, till it got to me. She told me why Dad went away once a month the way he did—so he wouldn't kill his family.

"Marlowe, the life you wanted could never be yours, even if Doris were still alive. Your father and I knew that because we went through the same thing. When you went to Vietnam, we were truly hoping you wouldn't make it, just so you wouldn't have to go through what he went through, and so Doris wouldn't have to live the kind of life that I've had to live. That's why we pushed her away. So she could move on. But it's too late for that now, isn't it?"

"This can't be happening," I cried.

"You should have died overseas. Doris would still be here. . . ."

"No. Doris is dead because of you. You instigated this whole damn thing. You drove me away. You didn't warn me, Mom. You let us go."

"Would you have believed me? I couldn't . . . How could I say these things to my boy? It should have ended with your brother. . . ."

"What do you mean?"

"Jeffrey didn't die," she said. "Your father killed him. Just took him out one night and didn't come back with him. I didn't want to know what he did. He was going to kill the *both* of you so it could end with him, but after he did your baby brother, he couldn't go on and kill you too. He was too weak. He loved you too much. He loved Jeffrey too, but he thought the both of you would be able to go off together. He was supposed to tell you about the curse. But he couldn't. He wanted to spare you this pain. You were supposed to die over there, Marlowe. Why didn't you die?"

"Mom, this isn't right. . . ."

"It's not," she said. Then: "There's only one right thing left to do. This has to end with you."

She left the room and came back with my father's loaded revolver. She handed it to me by the barrel. "Take it," she said. "Do what needs to be done."

I took the gun. It was heavy in my hand. Something inside me told me she was right. I should have just ended it, but I didn't. I couldn't.

"I can't," I said. "I've already died once. I don't want to do it again."

"There's no hope, Marlowe, and there's no cure. Believe me, your father tried. He really did. Wherever you go, death will follow. And it will never end."

"We'll see. There has to be someone out there who knows about this. Someone who can reverse it, *somewhere*. There has to be a cure. Someone who can help."

"There's no hope," she said. "Your search will be futile and painful. But if that's what you want to do, you'll need this."

She reached into her bathrobe and produced the eagle feather.

"It was the Indian's. It's the only thing that matters now."

There was no kiss good-bye, no parting words. Her son was dead, or at least a very human part of him was, and in his place was a walking, talking pestilence. A plague. A bike-borne disease named Vicious Death. In the space that died was a doorway to hell that would never fully close.

"There's no hope," she repeated.

"We'll see," I replied defiantly as I passed through her doorway and out into the night. The next time I would see her, she would be dead.

I walked through the door of my childhood home for the last time and left my mother standing in the doorway. Later that night, my mother burned the motel down to the ground. Doris's body was never found, and as far as her parents ever knew, we'd run off together, never to be seen again. They never knew what happened to their girl.

Strapped to the back of my bike was the bag that Doris had brought over. In it had been her clothes, some makeup, a couple of books, a small framed picture of her that she knew I couldn't live without, and her night-light. The one with the clown's head on it. The one she'd had since she was a little kid, the one she *still* had, because she was deathly afraid of the dark. They were the trinkets and charms of my Doris—the material objects that had meant so little to me the day before, but had now taken on such deep and abundant meanings because their existence was all I had left of our life together.

I had the clothes on my back and forty-eight dollars to my name. My useless name. A name that brought such astounding sorrow to the lives of those it touched, and, like a Pandora's box, would do the same twenty years later when I thought I could bring it back out of the closet I'd hidden it in, polish it off, make it mean something, and use it again.

I got on the bike and I cried her name. "Doris, I'm so sorry."

My life was no more. Nothing was left, save doom, and darkness, and bloody moons gorged ripe and red with horror. I was in hell, and from this hell, there seemed to be not a single escape, a saving refuge, a possible way out. But I couldn't give up that easily. The war, the blood, my love—it couldn't all have been for nothing. There had to be a cure. I had to try.

With that, I started the bike, and I was gone.

I got to Long John's a little after seven in the morning. Abraham's Buick was in one of the spaces. I hopped up the steps, went through the door, and heard the bell jangle above my head. Abraham was behind the counter, wiping it down with a cloth.

"Mind if I come in?"

"Of course not," said Abraham. "You owe me for that coffee."

I took a seat on one of the stools.

"How you doin', Abe?"

"Pretty good," he said. "How about you? Last time I saw you, you looked like you'd become intimate with an ugly stick."

With the full moon come and gone, I was back in tip-top shape. I felt like a million bucks. But I probably had somewhere in the neighborhood of a hundred.

"I have a history of resiliency."

"Got the recipe?"

"It's a family secret," I said. "Sorry. I just came by to tell you I'm skippin' town, Abe. I'm outta here."

"I kind of figured you would be."

"I think I wore out my welcome these last few weeks. I gotta start over again. Somewhere fresh."

"To be honest, you wore out your welcome the day you showed up."

"I probably did," I said.

"Is anybody going to be looking for you?"

"I hope not."

"I ask because I see you have a new ride out there. I recognize that car. Is there anything I should know?"

"Nothing you need to know, except I'm not a bad guy, Abraham. Everything else you might hear on the news at some point."

He went back to wiping the counter, then said, "But you're not a bad guy."

"That's right."

"In that case, you don't owe me for the coffee."

"Can I have another then?"

"Don't push your luck," he said. "Where are you off to?"

"I don't know where I'm going."

"Did you ever?"

"No, I guess not. It was nice working with you, Abe."

"I wish I could say the same," he said.

We shook hands, and the bell jangled behind me for the last time.

The hatchback pulled into the parking lot, all clean and shiny, and he came to a stop in the same place it was in the last time. Van Buren killed the engine, undid his safety belt, and opened the door. I snuck up behind the car. My right hand was curled up in a pretty little fist of fury.

His brown leather shoes hit the asphalt. He must've heard a footstep, for he turned to me before I reached him. It didn't matter though. My right hook knocked him down to the ground. His sunglasses flew away, revealing discolored eyes. I dropped to my knees and plucked the handgun out from the inside of his jacket before he knew which way was up, and I trained it to the side of his head.

"Higgins," he said, shocked.

He licked a trickle of blood away from the corner of his mouth, and struggled a second to uncross his eyes. His face was still a patchwork of browns and blues from our skirmish in the woods. His nose was covered with a white strip.

"Surprised to see me?"

"How . . ."

"You tried to kill me," I hissed. "That wasn't very fucking nice."

"Higgins . . ."

"You fucked up. People like you always do. If you're going to try to kill a man, you do it right, like I do."

"Please don't . . ."

"You're a scumbag, Van Buren. You're no kind of cop. Where did you get that car you rammed me with?"

"Impound," he said.

"You ruined my truck."

"I shot you . . ."

"Yes you did, you motherfucker."

"You should be dead. How . . ."

"You're a cop, Van Buren. You would know that they didn't pull a body out of that truck. Don't pull this shocked shit with me, and if you thought I wouldn't come back for you, you're a bigger fool than I thought."

"I thought you'd crawled into the woods and died, Higgins. . . . What're you going to do?"

I know what I would have liked to do.

I pulled an envelope from the back pocket of my jeans. It contained Van Buren's shield and a hand-drawn map I'd made for him. The map was crude, but showed exactly where in those thick and haunted woods off of Old Sherman Road there was a little ancient shack with a broken window, a body, stacks of incriminating photos, and the cameras that took them. It was a gift from me to him, even though he shot me. Twice.

I tossed the envelope into the car and said, "There's a treat in there for you and the *federales*."

"What's that?"

"Where to find the Rose Killer."

"You got him?"

I let the question go. It seemed redundant to me that he felt it necessary to ask.

"I can kill you anytime I want, Van Buren. But I won't. I want you to forget my name though. The contents of that envelope were stuck under your windshield wiper when you left the house this morning, you copy that?"

He nodded.

"Forget my fucking name. Forget I exist. If I ever see you again, I won't be merciful, and I won't fuck up. I'll do things to you so bad I won't be able to live with myself."

I threw his gun into the car, stood, and slammed the door.

"Your badge is in there too."

"Thanks," he said.

"Don't thank me. Quit. You don't deserve it."

I walked away. No one followed.

After dropping off the shield and the map to Van Buren, I paid Mrs. Pearce a visit. I had every reason to believe the house was still under the watch and guard of the police, but I couldn't leave without seeing her.

She opened the door and was much more cordial this time around. She invited me in, led me to the couch, and made me what must have been the best cup of tea I'd ever had in my life. I was never a big fan of tea, but Pearce liked it, and it was that part of him that was inside me that enjoyed the drink she made for me.

Her face looked not as exhausted as it did the first time I was there, and the aura that surrounded her seemed a little less gray.

When she finally got around to asking me what I was doing there, I pulled from a sleeve in my wallet a single piece of black, human hair. I gave it to her carefully, as if the fingers that held it were fine surgeon's tools, and once she held it tight between her fingers, I told her that it was a hair from the head of the man who was responsible for her husband's death. It was true enough for me.

She inspected it like it would answer her questions, like why her husband had to die so young, or what kind of man could have done such a thing. I just hoped it would put them down for her.

"Why are you giving this to me?" she asked, teary-eyed.

"There's never going to be a trial," I said. "No sense of closure for you. This piece of hair is going to have to do."

"How did you get it?"

"That's something you don't have to think on," I said, "and you shouldn't."

She felt her stomach and smiled.

"I am a cop's wife. I know when to leave well enough alone. Thank you."

"How's the baby?"

"Fine. Coming along. She'll be popping out just about any day now," she said. "I wish Danny were here for this. . . ." She stopped, brought a tissue to her eye.

"Me too," I said.

She cleared her throat and asked, "Any ideas for a name?"

"Yeah," I said, "actually, I do. I've always been fond of Doris."

Last, I pulled up outside Alice's little house on the north side of town. I felt bad that things had gone so sour between us. I knew that our relationship was just as much a figment of my imagination as it was real, and I had scared and offended her by thinking it was anything more than what it was—an arrangement. But I didn't regret following her all the times I did. Half the reason was because I wanted to make sure she got home safely. I always did. The other was because I loved her.

I blew the horn. It was not yet ten o'clock, and she was sleeping. By nature, her schedule was, sadly, nocturnal, like mine. I blew the horn again, and this time her face appeared behind the kitchen curtain. A minute later, she came out in her real jammies—a pair of boxers and a tank top. Her hair was down, and she came out to the curb barefoot. I loved her feet. She never looked better than she did outside of Mama Snow's house.

I got out and rested against the hood.

"Marlowe," she said.

"I'm sorry to wake you. You look great."

She smiled.

"And you look *okay*. A lot better than the last time I saw you. I guess everything worked out for you."

"It worked out good enough."

"Where did you get this car?"

"I traded it in," I said.

"Where? I've never seen that ride around here before."

Thank God for that.

I blinked, and just for a moment, I saw her through Raynor's eyes, the way he would have seen her. It made me sick. I blinked again to make it go away.

"It's from out of town," I said.

"What is it?"

"It's a '73 Mach 1. They don't make 'em like this anymore."

The Rose Killer's deathmobile would be my ride until I got out of Evelyn and got the cash together to pick up a new car for myself. I could only hope the tags wouldn't pop if I ever got stopped for anything.

"What happened to your accent?" she asked.

"It went the way of the Duke, Alice. I may not need it where I'm going, depending on where that is. I tried telling you that there was a lot more to me than people know, and this is one of those things. I'm not really a Bible Belt kind of guy. It's not my history."

"Well, that much I've always figured, Marley, you being who you are. . . ."

"I'm not a bad man, Alice."

"I know that."

"Do you?"

"I know it now," she said softly.

"I just wanted you to be okay. And I just wanted you to hear my real voice before . . ."

"So . . . is this it?" she asked.

"Yeah, darlin', this is it. I'm just about used up here. I'm gonna be hitting the highway in a short while."

"Oh," she said, looking down.

"I was wondering if you wanted to come with me."

She thought for a moment. She looked off into the distance, and finally said, "No, I don't think I will, I hate to say. We all have our . . . burdens . . . and I got mine. I can't go."

"I know," I said. "I'm sorry."

"But thanks for saying good-bye, Marley."

"I couldn't go without seeing you."

She smiled again, came up close, and kissed me on my mouth. I kissed her back. My fingers laced their way through her hair for the last time. A second later, she pulled herself away. That's all there could be. And all there was.

"Take care, darlin'."

"You too," she said.

She turned and started to walk back toward the house. I watched her pad away in her bare feet, away from me for the last time, and I couldn't take it.

"Wait," I said.

She stopped.

I opened the car door and rummaged through the trunk in the backseat.

I handed her the old, clown-faced night-light.

"What's this?" she asked.

"It's a little light," I said. "In case it ever gets too dark for you to see."

I drove through the opened gates of Wild Oaks Cemetery and up the main road that wove among the graves like an artery. After a few minutes of slow driving, I saw Pearce's grave up ahead.

I parked the car on the shoulder, and went the rest of the way on foot. The crime-scene tape had been removed, but all about the place was trampled grass from the most action the cemetery had seen since the War of the States. When I got to his grave, I took out a cigarette and rested it on the tombstone. He deserved one.

In my head, I remembered one of his last solid memories. He was sipping from a cup of coffee in his well-lit kitchen, and Martha was in the living room going through his jacket pockets because she was getting a load of laundry together. She discovered the note I had written to him in the guise of a rather trashy cross-dresser. Danny looked over to see what she was looking at with such disgust. "What's up?" he asked calmly.

"What the hell is this?" she gasped. "Who the hell is Tommy Candy?"

Danny walked over and took the note from her hands. He read it, then cursed under his breath. "That sonofabitch."

His wife's eyes were digging holes into him. Danny smiled and said, "It looks as if Marley's trying to help us get a divorce."

"Dear Christ," she said. "Why do you associate with that bum?"

"C'mon, Martha," Danny said. "He's not that bad. He just has a little bit of a devil's streak in him. He's trying, you know."

I looked down at the grave and tipped my invisible hat to him. "I did what I could," I said. "Take care, partner."

Like Bill Parker used to do, I drove a loop around Old Sherman, just to let me know, in some crazy way, that everything was going to be okay. I had no name and no destination, but there was always going to be a road to take, there was always going to be a full moon waiting for me, and no matter where I ended up, I'd keep on doing what it is that I do best.

I took a left where Main Street turned into a country road at Old Sherman and took it into the woods where it lay cracked and shaded under a tent of tree limbs. The town of Evelyn, the first place I'd had the chance to call home since I was just a boy, receded into the distance in my rearview mirror. Before long, I reached the St. Michael River and crossed Whitman's Bridge on my way to the west.

With that, I was gone.

EPILOGUE

Mick Hanson parked his stolen car on the corner and looked out at the long and winding residential street through the dirty windshield. There wasn't a soul in sight, and up in the cloudless sky the full moon shone, shedding enough light that he wouldn't have to worry about tripping over anything when he was stumbling through someone's backyard. He got out of the car, closed the door gently, and disappeared into the shadows.

He had been in San Antonio for just a couple of months. He'd never been there before coming in on one of the trains, but he knew it was a big city. There was no reason there shouldn't be a lot of work around for a guy like him, even if his record was less than perfect. Texas was supposed to be a religious kind of place after all, and if some shopkeeper there couldn't see past his faults, then who could?

So far, Hanson hadn't been successful in finding work, but he got by all right just the same. Locks just seemed to open at his will. And no matter where he ever found himself, there was always going to be a pawnshop close by that didn't ask questions about how he got all the jewelry that lined his filthy pockets.

He walked along the sidewalk. Up high, there was a sign nailed to a post that spoke of a neighborhood watch. He laughed under his breath, then caught sight of a nice-looking house a few doors down. There was a car in the driveway—a red Toyota Corolla with Texas plates. He peeped through the car's side window and covered his mouth when he saw what was there for all the world to see in the open glove box. There was a box of tampons in there.

His other hand disappeared into his pants pocket. Then he went around to the back of the house.

There was a bed of flowers that filled the air with a sweet scent, and past that was a small vegetable patch, a garden hose woven across the dirt like a snake that he would have tripped over if it wasn't such a bright night. He didn't like tripping. Nor did he like making noise.

Hanging on a line from between the two short trees was a clothesline, and on that clothesline were several tops of varying, garish colors, a pair of jogging pants with a racing stripe along the side, a tan nightgown, and a single brassiere, pink, that fluttered in the gentle breeze. Mick Hanson licked his lips and wiped the sweat from his brow with the sleeve of his dingy T-shirt.

He touched the female garment, felt the smoothness of the synthetic fabric as he rolled it back and forth between his fingers. Then he brought it to his face and rubbed his cheek with it. It might have just been in his head, but he would have sworn that it was warm, as if a woman had just taken it off seconds earlier. He stuffed it in his pocket, and then went over to the window.

It was opened just a crack, but as the curtains swayed back and forth in the breeze, he could see the woman pacing through a far-away room, talking on the phone. She was wearing next to nothing. A pair of men's boxer shorts, that's it. Her hair was golden and bounced around the top of her head in a thick perm. Mick Hanson liked straight hair, but wasn't the kind of guy that got picky about such things. The woman's breasts were small and lifeless. Tired-looking. One of them had a mole on it, just above the nipple, and it was that kind of fine detail that made Mick Hanson reach for his manhood again, made him pat it through his slacks like it was a dog waiting for a treat. Mick Hanson bit the inside of his mouth to keep himself from moaning.

The fact was that it didn't matter what she had been wearing, or even what she looked like. All signs pointed to her being alone in that house, and sometimes, if the opportunity presented itself,

Mick Hanson just couldn't help himself. Any valuables in the house that he could hock would be nothing more than a bonus at that point.

He stuck his fingers in the thin space between the open window and its frame with the intent of opening it enough so he could sneak into the house. As he did so, he heard a growling sound behind him.

His heart skipped a beat, and he thought of what it was like the last time he'd been attacked by a dog on someone else's property. He still had the deep, jagged scars on his forearm to remember it by.

He turned slowly, and when he saw what was standing in front of him, all seven feet of it, its teeth glistening with spit, its eyes as red as bloody pools, Mick Hanson lost control of his bowels, and the smell of his cheap, digested lunch filled the air.

The wolf raised its giant hand in the air so Mick Hanson could see it before he died. There, clutched in one of the beast's fists, was a sock. Mick Hanson's old, dirty sock. He took in a great big breath to scream, but the target never made another sound again.